Cover art by Vicki Leona

A Legend Of Wolves

No 1

The Task

By

Erin Gatten

Table of Contents

For my sister Tamara who instilled in me
a love of reading and nurtured
my love of stories.
Without you this book could not have happened.

Chapter I:
Secrets

He followed a wolf with fur the same polished iron color of his eyes. Cael's heart was pounding with fear, but he didn't know why. The canine leads him through the mouth of a cave. Inside, it was dry and hot and smelled of sulfur. The wolf seemed to illuminate the interior.

The cave was small; Cael could see the back of it standing just inside the entrance. There was movement off to his right. Cael turned towards it just in time to see a crimson lion leap out and attack the wolf. The canine snarled and retaliated.

Cael awoke in a cold sweat he sat bolt upright and pressed his hands against his face. It took him a full minute to re-orient himself. He was sitting up in his own bed at Purple House Orphanage. A pale gray light glowed from the window bringing some light to the much smaller figures in the other beds in the room. Cael was by far the oldest orphan at the manor. The director, Dorothy, was practically his mother, she was the woman who used her estate as an orphanage for him and just about every other delinquent who walked through her door. However, Cael had lived in the orphanage for so long (his entire seventeen years of life, in fact) that he felt that it was only right to call it home, and its owner his parent. Adoption was no longer a viable prospect.

Cael sighed and got out of bed. He looked out the window to see the light coming from the horizon even though the sun had not yet risen. He had run a hand back and forth through his rumpled, sleep-mussed hair and slouched out of the boys' dormitory. After getting dressed and combing his light brown hair evenly to each side with the part straight down the middle, Cael stepped into the light of a new day breaking. The air was crisp and fresh, a stark contrast to the air in his dream. Cael stood where he was, content to forget himself for a short time and enjoy the serenity of the moment. He let the anxiety from his dream melt away.

A movement off to his left caught his attention. It took Cael a little while to focus on the action enough to realize what it was. Dorothy was standing in a line of trees facing some kind of animal. It was too far away for Cael to make out what it was exactly, but he could tell that it was not naturally colored when he looked harder the animal had vanished. Dorothy turned around and started back towards the house.

It was not the first strange thing that had happened concerning Dorothy. In fact, strange things were pretty common around the orphanage director, she was a mage, and she had been teaching Cael to use his own magic for as long as he could remember. She was a capable teacher even though he was not a mage himself, Cael was an alchemist.

"Oh 'morning Cael, what's got you up so early? We're not due for sword practice for another hour or so." Dorothy had reached the porch and had hopped onto the railing and leaned her back up against a support beam.

"What was that thing you were with just now?" Cael asked avoiding Dorothy's question. "Was it something magical? It seemed to vanish quickly enough to be magical."

"Her name is Althea, but you don't need to worry about that right now."

"Althea," Cael said the word quietly, feeling the shape of the sounds and storing the information away for later.

"So, what got you up so early?" Cael should have known Dorothy would not let one of her questions go unanswered even if she did just that to so many of his own.

Cael shook his head, "just a bad dream, no big deal really."

"What kind of dream?"

He raised an eyebrow at the orphanage director, why was she so interested in this? Aloud he said, "Something about a fight between a wolf and a lion."

Dorothy looked surprised, "really? That's rather interesting. I didn't start having dreams about my task until I was told about it." This last was said so quietly that Cael couldn't be sure he heard her right. His first impulse was to ask her to repeat herself, in fact, he almost did, but he doubted he would get any sort of answer out of her.

Dorothy slid off the porch railing and rubbed her hands together, "since you're up, shall we get a start on sword training?"

"What! I don't even get to enjoy my morning? Just straight to the drills huh?" there was really no point in protesting, but he figured he'd voice his complaint anyway. Almost as soon as the last word had left his mouth, he had turned around and headed for the practice ring. Dorothy rolled her eyes and followed. They had been starting every morning with extensive sword training since Cael was eight years old.

The grounds at Purple House Orphanage were vast and covered with lush green grass and dotted with patches of thick wooded areas. The land was located just outside of a sprawling metropolis. Oddly enough the manor at Purple House was not, in fact, purple; it was a deep tan color with rich dark brown trim. The building itself was three stories tall and stood towards the front of the property. The practice yard that Dorothy and Cael used to hone their swordsmanship was at the back of the manor.

Wordlessly Cael opened up the tool shed where the thick leather armor and blunted, heavy, steel practice swords were kept. They wordlessly began strapping on sturdy sets of protective leather though even with that they still often walked away from their bouts with massive bruises. Cael was the first to finish suiting up, so he lifted out the hand and a half sword that was his favorite and the scimitar with a durable steel reinforced scabbard that Dorothy preferred.

"You're not going to pout throughout the whole lesson are you?" she asked when Cael silently offered the weapon to his teacher.

Cael had to grin; he was being more than a little childish. He had to admit that to himself. Seeing that slight improvement in mood, Dorothy moved over to the practice ring and opened the small gate of the corral like fence that enclosed it and motioned for Cael to go ahead of her. Instead of using the gate, however, Cael vaulted over one steel pipe crossbeam of the ring. Dorothy shook her head in an exasperated manner, but Cael didn't miss the small smile on her face.

They turned to face one another, with swords at the ready, sizing each other up in mental preparation. Dorothy was the first to move, a soft purple light glowed around her blade, and her quick, sudden slice almost caught Cael off guard. He managed to bring his sword up in time to protect his face, an answering iron gray light around his own sword. He cursed himself silently for letting her get the better of him.

"Come on Cael, wake up! I thought you said you couldn't sleep!" Dorothy went in for another strike, but Cael had learned his lesson. He swiftly side-stepped and slashed at Dorothy's back. The attack didn't hit home, nor was that what Cael expected. He was ready when his mentor straightened, spun out of the way and lunged at him once more. He knocked the scimitar out of the way and met the momentum of Dorothy's body with his shoulder. She hit the ground hard. The force of her fall caused her to lose grip on her weapon.

Cael backed up a few paces, "pick it up."

"I must say I'm impressed, and I'm almost convinced that you're ready." Dorothy stood and retrieved her sword in one fluid motion.

This time Cael was the first to advance, he came in high with a wide sweeping blow. The glow of the magical energy reinforcing his blade blurred in an arch as it came down. Dorothy blocked with the scabbard in her off-hand and slashed upward with her scimitar, purple magical energy trailing behind the sword's edge. The blow caught Cael in the chest, and the wind was knocked out of him. He went down on one knee, using his hand and a half sword for support. He stayed there for a moment gasping for air. Dorothy hung back, allowing him time to recover.

Cael shook his head clear and rose to his feet. In his peripheral vision, he noticed some of the children had congregated outside the fenced practice ring to watch their match. Morning sword practice had become something of a daily spectacle and was, in fact, the reason for the fence separating the combatants from the children; Dorothy was terrified that some stray pommel or crossguard would knock out someone's tooth, or worse. There was a cheer as Cael advanced; it seemed each child had their own favorite that they would root for. Dorothy liked to lord it over him that she was currently gaining in popularity.

Cael swiftly struck upward, but Dorothy locked his blade between her sword and scabbard. With a grunt that was almost a growl, Cael yanked it free and took a few steps back. Dorothy grinned, "I knew I wouldn't be stronger than you forever, but strength isn't the only thing that counts!" Halfway through her sentence, Dorothy stabbed forward with her scimitar and then whipped it around to strike Cael's shoulder with a speed that momentarily stunned the younger fighter.

Cael's brow furrowed and his expression darkened, it was time to stop playing around. He charged at his mentor with a yell and struck her across the midsection, knocking her back into the fence. Without hesitation he rushed forward, holding his sword in front of him. He met Dorothy's block head on and used his sword's superior reach to push through her defenses. He stopped the tip of his blade just under Dorothy's chin.

The older woman smiled, "Well done; I'd say that is enough for today."

Cael dropped his fighting stance and stretched out his neck and shoulders; a grin on his face, "That was a good match."

Dorothy laughed, "sure when you put your mind to the task. I certainly hope that since you insist on patrolling the streets with your friends, literally looking for trouble, that you fight with more focus than you did just now."

Cael frowned, it had been a few years since he and his pack of friends had started to roam around the city in an effort to catch and stop thugs from hurting people. Really it had started as an accident when they were on their way to lunch and had stumbled upon a mugging. Cael had taken one look at the terrified businessman, frantically trying to remove his watch, and punched the mugger square in the gut. The criminal doubled over and dropped his knife, allowing the businessman to safely get away. Of course, it had taken a little more than that for Cael to get safely away but because of all of Dorothy's training it wasn't really a problem, and Cael had explained this to his mentor time and again but she still insisted on worrying about him.

In response to Dorothy's lecture, Cael said, "it's different when I'm sparring with you, I have no desire what so ever to actually harm you, thugs and muggers are a completely different matter."

They opened up the gate to head back to the storage shed and were immediately swarmed by children. Dorothy hugged a few and told them, "I'll get him next time." and let an older boy named Peter carry her sword while she picked up and carried Jessica, the youngest child at the orphanage. Cael stuck his sword in his belt and knelt down to let a young boy named Tommy climb up for a piggyback ride.

"I just want you to be careful; Cael, you or your friends could get killed doing this. Sure you've been training with me this whole time but what about them?"

Cael was weaving back and forth to give Tommy a better ride, so he only heard about half of Dorothy's question, but he understood enough, they'd had this conversation several times before, "are you kidding me? I've passed along all the fighting stuff to them that you've taught me since day one. Not to mention, we've been going to those boxing classes on Sundays at the youth center for as long as I can remember. Heck, I'm pretty sure that, by this point, Abby's a better fighter than I am half the time."

Dorothy sighed as she set Jessica back on her feet and started removing her armor, "you know I'm just worried about you. It's a dangerous thing you're doing."

Cael, likewise, knelt down to let Tommy slide down so he could take off his own protective gear, "well what's the point of all this training if I don't use it to help people? You're the one who

15

always says 'those who are able should defend those who cannot defend themselves.'"

Dorothy gave a wry grin as she took her and Cael's swords and locked them away with their armor in the shed. "I hate it when you use that line against me. Though you shouldn't be in such a hurry, you'll have plenty of time to help lots of people with your skills very soon."

"You know these little hints about this super-secret task that will be expected of me isn't making me any less curious about what it is," Cael pointed out, "it has to be something big if you've spent all this time teaching me about magic and how to use a sword."

Dorothy actually did look sheepish for a moment, "I'm sorry, you have to believe that I do want to tell you but it is forbidden." They turned and headed for the house, and some of the children ran off to play and enjoy their Saturday while some trailed along behind Cael and Dorothy. The orphanage director called out to the children who ran off, "have fun but be careful," then she turned her attention back to Cael.

"That's another thing, forbidden by who? What on earth could possibly have you so determined not to tell me?"

Dorothy raised her eyebrow at him in annoyance, "Again I cannot say. But I will say this much; the reason why I cannot say is political and annoying in your case, but I'm not about to purposefully anger the magic users that put these rules in place. I'm certain that in many ways they are more powerful than I. And they do have good reasons for the law, but it doesn't particularly apply to you any longer. The second you started putting your training to use in the city you should have been considered ready to hear your task."

Cael sighed and threw up his hands in defeat, as he passed through the front door that Dorothy held open for him "alright,

alright, I'll let it go for now it's just aggravating to have something kept from me like this."

"I do understand I really do," and in an effort to change the subject Dorothy asked, "What are your plans for today then?"

Cael grinned, "Wander the streets looking for trouble."

The orphanage director rolled her eyes and turned toward her office "As if I needed to ask, just be careful, sweetheart."

Cael tilted his head back and to one side and gave her a lopsided grin, "always."

He turned and headed for the boy's bathroom. He was going to need a shower before meeting up with the Pack. Cael thought over his group of friends as he let the hot water loosen his muscles and dull the ache of his bruises. They started calling themselves the Wolf Pack after they began their patrols, hunting much like a pack of wolves for gangsters and criminals. Their actions had quickly gained the attention of the police department, and while the police didn't exactly condone their actions, they did not stop them or punish them either. Either way, Cael mused, he was grateful that they were permitted to continue. Setting his thought's aside, Cael scrubbed himself clean and quickly rinsed off before stepping out to dry.

As he pulled a black t-shirt over his head, he glanced at his reflection in the bathroom mirror to fix his hair into a part down the middle and let his bangs frame his forehead. He had a square jaw that was cleanly shaven and an average rounded nose. His eyes were the color of polished iron which would be unusual for any other man, but Dorothy had once told him that it was the mark of a magic user. He figured it was true; after all, her eyes were an amethyst purple.

Cael wound his way back through the house to his mother's office and leaned into the doorway, "Hey! Just wanted to let you know I'm headed out now."

Dorothy looked up from her paperwork and with a defeated kind of wry humor said, "Good hunting Cael."

With a chuckle, he left the house and grounds to travel down to the subway station. He hopped aboard a train that would take him downtown and found a seat in one of the less crowded cars. As the train rattled on, the car slowly began to empty of people. One by one the businessmen, the housewives, one nanny with three children in tow all filed out of their seats and into the world. As they neared the older downtown area of the city, the few people that remained, Cael's experience told him they were a fair bit more disreputable than the general population.

One block from Cael's destination the train screeched to a stop. He stood up and stretched, his hands high above his head, and marched out through the station and into the sunlight. There was a massive, abandoned apartment complex down the street from where Cael emerged. It was this apartment building that the Pack used as a base of operations and more often as a hangout. It dwarfed Cael as he approached the side door that was the only access point that wasn't nailed shut. The door opened directly into the stairwell. Cael announced himself with a very wolf-like howl and listened a moment afterward. There was a single answering howl; someone else was already here. The shaft went straight up, steps spiraling infinitely upwards along the wall. The footfalls of Cael's progress echoed off the diamond plate steel steps. His cacophonous journey led him to the fifth floor and a door that stood ajar down the hall.

He stepped through the frame while peering into the room. Gavin Shero sat leaning against a plywood and cinderblock desk, tossing a football up in the air and catching it. He graced Cael with a cursory glance before he turned his attention back to the ball. "Hey, what's up?" Gavin was built a lot like Cael; square jaw with broad shoulders and chest. Gavin was a little taller though, and he had jet black hair that he wore combed back.

Footfalls sounded in the stairwell, and another member of the Pack emerged from the hallway. Max Crawford's small face came into view. Max had long platinum blond hair that he kept pulled back into a queue. He carried his medium frame in a slouched, meek manner and he currently sported a fading bruise on his right eye. A week or so ago Max's dad had gone into another one of his rages. Max was a brave guy, but he hated fighting, he had yelled back at his father and had urged him to improve his behavior. That however only seemed to make the situation worse, so Max left and sought refuge at another member of the Pack, Brock's, house. He probably spent more time at one or another of their homes than he did his own, which as far as Cael was concerned was for the best.

Max smiled in a friendly greeting, "how's it going guys?"

Cael gave a lopsided grin in answer, "I actually beat Dorothy this morning."

Max moved over to one of the sofas in the middle of the studio apartment room and plopped heavily down on its tired springs. Cael leaned up against one arm of the couch while Gavin lowered himself on the edge of the seat across from Max on the opposite sofa. The Pack had found this couch and the one that stood directly across from it sitting abandoned on the curb in a residential neighborhood. The table that sat in between them they had fashioned out of milk crates and a plywood board.

"Huh, that's been happening more and more, I guess you are getting better," Gavin commented.

"There's no need to sound so surprised," Cael retorted wryly.

A few minutes later a thundering sounded once more on the stairs, this time accompanied by laughter and shouting. Jim Seinz who could best be described as short and stocky with brown hair cropped close in an almost militaristic flat top, and Abby Brooks burst into the room, Jim first with a triumphant yell.

Abby, unable to slow her forward momentum placed her hands on both Jim's shoulders and vaulted past his left side and into the room. Abby had a slender form with well-toned muscles, and her long, straight, black hair fell across her shoulders. Above her right ear was a streak of bright white hair that she had gotten when her much older brother came to pick her up from kindergarten after having a few too many beers with his friends. The shock of the resulting accident left her with the mark in her hair and fear of alcohol and those who partake in it. Despite this, she had a generally jovial demeanor. She continued bounding into the room to where the rest of the guys sat. "Hey! How's it going?"

"Just fine," Cael laughed, "how about you? You have yourselves a nice race did you?"

"Ah it was only up the stairs," Jim dismissed.

"Yeah, and you cheated!" Abby accused, "somersaulting forward at the top of the stairs like that!"

"I tripped! I was just trying to regain my feet!" Jim said after a bout of uproarious laughter.

Gavin laughed, "Maybe he just has acrobatic skills that you lack."

Offended, Abby demanded, "skills that I lack? Which one of us has studied ballet for nine years?"

"Well, it sure as profanity wasn't me," Gavin said leaning back.

"Ha! See? There you go," Abby bounded over to the couch and crashed into it between Cael and Max.

"What's got you guys all worked up?" came a voice from the doorway.

The Pack turned to see Brock Curtis stroll in with his hands in his pockets. Brock had a medium build with short red hair that he combed forward. He looked at everyone with a raised eyebrow and a confused expression.

"Abby's jealous of Jim's tripping skills," Max explained with as straight a face as he could manage.

Abby responded by making a face at Max, "Shut up."

"Don't worry Abby; I'm sure you improve your tripping if you just practice," Cael teased, "however it might have to wait, now that we're all here let's get to work shall we?"

With an excited whoop, the Pack jumped up in response. All six of them charged down the stairs like wild animals. The steps shook from the force of their descent. Cael sometimes wondered if anyone noticed or cared about their comings and goings, as they burst out of the side door. No one had come to inspect the derelict building in the four years that the Pack had been using it. They just assumed that no one cared anymore about the place; much like half the other buildings on the block that they ran past on their way down the street.

They never really followed any plan when they went out patrolling the city, the Pack just went out and got themselves horribly lost and then found their way out again in between stopping whatever attacks or robberies they happened upon. Today though the sun was shining and the air was still. In other words, Cael frowned, today was boring.

They had wandered their way through twelve blocks before anything remotely interesting happened. The Pack approached a group of four teenage boys who had blocked the path of a young woman. She looked very uncomfortable and was clutching her purse to her chest.

"Hey, sweetheart," one of the boys was saying, "That's a really pretty dress. It'd look even better on my bedroom floor."

Upon seeing this, Max charged ahead to stand at the woman's side, "leave her alone you cretin. Can't you tell she's not interested?"

"Who the hell asked you?" the boy snarled.

"Doesn't matter," Jim responded as the rest of the group caught up.

The boy's eyes lingered on each of the Wolf Pack in turn then scoffed in disgust and shrugged his hoodie up higher on his shoulders, "come on guys, it's getting a little crowded here anyway." and with that, they turned and slouched down the sidewalk and out of sight.

The woman turned to Max and laid a hand lightly on his arm, "Thank you."

Max smiled and gave a small nod, "anytime."

The woman crossed the street and continued on, and the Pack resumed their own path through the city. The sun climbed to the height of the sky, and they encountered nothing else noteworthy. Cael turned around to look at the rest of the Pack while walking backward. "I'd say that this is a bust. Who's up for lunch? I know I could go for some food."

"I'm game, where should we go?" Brock responded.

Gavin laughed, "Is that even a question?"

"Off to Tony's again today then," Abby stated and sprinted off down the street.

Brock, Max, and Jim bolted down the street after her. Cael and Gavin shared a conspiratorial look before Cael grinned and dashed forward to catch up. When he drew abreast with Brock, he bent down and snatched him around the middle before flinging him over his shoulder and continued charging down the sidewalk.

"Just what do you think you're doing?" Brock demanded.

"Stealing you, what does it look like?" Cael responded simply.

"You're ridiculous! Let me go!" Brock ordered.

By this time Cael's antics had caught the attention of the others in the Pack. Abby, in particular, slowed her pace to get nearer to the struggling pair, "I'll save you, little boy!" She then gave a quick jab to Cael's side, causing him to cry out in surprise and drop Brock.

Brock got back to his feet and dusted the dirt off of his pants while glaring at Abby, "'little boy'? Really?"

"Oh come off it! I free you from his clutches, and I'm the one you're mad at?" She exclaimed. She couldn't keep a straight face and burst into laughter, "I know I'm sorry I'm sorry." She waved her hand in front of her face in an effort to get more air. She clapped him on the back and led him off around the last corner to the front door of Tony's Pizzeria. They all filed through the glass portal that was emblazoned with the parlor's circular animated raccoon logo and congregated around the front counter.

The owner, Tony, had his hands full with used plates that he was taking behind the kitchen doors.

As he was pushing them open with his back, Tony spotted the Pack, "Ah! There are-a, my favorite-a customers! Find a seat any-a-where. I will be with you in a moment. Heh, we are-a a little shorthanded today."

Cael grinned as they found a table towards the back; he could never quite tell if Tony's accent was real or not. The restaurant they sat in though was probably the best in the city, or at least their side of it. The dining room was softly lit and filled with tables occupied here and there with families enjoying themselves. And most importantly, at least to the Pack, was the old pinball machine in the back corner.

The thing had to have been made back in the eighties, it had worn graphics, and some of the lights didn't work anymore, but there was an unmistakable charm about it. It had a jungle theme, with jaguars on the flippers. The track that the steel balls came out of was decorated with five toucans flying in a row. And, the primary goal was to get the ball into a cave in a mountain upon which a gorilla was seated.

Before he even sat down, Brock bounded over to the pinball machine and pushed a quarter into the slot. The rest of the Pack all gathered around to watch him as he expertly slammed the steel ball around the playing field. Each day when they would come in and wait for their pizzas, the Wolf Pack would go in and take turns at the game. The machine did not have a high score table, but each of them kept in mind their highest score, and they would frequently compare them to determine who had gloating rights.

After Brock's second ball, Tony approached their table with two steaming deep dish pizzas in hand. "I have a a-sausage, bacon, and mushroom for-a one, and a four cheese-a and pepperoni for the-a other!" He set the pans down on the table they had put their jackets on.

Cael walked back to the table, chuckling, "we don't even have to order anymore do we?"

"Well-a you do always order the same thing," Tony replied with a smile.

"We are in a bit of a rut," Abby came over as well, hands on her hips.

"But it's such a tasty rut," Max commented as he, too, returned to the table.

Gavin quietly slid into a seat and grabbed a slice and began eating. He eyed the rest of the Pack as they stood there, "I thought you guys were hungry, or do you just want to stand and talk all day?"

Abby put a hand to her chest, pretending to be offended. "I will do as I please, and I will thank you kindly not to question my actions, sir!" immediately after this speech she sat down and grabbed her own slice of pizza.

With a shake of his head, Cael smiled at Tony, "thank you; these look delicious." In response, Tony only smiled and nodded before walking away.

For a few moments, Brock attempted to continue his game as the rest of the Pack left to enjoy their meal. But after those few moments Brock quit, "Oh expletive, I give up." He took his hands away from the buttons and let the ball drop before finding a seat at their table and claiming his own piece of pizza.

After finishing two slices, Abby shook her head in amazement as she watched the rest of the group eagerly devour slice after slice. "Where do you boys put all that food?" she asked, the look of confused wonder never leaving her face. It did not take the group long to clear off the pans.

Cael ran his hands through his hair and stretched out his back with a grunt. He brought his hands back down and patted his stomach twice, "well what do you guys think should we get going?"

Abby had a faraway look in her eye for a moment, "yes, we should go, now."

Jim raised an eyebrow in her direction, "well alright, your majesty."

Cael, on the other hand, looked Abby right in the eye, a silent message passing between them. Wordlessly he stood up and moved to the front of the restaurant. After a second or two the others picked up and followed after him. They quickly paid and pushed through the door out into the sunlight once more.

Chapter II:
An Unprovoked Attack

Cael's brow furrowed and his jaw clenched almost of their own accord when he saw who was approaching. Kass Longhorn, a young man who had frequently opposed the Wolf Pack with ever-increasing ferocity, marched toward the group with fire in his eyes.

"I thought I might find you here!" Kass snarled.

"And what are you planning to do now that you've found us?" Cael's tone was guarded and had a sharp edge to it.

"I'm going to make you answer for your actions! That cop you tipped off last week came and arrested my older brother," Kass spat.

"So what makes you think we were the ones who tipped off the police?" Abby, who had been the one to actually make the call, asked.

Kass ground his teeth in frustration, "oh yeah like you wouldn't have after he gave you the slip when you attacked him last Thursday."

Gavin gave a derisive snort, "yeah after he robbed a store at gunpoint."

"You think you're so much better than us don't you?" he demanded.

Cael glared him down, "well we certainly behave better, don't we?"

This was the last straw for Longhorn. With an angry yell, he charged forward; heading straight for Cael who side-stepped Kass's advance and caught him by the throat. Cael pushed back on Longhorn's neck, forcing him to retreat while squeezing just enough to keep his attention. Kass snorted in frustration and punched Cael on the chin with a powerful uppercut that sent him stumbling back a few steps. Kass pushed the advance, bringing his knee up into Cael's stomach.

When Kass tried to strike that way again Cael was ready for him, He grabbed hold of Longhorn's leg and shoved it to the side. Unbalanced, Longhorn crashed into the sidewalk with a grunt. Cael barreled down on him, slamming his fist into Kass's face, and then he pinned him to the ground with a knee on his chest. "Whatever happened to your brother was the result of his own choices. Don't come here blaming us for your problems. If we hadn't called the police, I'm sure someone else would have. Now I suggest you take a good long look at your own life to make sure you don't suffer the same fate as your brother. Now get out of my face!" Cael growled before pushing up and giving Kass one last shove with his foot.

Reluctantly Longhorn got to his feet then took off down the street at a sprint.

"Well that could have gone a lot better," Max said with a frown looking off in the direction Kass had run.

"Yeah," Cael began with a sigh, "but it could have gone a lot worse too. I was lucky that he didn't try to drag that fight on longer than it had to." He ran a hand through his hair and looked over to his Pack.   "Well, nothing's going to top that today I'm sure."

"A guy specifically coming after us to exact revenge? No probably not, I say we call it a day," Gavin said rubbing a hand along his jawline.

They made their way to the nearest train station. As they were approaching their train car, Cael hung back to get a word with Abby before they boarded the steel behemoth. "You had another vision didn't you?" he asked in low tones so the others wouldn't hear. "I saw that faraway look right before we left Tony's."

Abby looked momentarily annoyed, "yes, okay I had another vision, I saw Kass coming up before he actually did, and if we hadn't gone to meet him, he would have broken Tony's door. So what? It doesn't change anything I want to stay away from all this magic stuff as best I can. It's just too weird for me and please don't tell the rest of the guys."

"I'm sure they would be supportive of you, the guys have never treated me any differently just because I'm a magic user. I don't see how you would be any different." Cael insisted.

"I'm sure they would, but just let me figure this out on my own. All this is still too new to me." Abby asserted.

Cael sighed and nodded, "alright, whatever you think is best, but remember, if you ever need to talk about it I'm here to listen. You're like a little sister to me, and I hate to see you struggling with this."

Abby smiled and patted Cael's arm as she stepped into the train car, "I know 'big brother,' and I appreciate it, but I just need more time."

With a shrug, Cael passed through the doors himself and grabbed a seat next to Brock and Gavin, who were carrying on their own conversation. "You just abandoned your last ball?" Gavin, ever the competitive soul, asked incredulously.

Brock shrugged it off, "I was hungrier for pizza than I was for a high score."

Gavin shook his head in mock disapproval, "so what was your score?"

Brock thought a moment before finally answering, "It was something like 760,000."

At hearing this, Jim, threw a triumphant fist into the air, "yes! Still the reigning champ! Aww yeah!"

Gavin pointed a finger at his gloating friend, "celebrate while you can. Next time it's my turn, and I will knock you off that pedestal of yours."

Jim gave him a confident grin, "well, we'll see if you can."

One by one the members of the Pack left their subway car on their journey home until no one was left but Cael. He stood and made his way to the surface; his pace was somewhat leisurely until he spotted the sun hovering low just above the western horizon. Cael then realized how late he was; his mother was going to kill him.

Cael quickened his pace; he was so absorbed in the sound of his worn-out sneakers pounding on the concrete of the alleyway formed by an office building and a Chinese restaurant that he didn't notice the man in front of him before it was too late. They collided. Cael stepped back a few paces, rubbing his head. He looked up at the man he ran into.

"Oh! I'm sorry, I wasn't paying any attention to where I was going," Cael tried to sidestep the man, but he blocked Cael's path in a purposeful manner.

"The collision was my intention, boy," the man had an unpleasant, almost cruel quality about him that made Cael shiver.

Cael took another step back, shaking his head, "I'm afraid I don't understand."

The man laughed, it was a chilling and ruthless sound, "if that is all you are afraid of you are either braver than most or a complete fool."

Cael narrowed his eyes suspiciously at the man. "Who are you? What do you want with me? What's the meaning of all this?" Cael demanded, stepping into a fighting stance and bringing his fists up in front of his face.

The man smiled, the sight was just as unsettling as the sound of his laugh, "you are a magic user, an alchemist if I'm not mistaken, and yet you challenge me with your hands like some mundane wretch? Perhaps I shouldn't feel threatened... As for your rather persistent questions, the laws of the benevolent magic classes," he gestured dismissively in Cael's direction, "like alchemists would rather I didn't answer most of those questions. Of course, the malevolent magic classes have no such law. Still, I think it more sporting that I play along for now. Not to mention it is quite amusing to see you blindly fumbling in the dark of your own ignorance. That is for at least another month. Until then be satisfied with this; I am the one," at this last, the man gave a small sneer, "who is going to kill you."

Cael took another step back, his eyes widening.

"Oh don't worry I can't actually do the deed now. I have yet to figure out how to get around that annoying protection of yours," the man's eyes narrowed. "I shall eventually though so don't get too comfortable."

"Why would you want to kill me?" Cael's casual tone did not match his racing heart or unsettled stomach.

"Again your law prevents me from answering you. Though don't misunderstand, I believe that comprehension is... vital; especially before death. When next we meet face to face there will be no question as to why you cannot live. You're a threat to me, and I do not enjoy being threatened. Goodbye." The man paused and summoned a ball of fire in his hand, "though, that does not mean you are completely safe from harm." He then flung the ball of fire right at Cael.

Before Cael could entirely avoid it, the blazing sphere caught him in his left arm. The flames burned away flesh and bone, leaving nothing but a cauterized shoulder. The man turned and strolled down the street, but Cael didn't notice. He lost touch with everything in the world except for the seemingly insurmountable pain that laced through his entire body. He wasn't sure how many seconds or minutes or hours slipped away from him as he sat slumped in that alleyway surrounded by discarded wooden pallets and plastic bags of garbage.

Finally, Cael picked himself off the ground and continued his journey home. As he walked Cael noticed that his sense of balance had not changed, he walked as though he still had two arms. Once, he thought he felt the fingers of his left hand brush up against the coarse fabric of his jeans. The absurdity of the whole situation threatened to overwhelm him.

He had never seen the man who had attacked him before. Cael didn't have the faintest idea why some random stranger would feel so threatened by his mere existence that they would be driven to such extreme intimidation tactics. The only possible connection Cael could see, as he hurried through the ever-darkening streets of Charnley IL, is that Dorothy was training him in both combat and use of his magic. Cael shook his head, perplexed; the stranger clearly had magical abilities of his own so the mere fact that Cael was an alchemist could not be the only cause for the stranger's consternation.

At last Cael reached the wrought iron gates of the fencing that enclosed the property of the orphanage. Cael pulled on one of the gate doors, but it refused to yield. He had been locked out, that sort of thing seemed to be the growing trend of the day.

"Expletive!" Cael barked as he kicked out at the stubborn portal. He let out a resigned sigh and went to the side of the gate where iron poles jutted out of a low stone wall. Cael jumped up on the stone wall and grabbed an intersecting crossbar with his one hand. Getting over was not an easy task, but Cael had climbed this wall about a thousand times. He wasn't going to let it beat him now. He swung his leg on top of the highest crossbar, hoisted himself up and jumped down on the other side with a dull thud.

Cael ran across the lawn, gripping his left shoulder because it seemed to lessen the pain that still laced every nerve ending in his body. The grass on the lawn was so long that it threatened to engulf his feet; he supposed before the next weekend came, Dorothy would have him drag out the lawn mower to take care of it. Cael hurried around the house towards the practice ring where Dorothy was no doubt waiting for him.

"You certainly took your time coming home Caelin Baldwin Ivywood! You're going to have to..." Dorothy's gaze found Cael's shoulder. "What happened to you?" Her face was washed with a worried expression. She came over to him an aura of purple magical energy materializing around her hands.

As Cael was explaining what had happened, Dorothy examined his arm, prodding at the flesh with her magical energy. Strangely, after her inspection, Dorothy looked slightly relieved. "Cael, try creating a replacement for your arm," she instructed, stepping back a pace.

"But Dorothy, you know that I can't create living flesh. The molecular composition is far too complex. I would expend all of my magical energy and pass out before it was anywhere near completion," Cael protested, frowning at his mother.

Dorothy looked thoughtful for a moment, "and even if you slept to replenish your energy, it would take weeks to complete it."

"More importantly, I'm nearly certain I wouldn't get it right," Cael pointed out.

"Then perhaps an elemental replacement would suit your needs," she suggested.

"Elemental?" Cael mentally ran through the periodic table. "Titanium would be light and durable, not to mention that it wouldn't rust every time I took a shower."

Dorothy nodded, "try it."

Cael summoned his energy and manipulated it into creating titanium molecules. He affixed the metal to his flesh and bones with covalent bonds that would have otherwise been scientifically impossible. He then shaped the metal in the form of his missing appendage. The titanium dully reflected the rapidly fading twilight.

After Cael had finished, Dorothy poked at the replacement limb hard. Cael jumped back, "Hey! That..." his eyes widened in surprise, "I felt that! I actually felt that! How is that possible? There aren't any nerves; there aren't even muscles."

Dorothy looked weary, "the part of your soul that is in your arm wasn't destroyed. It's because of your task which you..."

"I know I know 'I can't know anything about until I'm eighteen'" Cael finished exasperatedly.

"It's only another month, Cael. I know it's frustrating but hang in there," Dorothy encouraged.

Cael was reminded of something the man had said, "It has something to do with the man that attacked me, doesn't it? That's why you haven't asked about him. You already know who it is!"

"I've told you time and time again, Cael, I can't say," Dorothy sighed.

"It wouldn't be telling me anything, just answering a question," Cael persisted.

Dorothy gave him a look, the kind of look that clearly said not to argue with her, "you know I can't, our laws are very strict.

Though the fact that he was audacious enough to come right out and ruthlessly maim a... magic user, who hasn't been completely trained is maddening." She ran a hand through her wavy dark brown hair in an exhausted way, "come along I suppose we won't get any more training done today."

* * *

The next morning, Cael pushed open the door of the Charnley Youth Center. He was fairly early, but he was sure some of the Pack would already be there. He was not disappointed, in fact, he was the last of them to arrive, they were all standing to one side of the boxing ring that occupied the majority of the room.

Gavin watched his approach with a suspicious look on his face, "there's something different about you today."

Cael reached out with his left hand and pat one side of Gavin's face, "you're pretty observant aren't you?"

Gavin's eyes widened as realization struck, "what the vulgarity happened to you?"

"Well, I have a bit of a story to tell," Cael replied.

Max's innocent face deepened into a scowl "What happened, are you alright?" he said with a gesture toward the offending appendage.

"He's up, and moving isn't he? And he said he would explain, so why don't we let him speak before you start freaking out," Jim interjected.

"Okay, okay," Cael defensively put his hands up trying to forestall an argument, "you know how Dorothy is always dropping hints that there is some big dangerous thing that she's been training me to do?" He waited a moment for the Pack's nods of agreement before continuing, "Well I'm pretty sure that last night I met that big dangerous thing in a dark alley on my way home. It was some man, he was obviously a magic user, but I've never seen one like him before. He was sinister and, I don't know how else to say it, but he practically radiated a sense of dread.

"He stopped me, talked about how I was this huge threat to him and how he couldn't kill me yet but that he was going to find out how and then he threw a fireball at me that took my arm."

The outcry from the Wolf Pack was almost deafening.

"What! Some psycho is out there trying to kill you?" Abby exclaimed.

Cael's shrug was more than a little sheepish, "I guess I know what all that sword practice has been for at least."

Gavin's brow deepened into a scowl of concentration, "and you think you'll have to oppose this man somehow?"

"I'm sure that they are in some way connected, all that training can't be for nothing," Cael asserted.

"But what are you going to do about it?" Max asked, the earnest expression never leaving his face.

"Focus on my training even more, what else can I do?" the awkward silence that followed this proclamation was almost physically painful, no one quite knew what to say to make Cael's predicament any better.

Brock finally cleared his throat awkwardly, "well, we shall do everything we can to help you with that."

Cael grinned, "Just keep doing what you've always done, and you'll accomplish that."

And with that, the tension in the room dissipated. Gavin and Jim hopped into the ring with gloves on to spar a bit before their instructor arrived while the others found seats in the folding chairs that encircled the ring. Jim won the first round, so he stayed in place as Gavin went to where the others sat, taking Brock's seat as he jumped up for his turn to spar. They did this for nearly an hour with the victor of each round staying in to face a new challenger and only leaving when they were defeated.

Cael was a little wary of using his now metal left arm; he didn't want to hurt his friends. He mostly kept his left up by his face to deter anyone from striking his head and throwing punches with his right with a few strikes from his knees. But this became a bit predictable, and he did not stay in the ring for more than a round or two.

Time stretched on with still no instructor. The Wolf Pack was beginning to get worried until the phone on the wall rang. Abby rushed over to answer it, after a moment of listening to the person on the other end she said, "That's okay, we've been doing a bit of practice on our own. We'll catch you next week; hopefully, by then you'll feel better."

She hung up the phone and explained to the Pack's questioning faces, "that was Mike; he's got food poisoning and can't come teach us today. He was going to call earlier, but he fell asleep."

"At least that's all it is, I was beginning to fear something more serious had happened," Max responded.

They stayed and practiced a bit longer then decided to call it an early day.

"What should we do next then?" Abby asked.

"You guys could always come over to Purple House to hang out," Cael offered. Dorothy had frequently offered up her manor as something of a sanctuary for the Pack, so eventually, it became their default hang out when they weren't out patrolling the city.

With little ado, the Pack marched down to the subway and boarded a somewhat crowded train headed out of town. After a while, the train stopped at the station just a few blocks away from Purple House. As one, the Pack stood up and made their way past the gate, across the lawn, and into the manor. Like every other time the Pack came by, some of the kids ran into the foyer to greet them while one or two rocketed off to inform the orphanage director that she had company. The Pack had found seats in the living room by the time Dorothy came in to greet them.

She came up behind one couch and leaned on the back with one hand. "Hey, guys! I didn't realize you'd be coming by, but you are always welcome, of course. How has your week been?"

Max looked over at her with a shrug, "it was pretty quiet. So I would say it was pretty good, yesterday was fairly uneventful at least until the end of the day."

"Right? What with Cael getting attacked and with Kass coming after us," Brock commented.

Dorothy looked concerned, "Kass? Who's that?"

"You know that convenience store robbery a few weeks back?" Abby asked.

"You mean the armed robbery that the police were investigating?" Dorothy's eyes narrowed.

Oblivious to Dorothy's sharper tone Abby continued, "That's the one! Well, we had chased after the guy, but he had a gun so we didn't want to get too close and he got away from us. The best we could do after that was to call in the police and tell them who did it. We have had some dealings with the guy and his little brother in the past. Anyway, today his little brother came after us, but Cael stopped him pretty quick."

"You're telling me you went after an armed robber?" Dorothy demanded, incredulous.

Sensing the imminent danger Cael jumped in to do some damage control, "we were exceedingly careful, and aren't you the one who says guns are the weapon of the cowardly and unskilled?"

Dorothy pinched the bridge of her nose, "that doesn't make them any less deadly, Cael. That was horrifyingly reckless of you!"

"I'm sorry I really, really am. But you have to believe me when I tell you that we were super cautious about it, and brought the actual authorities in when we felt that we could do no more." Cael explained.

Dorothy sighed as she looked at him, "alright, fine, I'm going to have to start being able to trust your judgment sooner or later and you're going to do these things whether I like it or not, so I guess I don't have much of a choice do I?"

"But, isn't this what you're training him for?" Gavin raised an eyebrow at Dorothy "helping people?"

"That doesn't mean I have to like it," Dorothy responded flatly. "It's a fine line I walk between mentor and parent, and it hasn't been easy."

"I guess that I haven't made it easy on you," Cael conceded remorsefully.

"Oh honey, no. Don't think like that. I'm actually very proud of you. I'm not going to pretend that I don't fear for your safety, but you and your Pack here do so much good in the world. But I still have to say it; please be careful, particularly when they are armed," she said this last with an authoritative edge to her voice.

Cael grinned at that, "come on, mom, you raised me to be able to handle this."
Abby came forward and slung an arm companionably around Carl's shoulders, "in a small way you've raised all of us."

Dorothy laughed, "Well you know it really is like you all are my kids too."
Shortly after, Dorothy left the Pack to their own devices. The Pack, in a sudden wave of cabin fever, decided to go back outside.

"Alright, the air is fresh, the sun is shining, and there's a cool breeze, which is all well and good but what are we to do with this fine specimen of a day?" Brock asked with hands on hips to the rest of the group.

In answer, Cael bounded forward to smack Brock across the chest, "tag! You're it!" and with that, he was off dashing across the lawn and into the nearby woods.

"What are we, five?" Gavin demanded as Brock rocketed down the porch steps after Cael's cackling form, and the two disappeared into the trees.

"Evidently," Abby replied as she skipped off after them. The remaining members of the Pack shrugged almost as one and followed suit. However, only Max did so while skipping.

Cael was not surprised that he was Brock's main target. He laughed as he grabbed an overhead tree branch and swung himself onto a nearby rock; he then ran to its edge and performed a front flip off of it to land on the ground. He had to take a few hasty steps to regain his balance before continuing his escape from Brock's pursuit. Cael could hear the blood pumping in his ears, and his heart pounded in his chest and adrenaline flooded his system as he loped through the woods, dodging boulders and fallen logs.

He became so focused on his own flightpath that Cael lost track of where Brock was until the other boy dropped down in front of him from a massive pine tree and hurriedly struck him on the shoulder with a; "Tag! You're it!" and dashed away before Cael could counter.

Shifting gears from prey to predator was simple, almost natural, and Cael changed his tactic from an erratic path followed as expediently as possible to something more deliberate and methodical. He moved forward carefully, listening for the sounds of the rest of the pack. Off to his right, he heard footsteps in the fallen pine needles and leaves. Cael turned to find Gavin moving through the trees, and altered course to charge right at him.

It took Gavin a precious few seconds to realize what was happening, but as soon as he understood his predicament, he shot off like an arrow in the opposite direction. Cael chased him down with single-minded determination, vaulting over obstacles whenever it would close the gap even just a little. He overtook Gavin near the fence-line of Dorothy's estate and dashed away back towards the middle of the property before Gavin could retaliate.

The Pack stayed outside and chased each other for several more hours before dragging themselves back inside and collapsing in an exhausted heap on the couch in the living room.

They next decided on the much lower energy activity of watching a movie. Just as they had come to a consensus on exactly which film and had settled in to watch, there was a furious banging on the front door. The explosive volume reached such an extent that Dorothy came down the hall with a look of alarm on her features.

When Dorothy cautiously opened the door, a massive figure burst into the room, nearly knocking her over, "Damn it, boy! You were supposed to be home hours ago!" Alan Crawford roared, "I swear, Maxwell Crawford you are in for such an ass whooping when we get home!"

Dorothy immediately stepped protectively in between Alan and the Pack, "don't you dare think that you can come into my home and start threatening people I care about."

"He's my son," Alan growled.

"Which is not synonymous with a punching bag," Dorothy replied coolly, her eyes narrowing. She subtly shifted her posture into a fighting position.

"What I do in my own home is none of your business, woman."

"The same could be said for you, he is in my home and as such is under my protection," she spoke firmly and deliberately covering a barely contained ferocity.

Alan actually laughed right in her face, "and what 'protection' can a woman provide? There's no way you are as strong as I am!"

A sardonic grin twisted one corner of Dorothy's mouth, "try me."

The poor unwitting fool actually took her up on that offer and took a swing at her with a massive closed fist. Quick as lighting, Dorothy dodged the punch and grabbed hold of Alan's wrist as it passed harmlessly in front of her face. She then proceeded to twist his arm hard behind his back. He grunted in pain and attempted to break the hold by lunging forward.

Dorothy immediately let go, and Alan pitched forward out of control and crashed into the hardwood floor. He tried to get back up but was met with Dorothy's foot on his throat and the tip of a wickedly curved and razor sharp scimitar that appeared out of nowhere at his nose.

"Max will be staying here for the night, I will ensure that he makes it to school in the morning, and I swear if I see so much as another scratch on that boy again I will break every single bone in the hand that struck him. Is that clear?"

Given his current position, a fearful whimper was the only safe answer he could give, but that was enough for Dorothy. She let him stand and watched with no small amount of satisfaction as he scampered out the door.

She then turned to the Pack who were all staring at her in stunned silence and asked brightly, "so, sleepover anyone?"

The group did all end up staying the night and sleeping in a giant nest of blankets in the middle of the living room floor. All of them slept quite soundly with an overwhelming sense of security, knowing that Dorothy was herself sleeping just upstairs.

Chapter III:
Light through the Shadows

On the morning of April 23rd Cael walked into the kitchen and saw Dorothy leaning against a counter. She was gazing out the window above the sink and held a chipped mug of steaming coffee in both hands. The sound of Cael's approach tore her from her reverie; she looked over at him and gave him a bright smile, "Good morning and happy birthday Cael."

Cael tilted his head back and gave her a lopsided grin in return, "Thank you, and you know what this means?"

The orphanage director's smile took on an exasperated quality, "it means you're eighteen now and can learn the nature of your task."

"Exactly, so come on now, what is it?" Cael asked.

Dorothy gave him a mysterious smile over the edge of her coffee cup and then set the mug down on the counter behind her. "Follow me." without another word she moved to the kitchen door which leads outside back behind the house where the practice ring lay.

Confused, Cael wondered for a moment if she intended to start a sparring session as he hurried after her retreating form. She passed right by the weapons shed without so much as a glance, though. Cael hastened forward to catch up with his mentor, "where are we going?"

For a moment, Cael thought she wasn't going to answer him. Finally, she said, "we're going to meet a friend of mine, and it's high time I introduced you to your own."

This answer only served to confuse Cael more, so he merely focused on walking. Dorothy led him into the woods tucked in a back corner to the right of the manor. Her feet seemed to take a path Cael couldn't even see, moving confidently over rocks and fallen branches like they weren't even there. She wove around the maple, spruce and walnut trees that were densely clustered in the area as effortlessly as though she were walking down the street. A few times, Cael tripped and stumbled, but he forced himself to regain his footing and continue on quickly.

Dorothy finally slowed to a stop in the middle of a small clearing. From the opposite side of this clearing, a large hulking figure began to take shape through the trees. Cael's eyes grew wide as that figure drew closer and stepped into the open space. It was a grizzly bear, but its fur was a mottled purple with some white on its chest and snout. The bear dipped its head in acknowledgment as it came up to the pair and Dorothy reached out and wrapped her arms around its neck in an embrace.

Cael had to work hard to smother his astonishment as he looked to his mother for an explanation. She pulled away, "Cael, may I first introduce you my familiar; Althea."

"This is Althea?" Cael asked, incredulous.

Dorothy laughed, but it was the bear who replied, "Not quite what you were expecting?"

"Well, no, not rea-," Cael began. He stopped mid-sentence to stare, open-mouthed at the massive animal in front of him. After a minute he finally found his voice, "you can talk?"

Dorothy stepped forward, "allow me to explain, familiars, are the physical manifestation of a person's magical energy. They are tied to our personalities and our, strengths. They are a part of who we are."

"You're saying I have one?" Cael inquired.

In answer, Dorothy simply pointed to the area behind Cael. Cael turned around, at the edge of the clearing, just inside the circle of sunlight sat a large wolf. The sunlight shone off his polished iron gray fur. Cael immediately recognized the wolf from his dreams, the wolf that was already so much a part of him. The large canine stood up and slowly padded forward, coming to a stop in front of the stunned young man.

"Greetings, it is good to meet you face to face finally, my name is-"

"Darius," Cael finished the wolf's sentence in a hushed breath. The name came unbidden to Cael's mind. He knelt down, bringing himself to eye level with the beast. In a strange way, it was almost like looking into a mirror. It wasn't that their facial features were in any way similar but their very essences were the exact same.

The wolf gave Cael a panting laugh, "yes that is correct. I am your familiar."

Cael grinned, "So you're going to help me do whatever it is that is asked of me?"

"That's the idea," Darius replied.

"Well alright then," Cael stood and turned to Dorothy, "now all we need is to find out what that task is."

The orphanage director nodded and let out a shaky breath, "I know you're not going to like it but let me start by explaining who is giving out this task. Among the benevolent magic classes,

45

there is a guiding force; there are four Creation Temples that help to teach and govern our people. It's not really an actual government, as you know magic users find their own place in mundane society and are governed by the same laws as everyone else. The Temples simply offer support and protection, especially when dealing with the malevolent magic classes, but I'll explain those more in a little bit.

"Each of the four Creation Temples also serves their own purposes to help us function. There's Greenwood which trains and if necessary houses a standing militia of Runners, magic users who run missions for the creation temples. Sablewater facilitates the transfer of information among all magic users and monitors possible threats across the multiverse. Redearth keeps vast libraries, and the acolytes there engage in great amounts of research to help us better understand our abilities. The last; Argentcloud oversees and directs the other three and ensures that they run smoothly, they also if necessary, can teleport Runners to other planes of existence."

Dorothy paused and studied Cael and Darius's faces to make sure that they were following her lesson. "The second Temple I mentioned, Sablewater, also has another function. This temple gets its name from waters blessed with a special property that the temple master who is always a Seer can use to divine the will of his Majesty of the Highest Plane. That is where your task comes from, whenever malevolent forces rise up a champion must be chosen and trained. This happens rather regularly, unfortunately; about every generation or so, to the point where each champion is there to train the next."

Cael motioned for Dorothy to pause, "So, what you're saying is that you and I are champions chosen by the highest divine authority in the multiverse to fight evil?"

"That is exactly what I'm saying, and it will undoubtedly be hazardous," his mother replied.

Cael nodded, "so what was your task?"

Dorothy looked at Cael very seriously, "my task was to stop a coven of necromancers from resurrecting a powerful sorcerer."

Cael's eyes grew ever so slightly wider, "oh, what fun," he took in a deep breath, this was the question he had been waiting nearly all his life to ask, "So what is my task? Who do I have to stop?"

"I believe you have already met him actually," she gestured to Cael's left arm, "the man that attacked you. I am certain that it was Dartain, the demon king."

Dartain.

The very name chilled the blood in Cael's veins as he thought back to that excruciating and motiveless assault. Even a whole month after the event he still had nightmares about the attack and the sinister man who had threatened and mutilated him. Now Cael was being told that not only would he have to see this man again, but he would have to hunt him down and stop whatever malicious plan he was carrying out.

Cael swallowed hard, forcing down his panic in the process, "Alright, where do I start?"

Dorothy looked down at her watch, "school, you're going to be late if you don't leave now."

"Wait, what? You still expect me to go to school? Isn't it important to get on this right now to stop him?" Cael demanded.

"No," Dorothy shook her head, "He is unlikely to do much more damage in the time it will take you to graduate, and even though champions are awarded sizable compensation for their efforts, it's never a bad idea to have an education to help secure your future. You have three weeks until graduation I think you can wait that long."

Cael growled in frustration, "fine." He then turned to Darius, "come on let's go get ready."

"Perhaps that is not the best idea." Dorothy interrupted, "while it is not outlawed or even uncommon in this plane of existence for familiars to accompany their magic users in public. This city is not known, shall we say, for its high population of magic users, particularly those strong enough to have familiars. It may be a bit unsettling for mundane people to see a giant wolf walking around a high school. The general populous tends to get anxious when they think children might be threatened after all. In fact, a lot of familiars, including Althea here, actually make their home in the Illuminated Mists, the plane of existence between planes. They build communities consisting of familiars from magic users in each separate plane."

After a moment of thought, Cael slowly nodded. "You may have a point there it would probably just cause unwanted attention as well."

"I'll just stay in the Illuminated Mists with our group, I'm sure there is still more advice the elders can give me before we leave to complete our task," Darius offered, "I'll see you when you get back."

Cael let out an almost inaudible canine whine, "It's a shame that we have to wait to get to know each other when we've only just met." But all the same, he turned to walk back to the manor to collect his things. Dorothy walked beside him silently. He had a lot to process, and he appreciated the opportunity to think without a lot of conversation to distract him. By the time they returned to the back door Cael had broken the silence, "all in all, though, I think it is better to finally know what I'm up against rather than being kept in the dark."

Dorothy nodded in agreement, "honestly, judging by the way you've used your training to protect the streets whenever you can, I'm pretty sure you could have handled this information a long time ago. The Creation Temples' policy turned out to be quite inflexible, though. I understand that when so much is expected of someone, they want them to be able to enjoy their childhood as much as possible, but you actively sought to put your training to use in spite of your age."

"That's the whole point of it though, isn't it? Being a champion? To help people?" Cael inquired.
Dorothy laughed and wrapped her arms around him in a tight embrace, "oh my dear, the fact that that's the first thing you think of makes me even more certain that you are the right person for this task. I'm sure you'll do just fine, now get going Abby will be here any minute to pick you up."

Cael dashed back inside to grab a very tired looking backpack held together with an obscene amount of duct tape before running off to the front gate. Just as he reached the sidewalk, Abby's car came to an abrupt stop right in front of Cael. Abby drove a kind of patchwork car that she and her uncle had spent months putting together. Though, as Cael had understood it, Abby had been the one doing most the work with her uncle in a more supervisory role. Brock was sitting in the front seat, and he punched Cael companionably in the shoulder as he climbed in the back.

"Happy birthday Cael!" Abby said looking back before driving off.

Brock twisted around in his seat to look at Cael, "do you have any plans for today?"

"Dorothy wanted to have a little get together later this evening," Cael responded.

"Awesome, I was afraid I was going to have to give you your present now," he held up a small package, "but I will anyway." He lightly tossed the package into Cael's lap.

Brock twisted around to watch Cael open the brightly wrapped box as slowly as he possibly could. There wasn't a ton of paper on it, so this didn't take very long even at Cael's pace. Removing the paper revealed a mutilated fruit snack box. Cael laughed softly Brock always was very creative and meticulous about his gift wrapping, every December he would start hoarding boxes like a dragon with its treasure for Christmas. Inside the box were an mp3 player and a pair of earbuds.

"It's got eight gigs, I put a lot of the music that we've been listening to on it, and I also included some of the songs I've been working on as well," Brock explained exuberantly.

"Oh man, that's fantastic! Did you put that song you wrote last year on it, Wave Crash?" Cael asked eagerly.

"Yeah that one's on it and so is, Bloody Knuckles," Brock confirmed.

"Nice, thank you man this is great."

A short while later they pulled into the student parking lot. Before climbing out, Abby shot a look at Cael, "please don't leave that paper in my car."
Cael was already crumpling the wrapping into a dense wad, so his only response was to stick his tongue out at her.

"And you're supposed to be an adult today," Abby teased as he got out of the car

Cael followed, slinging his backpack over one shoulder as he went, "so you guys are coming tonight, right?" he asked.

Brock opened his mouth to say something, but before any sound came out, there was a sudden blur and something collided with Cael's midsection. He stumbled back a few steps but managed to keep his feet. Cael looked down to see that is was Gavin tackling him. He laughed briefly before reaching down and grabbing him by the belt and spinning around, knocking Gavin off balance. They collapsed onto the grass and Gavin maneuvered around to get Cael into a headlock. In retaliation, Cael punched at Gavin's sides repeatedly, forcing him to let go.

"Will you two knuckleheads cut it out before you get yourselves in trouble," Brock called out before Gavin could turn to strike back. Neither of them had been using anything close to their full strength, but the teachers who watched the grounds before classes started probably wouldn't care much about that.

Laughing, Gavin got to his feet and offered a hand out to help Cael to his. Cael paused and bent down to collect his bag, then they turned back towards the school and headed for the entrance.

"What I was going to say before I was so rudely interrupted," at this Brock glared at Gavin in mock anger, "is that of course I'm going to be there."

"There a party of some sorts tonight?" Gavin asked.

"Yep and if you're not there I will hate you forever," Cael responded with as straight a face as he could manage.

Gavin grinned, "Don't worry about that I'll be there."

"How about you Abby?" Cael asked, "Do I have to hate you forever?"

"Well I don't know, I was really hoping to clean my toenails tonight, and my nose needs picking. As you can tell my day is booked," Abby cast a sideways glance at Cael, a small grin on her face, "so what time should I be there?"

Cael let out a snort of laughter, "five."

"Llamas?" Max asked as he approached the group.

"Having fun out there in left field?" Abby asked with a laugh.

"No the time," Cael answered, and then tilted his head to the side, "why would I be talking about five llamas?"

In answer, Max simply shrugged, "so, what's at five?"

"A party, celebrating my continued existence on the orphanage front lawn, can you make it?" Cael explained.

"Oh," Max nodded drawing out the word, "for sure."

Abby was looking around the hall, "do any of you guys know where Jim is? I finally finished the book he lent me."

Gavin scratched the back of his neck, "Think he said something about going to make up a test he'd missed."

Abby shrugged, "I guess it can wait until lunch."

Above the heads of the Pack, a bell sounded and the throng of students around them began to move deeper into the building. The Wolf Pack followed suit, each heading off to their separate classes. Cael had history two halls down from the main entrance. He entered the classroom and immediately found his seat; this was one subject that he'd always enjoyed.

The teacher, Mr. Brown came in just as the last bell sounded. He said something, but Cael couldn't hear it over the rowdy kids in the room. "I said settle down!" It wasn't quite a shout, but he projected his voice so that it could be heard in the very back corners. He shrugged off his coat and continued speaking, "who wants to tell me where we left off yesterday?" Mr. Brown tossed the coat on the chair at his desk and rubbed his hands together with an attitude of anticipation, "anyone?"

Cael knew precisely where they had left off yesterday but that didn't mean he had any intention of answering the question. Mr. Brown continued to look around the room, "come on guys, now I know y'all are bright kids and I'm not just talking to myself up here if I were the nice men in white coats would have to take me away in a straitjacket." He pointed to a girl in the third row, "now Jasmine, save me from the funny farm, where did we leave off yesterday?"

With a giggle, Jasmine answered, "We were just starting to cover Puritan New England."

Mr. Brown clapped his hands once and pointed again to Jasmine, "there we go!" he exclaimed, "I knew I wasn't crazy! Yes, Puritan New England that's where we were. Now back then, the Puritan leaders in New England were, well let's say they were very heavy handed with the way they ran things, for example; open your books to page 287 and let me tell you about Mary Dyer.

"Mary Dyer lived in what is now Massachusetts in the 1600's. She started out puritan as anybody else but in 1637 she and her husband were banished to Rhode Island along with Anne Hutchinson at the end of the antinomian controversy. We'll cover more on that next week. Mary Dyer and her husband William later went back to England where Mary was actually born. There she met George Fox and converted to Quakerism. When they came back to the colonies, there was a new law in place outlawing Quakers in Boston.

"Neither the new law nor her banishment stopped Mary Dyer from going back to Massachusetts to preach the Quaker's nonviolent beliefs. For several years she went about doing this and became a Quaker preacher in her own right and was arrested several times for it by the Puritan regime. After a while of this going on," Mr. Brown leaned against his desk and folded his arms across his chest, "Mary and two other Quakers were imprisoned and sentenced to hang at the gallows. Despite avidly refusing to renounce her faith Mary was saved at the last minute by her husband and his upstanding reputation in Rhode Island."

"Mary wasn't satisfied with the work she'd already done though and went back to Boston to continue to oppose the anti-Quaker law in 1660. She was arrested again and once more sentenced to death by hanging. She walked toward the gallows with grace and dignity, her head held high." at this point Mr. Brown leaned forward and pushed the back of his hand against his own chin to emphasize his point, "with the noose around her neck Captain John Evered gave her one more chance to renounce her faith and save her life. She refused, saying that she had come to show them a way of peace and they only responded by killing innocent servants of God. With that, they hanged her. A man who was in the crowd that day, later told his wife, 'I saw the most beautiful woman in the world today, she hanged like a flag, and tomorrow I am going to become a Quaker.'

"The Puritans enforced all this persecution just because they didn't share the same beliefs of God. It was not even as though they worshiped different gods."

* * *

After morning classes Cael made his way to the cafeteria still thinking about Mary Dyer. He wondered if he would so willingly lay down his life if such a thing were called for. He supposed it wasn't much different from his decision to face any harm of injury it was just so much more final, of course, in only a few weeks he may very well be forced to make that choice, Cael thought with a frown.

He pushed from his mind these dark thoughts when he entered the cafeteria and his Pack came into his field of vision. It seemed as though he was the last one to make it to the table; his musings must have slowed his pace without him realizing it. Brock, Jim, Abby, Max, and Gavin were all gathered around their usual table laughing and carrying on. Cael quickened his pace as he neared the table and grabbed a chair.

"So, what's so funny?" he asked.

By way of answering, Abby asked, "did you hear about the ranger who was mauled by a bear?"

"I fail to see how that is in any way funn-"

"It was a grizzly spectacle!" Abby interrupted.

"Yes it was quite un-bear-able to look at," Brock chimed in.

"Things got kinda hairy when the police came to investigate," Max added.

"The scene even gave some reporters paws," Jim voiced.

"Alright, alright that's enough I think," Gavin put his hands up in the air defensively, ending the game before Cael could come up with a good enough pun.

"Fine, if you insist," Abby conceded. The table settled down somewhat before she spoke again, "Oh I nearly forgot," she rummaged around in her backpack for a moment before producing a small hardcover book and slid it across the table to Jim.

"What's this?" he asked picking it up, "oh I see never-mind. What did you think of it?"

"It was pretty good, I wasn't quite sure what to make of Vladimir in the beginning but now I think he's my favorite character," Abby responded.

Jim laughed, "I think that's kind of the point of Vladimir really."

Gavin turned to Brock, "well, I'm lost."

Abby shot him a look and stuck her tongue out at him, "Okay I get it shut up about the book."

Gavin shrugged, "maybe I should just read it too."

Jim offered him the small hardback, "You're certainly welcome to."

"Don't mind if I do," Gavin said taking the book and stowing it away in his bag.

Brock changed the subject by turning to Max, "hey I've meant to ask you; how do you make black when painting. I've been having a hard time of it in art."

Max quickly finished chewing before giving an answer, "it's simple really; all you have to do is mix two complementary colors together, like green and red."

"What are complementary colors?" Cael asked, tilting his head to the side.

Taken aback, Jim asked, "You don't know."

Cael shrugged, "I don't know anything about art."

Max nodded, "complementary colors appear on opposite sides of the color wheel."

Jim looked at Cael, still rather dumbfounded, "so you're telling me you've never had an art class."

"Maybe in grade school, but after that, I always just gravitated more towards science and history."

Jim shook his head in mock sadness, "you poor, poor deprived child."

"I get plenty out of life, thank you," Cael argued.

Without any apparent reason, Abby let out a high pitched squeal while looking out into the middle distance. The sound was alarming, its suddenness and pitch causing the guys around the table to stare at her in consternation. Cael turned in his seat to look at her rubbing his ear with one finger like it was hurting him.

"Son of an obscenity! What was that for?" he demanded.

Abby pointed to a girl's retreating back, "Did you see how cute her backpack is? It's a panda!"

Jim and Cael looked at each other, and simultaneously said, "Estrogen."

"Oh shut up!" Abby punched Cael hard in his right shoulder.

"Hey! Why'd you hit me and not him?" Cael snarled.

"You're closer," Abby replied simply taking a bite of her sandwich.

"Talk about a breach in the justice system," Gavin laughed, and Abby stuck her tongue out at him.

* * *

Cael ran up the lawn of the orphanage with Gavin on his heels. Abby had dropped them off then rushed home to pick up Cael's present. Gavin caught up with Cael and gave him a small shove to the side before sprinting on ahead. Not willing to let Gavin win their impromptu race, Cael charged forward and gained the lead. With a laugh, he pushed Gavin back and pelted ahead to where

Dorothy was setting up large folding tables on the front lawn in front of the manor.

Cael slowed to a stop, his feet thudding softly on the grass. Gavin, however, came barreling down on Cael, tackling him to the ground. "You don't have breaks, do you? You have to crash into something before you can even think about stopping."

"Having fun are we?" Dorothy asked, pausing in her work. "Oh sure, is there anything I can do to help Miss O'Donnell?" Gavin asked disentangling himself from Cael and getting to his feet.

"Could you help with the tablecloths? With this wind, I can't seem to keep them in place." Dorothy responded pointing to some plastic red and white checkered bundles lying, discarded in a heap, on the porch steps. "Maybe we can tape them down?"

Gavin slung his bag off his shoulder and began rummaging through it. After what seemed longer than necessary he produced a depleted roll of duct tape and smiled up at Dorothy, "we can make that happen."

Cael and Gavin got to work securing the tablecloths and setting the plates and plastic ware and Dorothy grabbed the dolly of chairs. Within fifteen minutes they had three tables set up and ready. It was at this time that all twelve of the children of the orphanage burst from the front doors, some carrying plates of food. Almost as one, they shouted, "Happy birthday Uncle Cael!"

Cael's face lit up with an expression reserved solely for the children, "What is this?" he exclaimed, "Did you guys cook me a whole feast all by yourselves?"

Tommy giggled, "No, Miss O'Donnell did most of it."

One girl, Sara pointed at Gavin, "and he brought the cake this morning."

"Oh, of course, how could I be so silly," Cael picked up a heavy tray from Ben who was standing next to Tommy and gestured toward the tables, " well don't just stand there with your arms getting tired, let's get this stuff on the tables!"

As the children relieved themselves of their tasty burdens, the rest of the Wolf Pack bounded across the lawn. They all settled down at one table or another. The Wolves all grouped around Cael. The food was delicious; Cael couldn't remember a day when he had eaten so well.

Between mouthfuls, Jim asked, "so, Gavin what did you make?"

"The cake," Gavin pointed at Jim, "that you don't get to eat yet." He looked around and saw the doubtful expressions on some of the Pack's faces, "and no, I didn't do any culinary experimentation on it. It's just a regular cake."

Max looked slightly disappointed, "not all of those came out bad; I really liked the Italian cream cake."

"That was a good one," Jim conceded.

"I'm sure this one will be just as good, Gavin is a very talented cook," Dorothy affirmed.

Gavin nodded genteelly, "thank you."

After everyone had cleaned their plates of food and sampled the now infamous cake, Dorothy shepherded the children off to bed for the sun had sunk well below the horizon. The tables were now illuminated with a circle of lawn torches. Cael sat back in his seat. He would have been content to relax and let the food settle in his stomach. Abby had other plans; she stood up, yelled, "presents!" and lobbed a small package at Cael's face.

Cael nearly tipped his chair over as he leaned back to avoid a broken nose. Getting the hint, Cael ripped open the package, though he knew what he would find. Cael was the youngest besides Abby herself and for the past year, she had constructed powerful video communicator watches for each of their birthdays. Cael smiled as he strapped it to his titanium wrist, "thanks a lot Abby; I was beginning to feel a little left out."

Abby grinned, "And I modified the design just a little bit to make them more durable and waterproof. After Brock shorted his out in that rainstorm two months ago, I figured it was a good idea." she turned to the other members of the Pack, "I can fix you guy's ones with the upgrade as well."

Almost as soon as these words left his mouth another box sailed toward him, this one fell short of threatening Cael's person, however. He hadn't seen who had thrown it but the tag tapped to the box told him it was from Max. Inside, he found a set of six well-balanced single edged throwing knives. Cael raised an inquisitive eyebrow and looked up at Max, "honestly, these are not the sort of thing I would expect from you, I must admit."

Max shrugged, "I may not particularly like fighting, but it is clearly going to be expected of you, and those will help keep you safe. The leather-wrapped handles are comfortable enough you can use them as regular knives as well as throw them." This last was said as if he were trying to change the subject.

"That means a lot to me, brother, thank you."

Gavin, in purposeful contrast to the others, stood up and carefully set his present down in front of Cael before returning to his seat.

"I know you didn't have this when we got here earlier," Cael said.

"I dropped it off before school with the cake; I didn't want to walk around all day with it in my bag."

Abby narrowed her eyes at Gavin, "then how did you get to school before us?"

"I didn't, my uncle dropped me off right as you parked," he explained.

Curious, Cael tore through the bundle before him to find exactly why Gavin wouldn't want to be caught with such a package in school. A large saw-back fixed blade knife rolled out onto the table, along with a magnesium fire-starter block, a flashlight, a compass, an emergency blanket and a small case with a mirror on the front. Upon further inspection, the case held a length of fishing line and hooks, a small sewing kit and a bundle of thick string. Cael was beginning to get the impression that his friends were worried about him and this ominous task hanging over his head. "This looks like it will come in handy, I appreciate it."

Jim, who was sitting right next to Cael lifted up something that looked quite heavy bundled up in plastic grocery bags and set it down on the table next to Cael. "Don't you just love my wrapping job?" he asked.

"Oh it's quite lovely," Cael said in as sincere a voice as he could manage. He opened up the bags, but, before he got all the way through, the weight of what was contained in the bags broke through the last few and it spilled out onto Cael's lap with the sound of raining metal. Confused, Cael held it up for a better look, "Chainmaille?"

"I suggested it, you're going to need it trust me, almost as much as you're going to need this," Dorothy had come back and was now holding out a long slender box. She came to stand by Cael and set the container down in front of him.

Cael lifted the lid of the box to reveal a gleaming hand and a half sword. The hilt of the weapon was fashioned into two howling wolf's heads, one on each side of the blade to form the hand guard. The handle has made of two tones of wood separated by a brass spacer, the majority of the wood was a rich brown and the lesser part near the round pommel was a deep red. Next to this was a pair of half gauntlets with a foot long blade extending from above each knuckle like claws.

He reached out and took hold of the sword's hilt. It fit in his grip better than anything he had held before. He lifted the blade out of the box and swung it a few times to test its balance and found it to be superb. "So where did you get these?"

"Get them?" Dorothy laughed, "I conjured them."

"You made these?" Cael looked back over the blade in awe.

"It took a while to get the hilt and the balance just right, I had to try a few times," she grinned sheepishly.

"You did a great job," Cael spoke in hushed tones as he took his seat once more, "these are amazing."
It was at this point that Darius chose to make his presence known; he bounded up to the table and jumped to put his massive front paws on Cael's lap. There were a few surprised shouts around the table. When Althea came lumbering up a few moments later, the shouts increased exponentially in volume.

"What the expletive is that thing?" Jim demanded.

"I am neither a what nor a thing, thank you. I am a who and a wolf." Darius retorted.

"And he talks," Abby exclaimed as if she should have expected the development.

"Guys! Guys! It's okay this is my familiar, Darius," Cael stood up to put himself between his familiar and his pack. "And this is Althea. She's Dorothy's familiar."

"So, when did this happen?" Gavin asked.

Althea pressed forward, "it has always been, though they just met each other today."

"And this is... normal then is it?" Abby asked, apprehensively.

"Kind of," Dorothy began, "particularly powerful magic users have so much magical energy that it can manifest physically."

"Well we always knew you were kind of a weirdo," Brock teased.

Max fixed Dorothy with a questioning stare, "so this wolf is going to help Cael with his task?"

Darius, in response, gave a very human-like nod.

"Speaking of which," Gavin began, "what is this big dangerous task that we've heard so much about since we were little kids?"

"I apparently have to stop the king of demons," Cael answered.

Dorothy shook her head, a small smile tugging at the corners of her mouth, but the subject of their discussion forced her to quickly sober. "Well he is a king of demons, and that brings me to the details of what you're going to have to do. In the lowest plane of existence, there are six demonic kingdoms. From these kingdoms spawn the darkest forms of magic and the kind of vileness that likes to influence the mundane world. Each domain exerts a measure of control on its own cluster of dimensions.

"It is essential to the balance of magic and really the entire multiverse that these kingdoms have an equal amount of power. It keeps them gridlocked and squabbling with one another enough that they are more focused on that than threatening other dimensions. This is where you come in, Cael; Dartain has been moving to take power and land from the other demon kings. He has gained several key points of territory from the other kingdoms and this must be stopped. The balance of power must be preserved among the malevolent magic classes or our side might soon be facing a siege."

Cael crossed his arms and scowled at his mother, "all this and you still want me to stay here and finish high school?"

Dorothy did not seem intimidated by Cael's scowl the slightest bit, "Dartain has been slowly moving since before you were born. Politics and warfare, especially among powerful malevolent creatures, are slowed by all kinds of in-fighting and maneuvering. The three weeks it will take for you to get your degree will not make a significant difference."

Cael huffed in irritation but he knew that this was one fight he would never win. He looked over to where the rest of his pack had been sitting silently ever since Dorothy had begun speaking. They were all looking back at him with the same wide-eyed and worried expression. Cael felt compelled to reassure them; he couldn't stand to see his brash and courageous friends in such a severe state of concern.

"Come on guys; don't look at me like that. We always knew this was going to be dangerous, but I've been training for this my entire life. It's not like our patrols are really any different."

Gavin crossed his arms over his chest and frowned up at Cael, "That's where you're wrong, we won't be there to watch your back while you're running around fighting demons."

Cael tilted his head back and gave his brother a lopsided grin, "oh no? I disagree, whenever we spar or rough-house you guys are preparing me for what's ahead. You all have my back in more ways than you will ever know."

Abby and Jim grinned at each other.

"Sparring huh?" Abby asked.

"Good idea!" Jim leaped forward and tackled Cael to the ground.

For the next few precious hours, Cael didn't worry about what was ahead of him; he only focused on those who were around him.

Chapter IV:
This is Not Farewell

Cael wove in and out of the crowd that flowed off the football field that had been used for their graduation ceremony. He had not actually bothered to attend the ceremony itself, he had gotten his diploma and that's all he cared about. He was on his way to meet the rest of the Wolves if only he could find them. The multitude of people made his search rather difficult.

Frustrated, Cael gave a short whistle and then a long howl that began high and ended a few notes lower. Off to his left, the call was returned. Cael turned in that direction and pushed forward, dodging the horde of graduates. At last, he reached the Pack, who were waiting for the crowd to disperse.

"So, did you guys have fun?" Cael asked.

"It wasn't so bad," Jim began thrusting a thumb in Gavin's direction, "we got to sit together."

"Yeah, Brock and I were close enough to talk at least," Max interjected.

"Man I'm jealous of you guys I was stuck all alone up towards the front. It was so boring," Abby complained.

"I would have been all alone too, something tells me I didn't miss much," Cael laughed.

"Still," Gavin began, "I think some measure of ceremony is nice."

"That may be true," Brock conceded then checked his watch, "though we need to get going our appointment is in fifteen minutes."

They managed to navigate the now much thinner crowd quickly and headed for the train that would take them near their destination. For the last two years, the pack had discussed the idea of all getting a tattoo to remind them of their unity no matter where life decided to take them. The entire first year had been them trying to come up with a design on which they could all agree. They had settled on a blue rampant wolf with black accents; Max had painted it soon after. Then it was just a matter of waiting until they could consent on their own. Since Abby had turned eighteen a few days ago, they figured after graduation was the perfect time.

The Tattoo parlor they had selected was one of the largest in the city. They had enough artists on staff that all six of the Wolves could get their tattoos done all at once. As they stepped through the doors, Cael was struck by just how clean everything was. The counters were sparkling stainless steel; the chairs were upholstered with black vinyl that was obviously well taken care of. Sample tattoo designs covered the walls behind glass panes. The art that surrounded the pack was quite astounding, and the artists had even impressed Max when he had presented his design when the Pack had made the appointment. Each of them had copied it flawlessly.

The pack sat down each in a black vinyl chair, and the artists got to work. "This your first tattoo?" the man asked as he laid the transfer paper out on Cael's upper right arm. He had a shaved head and tattoos all the way up to his jawline, below that Cael saw very little of the man's natural skin color.

"First and only probably," Cael responded.

The man let out a breath of laughter, "that's what I said when I got my first one."

Once he started working, the artist spared little concentration on small talk. Cael was more focused on the needle repeatedly stabbing into his flesh to really notice the lack of conversation anyway. It stung a fair bit initially, but the skin soon became numb from the relentless injections of ink. Cael tried not to tense up and settled in for the long wait for it to be over.

It was several hours later that Cael's artist shut off his machine, wiped off the last of the blood, and said, "you're all done, just let me cover it. You'll want to keep this on for an hour or so." he wrapped Cael's arm securely in cellophane.

One by one the rest of the Pack were allowed to get up from their seats. None of the Wolves had gotten their tattoo in quite the same place, Cael noticed. Abby had decided on her left shoulder blade. Gavin had gotten his on his chest right over his heart. Jim had chosen to get his over his right deltoid. Max's tattoo was now on the inside of his left forearm. And it was Brock's right calf that was now emblazoned with the proud azure rampant wolf.

As they were leaving the parlor, Jim grumbled, "I didn't think it was going to hurt that much."

"Oh yeah?" Gavin asked feigning a punch to Jim's shoulder.

Jim jumped back out of Gavin's reach, "do and I will kick your rump eight ways to Sunday!"

"Good luck with that," Gavin scoffed but made no actual attempt to attack.

Abby checked her watch; it was only about seven in the afternoon, "so, what should we do now?"

"Food," all of the boys responded at once.

She blinked in surprise, "well that answers that question."

They hopped on the train and headed off to Tony's place to ease the pangs of hunger that built up while they were confined to the chairs of the tattoo parlor. Once they arrived, they spotted a few of their now former classmates enjoying their own dinners.

Not long after the Pack settled in around a table, Tony came rushing towards them. "There they are my-a favorite high-a school graduates!" He beamed down at the group, "any-a-thing you want today, it's-a on the house, my-a graduation present to you! You kids have-a made me very proud."

Cael was a little surprised, Tony had always been friendly and they joked around now and then when he wasn't too busy, but giving away free pizzas was terribly generous. Especially with as much as the five boys ate.

Tony was still talking, Cael focused back on his words, "I will-a get you your usual order, and hey do you-a want a dessert pizza? I will bring you a dessert-a pizza!" he bustled off to the kitchen whistling to himself

Jim and Brock exchanged a disbelieving glance. Before anyone could say anything, someone plopped down in an empty seat next to Gavin, "So, pretty exciting right? We're off to the great unknown; our whole future is ahead of us. And we get to strike out on our own! I'm so stoked to get out of my parent's house." It was Kyle; he played on the football team with Gavin. "So, what are you guys' plans?"

"Well, hey Kyle how's it going?" Max asked.

Kyle looked over at him and burst out laughing, "sorry I guess I didn't say hello did I?"

"Anyway, to answer your question," Gavin began, "I'm enrolled in a culinary school upstate."

"Oh heck yeah! I remember those cookies you made for the football players' dinner this year; they were awesome!" Kyle exclaimed.

"I'm staying here I'm gonna study music theory," Brock said.

"Yeah I'm staying here too but I'll be studying studio art," Max added.

"I'm going to work full time at my uncle's mechanic shop, I've been working there part-time for a good five years now," Abby explained.

"Kinda like Abby, I've been working part-time at this jewelry company, that's owned by a friend of the family. I'll be going on as a full-time worker there." Jim piped in.

Kyle had been giving each his full attention as they had spoken, now he turned to Cael, "what about you man? Any big plans?"

Cael shifted uncomfortably in his seat for a second, "I plan to become a private investigator eventually, but there are a few things I have to do first." he added quickly, "what about you? Kyle, what's on your horizon?"

Kyle pointed at Cael earnestly, "I'm gonna play ball here and impress the talent scouts, then I'll sign with them and play professional football, be on TV and everything." He said dreamily sweeping a hand across the air in front of him.

"That's a big dream," Gavin noted.

Kyle laughed, "you gotta dream big to make it big, brother." He clapped Gavin on the shoulder, then pointed to a group of girls who had just sat down, "speaking of which; I've gotta go."

After a moment of silence, Max looked over at Cael and Gavin, "that's right you two are leaving the city." He stopped there letting the implications hang in the air.

"Oh don't worry about it, I'll be down, like, every weekend," Gavin assured, waving a hand dismissively.

Cael looked at Max reassuringly, "and I'll be back as soon and as often as I can."

Max clearly didn't know what to say so he merely nodded.

"Here we-a go!" Tony appeared at Abby's elbow carrying a tray with three steaming hot deep dish pizzas and set them one by one down on the table. "I will be-a back with the dessert pizza a little-a later!" and he was off again just as quickly as he appeared.

The Pack was silent as they turned their attention to their meal. The warm pizza was topped off with sausage that had just a hint of spiciness and rich mushrooms that echoed the flavor of the sausage and cheese. The tart sauce that oozed from between the two crusts made the process of eating rather messy, but Cael thought it was a small price to pay for the most flavorful pizza in the city.

Tony next jovially brought out the dessert pizza. It had a sugar and cinnamon icing and was made of sweetbread dough. It was the perfect end to the perfect meal. Cael sat back and waited as Max and Jim finished their meal. Max gave an apologetic smile when he realized he was one of the last to still be eating. "Sorry guys," he said around a mouthful.

Brock waved him off, "it's not like we have anywhere we need to be."

Max looked over at Jim who had just finished his last piece, "still, I don't want you to have to wait on just me." He quickly shoveled down the rest of his food.

Jim shook his head laughing, "well that's one way to do it, I suppose."

Cael shook his head, a small smile playing across his lips, "so does anybody have any ideas on what to do tonight?"

"You know," a wide grin spread across Brock's face, "My Daughter's Twelve Gauge is playing tonight at the Revolution. We could go check them out."

"That's the new band you're always talking about isn't it?" Jim asked.

"Yeah I know I said it before but they're incredibly talented," Brock said enthusiastically.

"Sounds like it could be a lot of fun," Max agreed.

"We should probably say goodbye to Tony at least before we go," Abby twisted around in her seat to look over at the kitchen door that the pizza maker had just disappeared behind.

The group stood and filed towards the front of the restaurant. It was a minute or two before Tony reappeared from the kitchen with two steaming pizzas in his hands and rushed over to the dining area.   Apparently, graduation was particularly beneficial for the food industry. Tony set the pizzas down in front of his customers there was a big smile on his face as he joked with the people sitting around the table. He patted one man on the back as he turned to leave and made his way over to where the Pack stood. "You are-a taking off huh?"

"Yeah we gotta get going," Cael said.

"Thank you again so much for dinner, Tony," Gavin added.

"Ah no-a problem guys, it was-a my pleasure," Tony enthused and waved as the Wolf Pack filed out the door.

Max shook his head, amazed, "that guy is something else isn't he?"

Brock chuckled, "without a doubt," he agreed.

The Wolves made their way back towards the subway station. Abby let out a whoop and darted down the street after giving Jim a playful shove. Jim, in response, pelted after her. Abby was faster than him on most days and as soon as she heard his sneakers pounding on the concrete, she ran full tilt down the sidewalk all the way to the station. Jim did not even come close to catching her.

The rest of the pack jogged lightly up to the subway station to see Abby casually leaning against one wall. Jim was situated in front of her stooped over with his hands on his knees. He was breathing heavily and Abby was doing absolutely nothing to hide her laughter. "Alright you win," Jim conceded.

The black and white-haired woman pat him on the back somewhat condescendingly, "that was obvious, I'm afraid." She skipped off toward their terminal to wait for the next train with the others close behind. With one last huff of breath, Jim straightened and turned to join the others in their wait.

Trains roared all around them coming and going in and out of the station. The wheels rattling along the tracks rumbled in Cael's very bones. Even over the din of the metal monsters around him, Cael heard the first signs of trouble brewing. Instantly alert, Cael scanned the area slowly until his eyes rested upon two young hoodlums flanking an elderly woman. One reached out and swiped the pillbox hat from her head and put it on his own head mockingly to the jeers and laughter of his companion.

Scowling, Cael stalked off toward the scene. The rest of the Pack was familiar with this kind of behavior and recognized when something was amiss. They cautiously followed a few steps behind Cael's approach.

"I believe the lady would like to be left alone today, gentlemen," Cael interjected as a way of announcing himself.

The one with the hat still on his head regarded Cael contemptuously, "oh yeah? And what are you? Her great protector?" he sneered.

He glanced at the woman who looked at him pleadingly with fear filled eyes. He turned his attention back to the two hoodlums. "If I have to be," he answered.

No-hat looked over to the rest of the Wolves, "you gonna get your friends to jump us then?"

Cael's eyes slowly roved over the two before him, he folded his arms across his chest and shifted his weight casually to one foot. "No," he said drawing out the word, "you don't have any weapons on you that I can see. We have a rule about that, only one of them will help me fight you if it has to come to that."

"So the question is," Gavin began, stepping forward and adopting a stance very similar to Cael's but far more threatening, "are you two going to be smart and walk away, leaving this poor woman to her business, or are we going to have to make you leave?"

The first one scoffed and took the pillbox hat from his head and tossed it carelessly at the old woman's feet. "Do you honestly think you punks scare us?" he stepped forward and puffed out his chest in an effort to make himself look more intimidating.

Cael looked over at Gavin with a small knowing smile tugging at the corners of his mouth, then turned back to Mr.-hat-thief. "If you were smart we would. We would scare the profanity out of you, but that's obviously not the case."

"Yo man, I think he just called us stupid," No-hat pointed out, also stepping forward.

In answer, Cael simply grinned and shifted his stance, spreading his feet apart and bringing his hands up. The hat thief was the first to move; he rushed forward almost heedlessly. Cael met the man head-on, blocking his wide swing and answering with a hard jab to the hoodlum's chin that knocked his head back violently. Hat-Thief's friend charged low like a bull at Gavin who dropped even lower down on one knee. As soon as they made contact, Gavin surged upward using his opponent's momentum against him. No-Hat flipped head first over Gavin's shoulder and landed hard on his back on the other side. Gavin took advantage of this development by bringing his foot down with crushing force onto the hoodlum's stomach. No-Hat curled up, his hands covering his abdomen and then proceeded to puke his guts out.

Gavin turned to give Cael a look that plainly said, "I'm done with my fight, what's taking you so long?"

That look went ignored as Cael was too busy trying to get free of the full-nelson the hat thief had locked in. With a frustrated snarl, Cael viciously stomped down on his adversary's instep and flexed his arms down as hard and fast as possible. Cael rushed forward, away from his opponent. Then mule kicked him hard in the chest. The hat thief reeled backward and slammed into a bench behind him, the same bench the woman was still sitting on. When the hat thief went down the elderly lady began beating him about the head with her purse. Cael spun around, fists raised, only to find the hat thief running away completely abandoning his friend.

Seeing this, Cael dropped his fighting stance and went over to the old woman who was dusting off her hat. "Are you okay ma'am?" he asked.

"They didn't hurt me none, thanks to you. Who knows what would have happened if you hadn't shown up," she replied.

Cael sighed, "would have been better though if our numbers alone had been enough to scare them off."

Meanwhile, Gavin nudged No-hat with his foot, "hey your friend ran off, you might want to follow him." The hoodlum struggled to get to his feet and stumbled after the hat thief with a groan of pure misery.

Cael walked back to the rest of the pack, a lollipop in his mouth. "Anybody else want a hard candy?" he asked pointing back towards the old woman. "What?" he asked Jim who was giving him a bemused look, "she wants to thank us, besides," he said pulling the lollipop out of his mouth and brandished it, "it's apple flavored."

Brock bounded forward, "that's good enough for me!"

* * *

A half hour's train ride later, the Pack stepped through the doors of the Revolution, a small CD and record store that frequently hosted live music events. The band was already well into their set with a small crowd gathered around them in the corner. Brock rushed forward to stand with the crowd.

"You think we're late?" Jim asked

"Yep," said Abby looking over at Cael, "I wonder whose fault that is."

Cael raised an eyebrow at her, "I blame the hat thief, personally."

"Me too," Max interjected.

"And maybe me, a little," Cael added.

Abby shook her head, smiling, "no, we couldn't stand there and do nothing." she wrapped an arm companionably around Cael's shoulders, "the day Cael Ivywood stands by and lets somebody suffer is the day the world comes to an end."

Cael laughed, "that bad huh? I'll keep that in mind."

The rest of the Pack turned their attention to the band. They really were quite good; Cael thought to himself, he could see why Brock liked them so much. The sound of their instruments slightly overpowered their vocals but they were clearly very skilled and very passionate about their music. Halfway through one song, Cael noticed something bright red blossom on the white part of one musician's guitar. It wasn't until they had finished the song and the man paused to wrap electrical tape around his hand that Cael realized that the musician must have cut himself. The guitarist hadn't even reacted; he had just kept playing with a busted up hand until the song was done.

Cael looked out to the crowd to see if anyone else had noticed, but the only thing he saw there were people listening to the music some even had their eyes closed, some were dancing, some were bobbing their heads along with the music.

Brock looked back at the rest of the Wolves with a playful glint in his eye. He dashed back and grabbed Max and pushed him through the crowd over to where everyone was dancing. Max did not seem too pleased with the idea and stood there looking lost while Brock danced around him and tried to goad Max into joining him. Eventually, with an exaggerated rolling of eyes, Max began to follow along with Brock's goofy dance moves.

Abby pirouetted forward to join the two boys in their frivolity. With a laugh, Cael motioned for Gavin and Jim to follow, as he too rushed through the crowd to join the dance. Gavin made an excellent impression of Max as he too rolled his eyes at Jim. They also strolled towards the dance floor, however.

Cael felt the drumbeat reverberate in his chest. And lights overhead flashed erratically as the Wolf Pack bounced and kicked from foot to foot in time with the beat. Most of them were not particularly graceful, with the possible exception of Abby, and maybe Brock, but it was pure, raw, enthusiasm and exhilaration and Cael could not have enjoyed himself more.

By the time the music ended and the band started packing up their equipment, Cael found himself exhausted and short of breath. By the look of the sweat-dampened faces of the rest of the Wolves, they felt the same. After they had let go of the initial awkwardness, The Wolf Pack had thoroughly enjoyed themselves. They danced non-stop the entire time the band was playing.

After the show, Brock got each member of the band to autograph a picture for him. While he had their attention, Brock also asked them a few questions about getting started in the music industry. Eventually, the Pack made their way out the door with everyone else and stepped out into the warm night air.

"You were right Brock, their music is outstanding," Jim conceded.

"I told you!" Brock exclaimed, "when will you guys realize that I have fantastic taste in music?"

Cael grinned, "I think we've learned our lesson in that regard."

Gavin let out a loud but contented sigh, "I don't know about you guys but I'm bushed. I'm ready to go home."

Max yawned, "yeah, I'm about asleep on my feet."

As they spoke, their feet followed the familiar path to the subway station. This late at night the station was almost silent, though the trains never stopped running even when there was no one to ride them. It was several sleepy minutes before the Wolf Pack boarded a car that then rattled its way home.

The car they sat in was empty but for them. In the quiet, Cael absently fiddled with a dial on his communicator watch. "Do you think this thing will work in another plane of existence?" Cael brandished the timepiece to clarify his question.

Abby considered a moment, "hmmm I'm afraid I have no way of testing that kind of range, we'll just have to see."

Cael looked back at the watch on his wrist, "I hope so." he found himself wanting to say more but he couldn't seem to find the words. He wanted to tell them that he wished he didn't have to go on this great mission alone. He wanted to say that he was going to miss them, but he couldn't bring himself to start. A second later the moment was gone, and Cael had missed his chance.

That next moment was filled with Brock dashing to one end of the train car and swinging back on the handrails that stretched from floor to ceiling at regular intervals next to the benches. He spun around on each rail passing from one to the next until he got back to the Pack.

"How do you still have the energy to swing around like a monkey?" Gavin demanded.

"Are you kidding? Tonight was great! I'm pumped up!" Brock laughed. He jumped up and down in place a few times and then did a somersault in the middle aisle. It was a rare day when Brock got into one of these moods that his energy was not infectious. Today was one of those days, the rest of the Pack was just too tired. Instead, the Pack's lethargy seemed to drain Brock of his energy.

When the train, at last, rolled to a stop in the Pack's neighborhood they slowly filed out into the station. They looked at each other for a long moment. As the silence stretched to an almost uncomfortable level, Cael once again struggled to find the right words. Before he'd found them he began anyway, "look guys...I... I know I'm really gonna miss you all," he started rather lamely. "But no matter what happens I refuse to let us lose contact; you guys mean way too much to me to let that happen. We call ourselves the Wolf Pack right? That's not just because we hunt like wolves it's because we are a family and that is never gonna change."

Max nodded, "we may be going off in different directions after today, but I vow here and now, that we will always be the Wolf Pack."

Abby laughed, "that's what the tattoos were for after all isn't it? To unite us."

Cael gave a quick, sharp nod, "exactly, we may part ways here tonight, but that does not change who we are." he put a fist toward the rest of the group. Gavin pressed his own fist up against it. One by one the other Wolves followed suit. They stood that way for less than a minute, but they had said what needed saying.

"I'll see you guys later," Cael said finally before turning to exit the station and began the trek back to Purple House.

The night air was quiet and still. Cael made his way down side streets and alleyways that were as familiar to him as his own name. He enjoyed it as much as he could because it was probably the last bit of familiarity he would experience for a good long while. There was where he had fought two bullies teasing a little boy, and there was where he, Jim and Gavin had gotten pretzels on their way to Purple House after school one day. And...

There.

There was where he had first encountered Dartain. He stopped for a moment staring at the spot, his heart racing. He half expected the demon king to show up again, looking for a fight. He hadn't done so well the last time they'd clashed. Cael reached up and touched his shoulder where the titanium met with his flesh in a ragged scar. He could practically feel the fire on him still. That wasn't a readily forgotten sensation.

In a very purposeful manner, Cael strode away from the scene. If he was going to complete his task successfully, he couldn't dwell on past failures. He just hoped that when the time came, and everything was on the line he could put the encounter behind him once again.

This time Dorothy had left the gates of Purple House open just a crack for him. He slipped inside and closed it as quietly as he could. His hand lingered on the handle as Cael turned back toward the manor. With a huff, he marched across the trimmed lawn and leaped up the steps to the front door. There was not even the quietest of sounds throughout the entire house. Cael carefully stepped down the hallway to the boy's dormitory.

There was a tense moment as Cael was dressing down for bed when Tommy stirred and murmured discontentedly. Cael froze, even holding in his breath until the young boy settled back into his pillow and Cael climbed into bed. He lay for a long time staring up at the ceiling with his hands tucked behind his head. Exhaustion finally caught up with him and he was able to drift off to sleep.

Chapter V:
A Single Step

Cael took a long swig from his mug of coffee and stared out of the window. He and Dorothy were sitting at the kitchen table. Dorothy had wanted him to have a good breakfast before heading off into the unknown. She had heaped bacon, eggs, muffins, bagels, and sausage all on to his plate. Cael wondered if she wasn't trying to keep him home in a food coma.

They had already gone over the basic plan of attack; Sablewater had discovered Dartain's presence in a different plane of existence. Cael would go there and gather information by scouting out his position. There were also a few more things he could learn along the way at each of the Creation Temples. It would be a good idea to stop by if he found the opportunity.

With a sigh, Cael pushed his chair back from the table and stood up. "I think I'm as ready as I'll ever be to move out."

Dorothy raised an eyebrow, "for as long as I can remember you've been chomping at the bit to get your task done, why the sudden reluctance?"

"I guess I'm just... nervous," Cael admitted.

A small knowing smile found its way slowly across Dorothy's features, "a little scared?"

"I believe the word I used was nervous, not scared. I never said scared," Cael protested.

Dorothy nodded in that same knowing way, "well, it's completely understandable to be a little nervous in light of what's ahead of you. I was terrified when I set out on my task; I don't mind admitting. But you're a naturally courageous person Cael, and courage is nothing more than fear tempered by purpose."

"Hmmm," Cael grunted noncommittally as he moved to the other end of the table where his gear had been piled up in a slightly haphazard manner. He picked up the chainmaille Jim had given him and slipped it over his head. It pinched slightly as he straightened it on his shoulders, but its snug weight had a comforting effect. Next, he grabbed the sword; that he had decided to name Howling Wolf, in its sheath that Dorothy had given him.

Dorothy's smile grew mischievous as Cael lifted it from the table, "push the blade all the way into the sheath."

Confused, Cael did as instructed and as the blade locked into place, it vanished. Well, that wasn't exactly accurate, it vanished from his sight, but he could still feel the hilt in his hand. Cael looked up at his mother his surprised question written plainly across his face.

The orphanage director laughed, "I enchanted the scabbard. When your sword is completely sheathed, it's like a circuit completing that puts a spell on your sword, masking it from detection by anyone but you. I did the same with your gauntlets, and I also added the throwing knives that Max gave you to your baldric. It will help prevent you from ever being disarmed."

Cael grinned as he strapped on the baldric and belt, followed by the loose climber's harness that held his bladed gauntlets, "very clever." Last Cael picked up his slightly dilapidated backpack that contained all the other gifts from his birthday, a blanket, rations of food, and several other supplies that might prove useful, once that was also settled on his shoulders, he faced his mother once more.

She was holding up an oval medallion on a sturdy chain, "I have one more thing for you. This medallion will enable you to easily communicate with anyone you meet on your travels, no matter what language they are speaking, just make sure it is always in contact with your skin."

"So I just speak plain English, and they will hear their language and no matter what they say I'll hear it in English? I hadn't thought about that, but without this, it would make my job very difficult wouldn't it?" he slipped the chain over his head and tucked the medallion under his chainmaille and T-shirt. "Alright, let's go meet with the animals."

They marched out the back door and headed towards the woods. The sky was clear and bright; it would have been the perfect morning to play hide and seek with the kids. Cael wondered what the weather would be like wherever it was he was going.

They entered the clearing where Althea and Darius sat waiting. The Iron furred wolf looked impatient and just a little anxious. In contrast, Althea was the picture of calm and serenity. Darius stood up and padded forward, "are we ready to get going finally?"

Cael let out a huff of air, "yeah I think we're finally ready to get on our way." he turned to his mother who was smiling at him sadly. Her eyes were bright with suppressed tears.

"I'm so proud of the man you've become, I know you're going to be great out there, but please be careful," she stepped forward to hug him. Cael did not expect the lump that formed in his throat as he moved in towards his mother's embrace. He didn't trust his voice, but he forced himself to speak.

As he'd been afraid of, his voice was thick with emotion, "I want you to know how thankful I am for you. I honestly don't know where I'd be if you hadn't taken me in. There are plenty of orphan's in the world who are nowhere near as lucky as I am. And I am the man I am only because that's how you raised me."

Dorothy squeezed him tighter before letting go. "I don't know if that is entirely true," she laughed. "I love you. Please be careful out there."

Cael nodded, "I will, I love you too Mom."

He turned back to Darius and nodded to him. He gave a wolfish grin and swiped at the air with one fore-paw. There was a sound like metal clanging together and in the area where Darius had struck there appeared a faint illumination about the size of a doorway. "After you."

"Is it some kind of portal?" Cael asked stepping forward to inspect the illuminated area.

The iron-gray wolf actually nodded, "exactly."

With one last look to Dorothy who gave an encouraging if somewhat sorrowful nod, Cael stepped forward; and was immediately assaulted by a glaring white light that seemed to come from everywhere at once. Squinting, Cael attempted to survey his surroundings. This endeavor yielded no real results, however, as there was nothing around him but the white light. He slowly turned in a circle, and there was the distinct crunch of gravel beneath his feet. When he looked down, though, he found nothing but more white light. What was this place?

The clang of metal sounded again, and Darius materialized at Cael's side. "Alright follow me!" Darius exclaimed and bounded forward.

"Follow you where?" Cael demanded.

Darius turned to look back at Cael, a confused expression on his lupine features but said nothing.

"I can't see a thing in this place," Cael clarified.

"You mean to tell me Dorothy never taught you how to magically sense your surroundings?"

"She may have briefly covered it. I was never quite as good at the things that weren't simply conjuring and manipulating molecules." Cael ran a hand through his short brown hair and let a quick puff of air.

Darius sat down to briefly scratch behind one ear with his back paw. He seemed to consider a moment, "how do I put this into words? What you have to do is…"

"I know what to do," Cael interrupted, "I'm just not good at it."

If wolves could scowl, that's exactly what Darius would be doing, "I'm going to have to carry you aren't I?"

"Well maybe I can figure it out," Cael focused his energies and tried to internalize them but it just kind of seemed to fizzle out before he could.

Darius had his head tilted to one side as he was regarding the spectacle the wolf had an incredulous expression on his face. "It's your energy! How can you just lose it like that?"

"I don't know," Cael snarled.

"You would think that it would be second nature to you it's no different a process that you employ to be able to move that arm of yours," Darius actually rolled his eyes as he spoke.

"Wait really? I didn't even realize I was doing that," Cael raised his hand to his face and stared at it for a moment he could almost feel the barest hint of the magical energy around it. "I think I understand better now but Darius we're losing time I don't think I can get this fast enough."

The iron-gray wolf let out a huff of breath, "alright climb on." He crouched down in order to let Cael more easily clamber onto his back. Cael worried that he was going to be too big for his familiar to bear. That fear was quickly assuaged as Darius suddenly grew to the size of a horse. The wolf glimpsed back to see Cael's stunned continence and let out a bark of laughter, "don't look so surprised," Darius mirthfully began, "I'm pure magical energy. I don't actually have a true corporeal form; my size and even my shape are only what they are because you identify with them." As Darius spoke, he had begun running at a mile-eating pace off in what seemed to Cael like a random direction.

While they were traveling Cael tried to grasp some of the raw magical energy within him and extend it out to sense the landscape around him. He caught "glimpses" of a bolder here and a tree there, but he could never seem to get a clear picture. He was sure some of this had to do with their somewhat quick pace, but Cael couldn't fool himself into believing that was the only thing stopping him.

It was all too soon that Darius slowed to a stop and shrank to a standard wolf size. Taking the hint, Cael swung his leg over the wolf's head to dismount. He shook as if to get water off his fur and opened another portal with the increasingly familiar sound of metal clashing. On this side looking at the portal, it seemed almost as if Cael were looking at pure shadow.

He took a breath and stepped through. It took a moment for his eyes to adjust but after while he was able to see again. On the other side, he found himself in a forest, right next to a dirt road. Darius appeared once more next to him with the clang of metal.

"Alright, we're here, what's next?" Cael asked.

Darius laughed, "I know the Illuminated Mists like the back of my paw, but the other plains of existence? Not so much."

"Is that what that place is called?" Cael asked, pointing a thumb in the direction they had come.

Darius nodded, "it is the plain between plains. I'm certain Dorothy told you that already."

"Sorry, I've had a lot of information to process over the last month. Anyway, is this the general area that Sablewater indicated? Maybe we can find a town nearby and see if anyone has seen something that might lead us to Dartain," Cael started picking through the underbrush to the road.

"What are you going to do if Dartain catches us?" Darius asked as the made their way down the path.

"Last time he caught me by surprise when he attacked me, this time..." Cael's brow furrowed and his voice took on a savage edge to it, "I'm ready for him."

It wasn't long before they crossed a sign-post that had Crossroads written on it. Crossroads, as it became apparent after a few more minutes of walking, was not just a fork in the dirt road beneath their feet but rather a whole village of thatch-roofed cottages. In the center of town, there was a bronze statue that depicted a minotaur smiling up at the small child on his shoulders who appeared to be placing a horned helmet on his already horned head. At the base of the statue was a plaque that read; Counselor Ferdinand the All Brother and Mido the brave halfling youth.

Cael turned to his companion, "so this is a real person? Minotaurs really exist?"

Darius tilted his head to one side, "this bewilderment coming from the alchemist who just came here from another plane of existence?"

"You may have a point."

From somewhere off to Cael's right there suddenly came an angry scream. Cael was off like a bullet in that direction with Darius struggling to keep up. The noise led Cael down one of the central roads to the edge of town. The commotion turned out to be a brunette woman. She had an ash wood bow; the string pulled tight up to her cheek. Her target was one of a pair of hobgoblins who were waving their swords menacingly and quickly closing the gap between them and the archer.

"Why don't we even these odds?" Cael snarled. He leaped forward between the hobgoblins and the woman while drawing Howling Wolf. One hobgoblin turned to the other and gestured toward the woman, then to himself and finally to Cael. The second hobgoblin rushed the archer while the first advanced slowly on Cael.

Cael smirked and tightened his grip on the hilt of his sword. The hobgoblin came within striking range and swung his sword at Cael. It was simple enough to dodge the blow and counter with one of his own. The hobgoblin blocked with the flat of his blade and tried to push Cael's sword down and stab at the alchemist's midsection but he was stronger than the hobgoblin anticipated. Not only did Cael manage to keep Howling Wolf trained on the foul creature but he was able to knock its crude weapon aside and strike down on the hobgoblin's shoulder. Cael's sword bit deep into the creature's hairy brown flesh and it yowled in agony.

The brunette archer seemed to be faring just as well. She was jogging backward out of her opponent's reach while rapidly firing at him from her bow. The dexterity with which she accomplished this left Cael quite impressed. It was not long before the second hobgoblin fell to the ground, its body bristling with arrows.

While Cael was momentarily distracted, the first hobgoblin pressed his advantage. He quickly advanced on Cael causing him to stumble backward. As he landed hard on his back, Cael heard a snarl from Darius behind him and the wolf rushing forward. The hobgoblin was barreling down on him far too quickly, however. The only thing for Cael to do was to bring his blade up into the creature's chest as it came down on him. The hobgoblin only widened its eyes slightly in surprise before it slumped forward, motionless.

Cael shakily got to his feet after rolling the hobgoblin off of him. He stared down at Howling Wolf and the hand that gripped its hilt. Both were covered in blood as red as any human's. He had never killed anything intelligent before. Dorothy had taken him hunting for deer once when he was fourteen, and they had each brought home a buck, but that had done nothing to prepare Cael for the sick feeling that now assaulted his gut.

"Are you okay? You look like you're about to lose your breakfast," the archer had come over to lay a hand on Cael's shoulder.

Cael didn't trust himself to be able to open his mouth, but luckily Darius took it upon himself to answer, "He's never slain anything until now."

The woman's eyebrows shot up in surprise, "you certainly were in a hurry to join that fight for someone who's never spilled blood before. Come to think of it, how have you managed to survive this long without having to spill a little blood? You got to be what? Sixteen?"

Cael took a great gulp of air before managing, "eighteen, and I'm not from around here."

The brown-haired woman regarded him for a long moment before finally saying, "huh, must be a nicer place than this."

Before Cael could respond, something came crashing through the trees to their right. Cael straightened and readied his blade, but the woman pushed down on his arm, forcing him to lower the weapon. A massive brown furred minotaur burst into view. He was holding a short sword in each hand. He was wearing a brown leather chest piece with thick straps over his shoulders and dark gray leather shorts that looked like they might have been pants at one time. On his head in addition to the curved horns that protruded from the sides of his head was a horned skull cap. "Mavis! I heard you cry out! Where's the danger?"

"Ferdinand, you're a little late to the party, wolf boy here beat you to it," the archer, Mavis, replied.

"Wolf boy?" Ferdinand turned to Cael, "you okay there, kid?"

Cael fought for composure, it took him a minute, but he finally managed to force down his nausea. "I uh... I think I'll be alright."

The tall minotaur eyed him briefly then reached into a pouch at his belt and withdrew a cloth that he tossed to Cael. "Wipe off your hands and your blade; I'm sure that will help. Then we'll go down to the Golden Hound, and we can talk it over."

Cael gratefully began cleaning up. He started with his hands then methodically wiped down his sword. The somewhat grizzly task brought back some of his nausea, but it also went a long way to making him feel much better about the situation.

Once he had finished, Cael and Darius followed Ferdinand and Mavis back into town. The minotaur wove through the crowd with ease, and here and there he greeted the townsfolk with a smile or a wave. It was only when they passed by the big bronze statue that Cael realized that he had seen that horned helm before.

"So you're 'Counselor Ferdinand the All Brother' then?" Cael asked as they passed under the statue's shadow.

Ferdinand rubbed the back of his neck, "heh, yeah I picked up that name along my travels. Though I really only pursued the seat on the city council so I could open up an orphanage for all the kids affected by the war with Wolfheart."

Cael grinned, "an orphanage, huh? That's important work."

"And all too often overlooked, unfortunately," Ferdinand replied.

"I don't know where I'd be if it weren't for an orphanage," Cael remarked.

The minotaur's pace slowed, "oh really? You grew up an orphan?"

Cael shrugged, "I had it better than most, the director of the house I grew up in raised me like her own son."

Ferdinand came to a building and held the door open for the rest of the group. He clapped Cael companionably on the back as he passed and laughed, "we come from a similar background you and I. My sister, Prinn, she's an elf, took me in when I was but a minitaur and gave me a home after my parents were killed by the bandits they had been hunting down."

Inside, there were tables and booths spread out through the room. There was a bar that took up much of the center. One matronly woman moved from table to table chatting with the people seated there and bringing them drinks or food. A middle-aged man stood behind the bar and served drinks as well. Cael strained to see behind the bar into the kitchen, and there he saw a younger man stirring something in a large metal cauldron that sat over the fire.

Mavis pointed off to their left, "we can sit at that table over there."

Once they had settled into their seats, the matronly woman bustled over to them, "well what can I get you and your friends, counselor?" she looked over at Darius, who was sitting on one of the chairs right at the table and raised an eyebrow. "Interesting pup you have there, can't say that I've seen one so well trained."

Cael noticed something as the woman spoke; her voice didn't seem to match up quite right with how her lips were moving. It was like Cael was watching a poorly dubbed foreign film. He supposed that was the side effect of the medallion that Dorothy had given him to translate the languages of other dimensions. In answer to the woman's comment, he replied, "Yeah, he's smarter than most."

"Only most?" Darius asked with a scowl at Cael who shot him a mischievous grin.

Ferdinand gave a snort of laughter, then turned to the barmaid, "I'll just have a tankard of ale, June, thanks."

"One for me too," Mavis added.

"Uh," Cael began suddenly uncomfortable, "I'll have some water?" he posed it as a question, not even sure it was an option. "And one for my wolf if that's possible."

June gave him a kindly smile, "sure is possible, sweetie, we got a spring out back. The water comes out fresh and clean." To the rest of the table, she said, "I'll be right back with everything." She bustled off back behind the bar to fill their orders.

"A little bit of alcohol might help your nerves," Ferdinand told Cael.

The champion shook his head, "maybe, but to partake in such beverages would betray a dear friend."

Mavis raised an eyebrow at that, "you're a strange one I'll give you that, Wolf boy."

"The name's Cael, actually."

"So Cael, how are you feeling now?" Ferdinand asked, effectively cutting off the snarky remark that Mavis had ready.

Cael let out a slow breath, "Better, though I have to admit I'm still a little shaky. I've been in plenty of fights before, but I've never taken a life."

The minotaur nodded slowly, a contemplative look in his eyes, "If it helps, the creature you killed was a part of a group of marauders that have been attacking Crossroads for the last month or so. They have been stealing supplies and killing anyone who gets in their way. Sometimes they end up killing unarmed villagers. You probably saved some lives today too."

Before Cael could respond, June came back with their drinks. She slid two great big wooden tankards with foam spilling over the rims across the table to Ferdinand and Mavis. She handed Cael a similar tankard filled with crystal clear water. Lastly, she set a soup bowl down in front of Darius also filled with water. "Anything else I can get you? I've got some of those hazelnuts you enjoy so much, counselor."

The minotaur's ears perked up in interest, "hazelnuts? Maybe I could have a few so long as you're offering."

With a chuckle, the barmaid bustled off once more back behind the bar. She returned almost immediately this time and placed in the middle of the table a wooden bowl heaped with the small brown nuts. Ferdinand eagerly reached for the dish, he cracked one shell with his strong teeth and turned his attention back to the young alchemist.

Cael was thankful for the moment to gather his thoughts, he shook his head, "I could have saved those people by simply incapacitating that hobgoblin."

Mavis snorted, "are you kidding me? If you had let that hobgoblin go it would have just come back with reinforcements endangering even more people."

Cael frowned, grinding his teeth as he thought it over.

"You can't beat yourself up over decisions you're forced to make in the heat of battle. I'm sure you didn't have time to go over the morality of what had to be done when that hobgoblin was coming after you," Ferdinand interjected.

"I didn't have much of a choice at the time, you're right. I guess I just didn't think taking a life would affect me this much," Cael admitted.

"Haven't you known you would have to eventually? Isn't that the whole point of why we're here?" Darius questioned.

"Yes," Cael grudgingly admitted.

Mavis raised an eyebrow at the two. "Explain," she demanded.

Cael shot her an annoyed look, "I'm... hunting something."

"Someone," Darius corrected.

"And you're squeamish about killing? You didn't think this through did you? What was your plan? Throw flowers at this someone until he surrendered?" Mavis ranted incredulously.

Ferdinand laid a restraining hand on the girl's shoulder. "Mavis, take it easy do you remember the first time you had to spill blood? He just needs a little time to adjust."

Cael wasn't sure he wanted to adjust, but he knew better than to say so.

Mavis on the other hand actually spat off to her side like she had a bad taste in her mouth and took a long pull from her tankard. When she finished she wiped her mouth with her arm, "you want to know how I felt the first time I spilled blood, counselor? I felt relieved. I felt elated, triumphant even when I finally took down those bastards who burned my parents alive inside their workshop!"

Ferdinand regarded her sadly, "is that what happened? You've never said before... I'm sorry you had to live through that."

Mavis waved him off, much more calmly than she had been a moment before, "it's in the past. I've come a long way since those days."

Cael shook his head to clear it and took a pull from his own tankard and tried to imagine how he would react if someone killed one of the Pack in such a horrible fashion. The mere thought was enough to set a fire in his gut. He certainly could not condemn this woman for her passionate response, and he was that much closer to understanding how to deal with this task ahead of him.

Ferdinand removed his helmet and rubbed a hand across the top of his head between his horns before returning the helmet to its place. He leaned back in his chair and regarded Cael solemnly, "so who exactly are you hunting? Maybe I can help, I can even call in a few contacts if necessary."

Cael considered for a moment. No one ever said his task had to be a secret. "I'm hunting a powerful demon."

The minotaur's jaw clenched at Cael's revelation. "Demons, I've dealt with before. Nasty monsters, they'll destroy and subjugate anything or anyone to accomplish their goals."

Cael brandished his left arm, the titanium glinting in the light from the roaring fire in the hearth on the back wall. "That, I already knew."

"Well, what are your leads to finding this demon?" Mavis inquired, her voice muffled by the tankard in front of her face.

Darius answered, "just that his energy signature was located in this area."

Ferdinand rubbed his chin, "if you need a place to stay while you search you are welcome to stay at my estate."

Mavis slammed her empty tankard down on the table, "so long as you're here, we may as well welcome you in true Golden Hound fashion! Another round June!"

* * *

Hours later Cael had the massive minotaur's arm slung over his shoulders, and was leading him through the streets of Crossroads as the bull gave him slurred and half-coherent directions to his estate. They seemed only to be going around in circles. Every instruction from the inebriated minotaur seemed to get them more lost. Cael finally found a signpost that said: Crossroads' Orphanage. Cael trudged down the road the sign indicated, dragging Ferdinand along with him as Darius followed behind.

The windows of the manor were completely dark. Cael tried the door and found it unlocked. Inside, Cael dragged his burden over to an armchair that sat beside the cold fireplace. Ferdinand attempted to walk the distance but did little more than trip over his own hooves. Once he was settled in the armchair, he pointed over to the fireplace that had a few logs ready and waiting.

"Could you... fire... thing?" Ferdinand asked and then frowned in confusion at his own words.

Cael looked at him with a bemused expression on his face, "let me see what I can do."

Darius was studying the hearth and looked to Cael as the young man crouched down in front of it. "looks like the only thing here to light it is this flint and steel."

Well, that was going to be a challenge, Cael frowned as he turned the implements over in his hands. "Yeah, that's not going to work," Cael said, setting the tools back down. He shrugged his backpack off and began rummaging around until he found the magnesium block that Gavin had given him.

His gaze drifted over to the wood basket sitting off to one side. Next to it sat a small brass tinderbox, he opened it and began shaving off little bits of magnesium above the charred material. He was careful not to move his knife too quickly; he didn't want to send sparks down until he had a good pile of shavings. It took several minutes but, soon he had an ember glowing, and he gathered some of the soft fibrous tinder from the wood basket and placed the two close together while gently blowing on them. Cael was rather proud that the kindling lit quickly. He dropped it in the recess with the wood already arranged in there and began adding twigs, then larger and more substantial fuel until he had a nice roaring fire going.

He looked up at Ferdinand who had been oddly quiet during the whole process. The minotaur was fast asleep, his chin resting on his fist. Behind the armchair at the beginning of one hallway: stood a small child. He was rubbing one eye tiredly.

"Ferdy, the door woke me up, now I can't sleep. Can I have a tumbler of water?"

Cael paused for just a split second, "uh, Ferdy fell asleep himself, kiddo, but where do you get water? I can fetch you a glass."

"The pump out back," the child answered, then his eye's fell on Darius. "Is that a real wolf?"

Cael and his familiar exchanged a quick glance, "well, yeah... kind of. Do you want to pet him?"
The boy seemed a bit shy, but nodded and shuffled forward and extended a hand. Darius dipped his head so that the boy could reach out and pat it tentatively.

"Alright, you stay here with Darius, and I'll get you that water." he moved toward the door, then paused and turned around, "and where do you keep your cups?"

The kid gave him a slightly exasperated look and pointed to a cabinet in the corner. Cael gave him a quick grin and retrieved a small clay vessel before stepping out the door. He quickly filled it with water from the pump before coming back inside to hand it to the child. Cael was rewarded with a slightly gap-toothed smile as the kid took the offered tumbler and drank it as he went back down the hallway where Cael assumed the dormitories were.

"Now what?" Darius asked.

Cael surveyed the room, while the chairs and benches in the room looked comfortable enough for sitting, sleeping was another matter entirely. There was a plush sheepskin rug spread out before the hearth that seemed much more inviting. He stretched out next to Darius on the pelt. The wolf curled up on one end, and Cael rested his head on his familiar's flank. Hopefully, Cael thought as he drifted off to sleep, they would make more progress in the morning.

Chapter VI:
In the Middle of Things

Cael awoke the next morning to the sound of thundering feet on the floorboards. For a moment he merely assumed he was still at Purple House and rolled over to go back to sleep. Surely Dorothy would be in to drag him out of bed shortly.

Instead, he breathed in deep the smell of sheepskin and Darius stretched underneath his head. He slowly sat up and surveyed his surroundings. The fire had died in the night; the hearth lay cold and full of ashes. He glanced at the armchair next to the fireplace and found Ferdinand leaned forward rubbing his temple. His hoof had knocked over the basket of knitting that sat on the floor.

The thundering on the floorboards grew increasingly louder, and the parlor erupted in a burst of noise and activity. More than a dozen children came pouring into the room followed by a woman with auburn hair, delicate features, and ears that ended in sharp points. The minotaur squeezed his eyes shut tighter and snorted out of his nostrils. He stood up abruptly and turned to face the crowd of kids.

Cael felt a moment of panic and surged to his own feet to intercept the massive bull. Cael didn't make it in time to stop him as Ferdinand rushed forward and lifted one of the children into the air. A knot clenched in Cael's gut and was about to growl a command for the minotaur to put the child down when Ferdinand laughed jovially and spun the boy around.

"Now what's with all this yelling?" Ferdinand asked, a smile still gracing his bovine features as he set the boy back down on the ground.

A little girl who had climbed to the back of the armchair answered, "Miss Prinn promised to make us griddlecakes!"

"Griddlecakes!" Ferdinand exclaimed, "Why didn't you say so? Let's go set the table!" the minotaur charged off into another room with the pack of squealing children right at his heels.
Relieved, Cael chuckled and watched them go.

"So are you another stray Ferdinand dragged in?" The question came from the elegant featured woman with pointed ears.

Cael couldn't help laughing a little bit before giving his answer, "I suppose you could say that, yes. I had nowhere else to go, and I should only be in town for a little while."

The woman nodded, "my name is Prinn by the way," she held out her hand for him to shake. "wanna help me make breakfast?"

Cael grasped the offered hand, "I'm Cael, and I'd love to help." He followed Prinn to a large room where one wall was wholly consumed by a brick oven, a cheerful fire already crackling and popping away in it.

Prinn pulled a griddle pan down from the wall where it had been hanging. The heavy cast iron cookware had feet on one side, one at each corner. She set the griddle on top of the fire to heat up and then began gathering ingredients from the larder. "Cael, could you grab some eggs from the spring house? It's out that door and to the right." She pointed to the rough cut door in the corner.

Eager to be helpful, Cael rushed forward through the door and out into the shining daylight. There was a small stone structure off to the right just where Prinn said it would be. The grass under Cael's feet was soft and springy, cushioning his steps as he jogged to the door of the spring house. The air inside was cold and damp; the structure was built over a small creek that ran from one side of the building to the other. It took a moment for Cael to find the eggs. They were in of all things a wooden crate full of ashes marked with eggs in a basket. Crate in hand, he made his way back to the kitchen at a more careful pace.

Prinn was already whipping up some batter with a wooden spoon in a large bowl when Cael made it back in the house. "Great! There are those eggs!" she brandished the bowl at him, "crack about six of them in here." The first two eggs mostly ended up all over Cael's hands but the rest made it in the bowl with minimal disaster, and Prinn smiled like she was trying not to laugh at him. She took the bowl from him when he was done and stirred the eggs into the batter.

In no time at all Prinn had transformed the batter into several heaping stacks of griddle cakes. She handed one platter to Cael to take out to the dining room. Ferdinand seemed to be leading the children in a chant of; "griddlecakes, griddlecakes!" while pounding on the table with his fork. A cheer went up as Cael placed the platter in the middle of the table. Prinn came in behind Cael and set down her own burden, before taking her seat.

Cael slid into an empty seat next to Darius that he suspected his familiar had saved for him. The platters were passed around, and everybody claimed their share of the much-anticipated breakfast food. Cael had to admit as he took his first forkful that they were worth every bit of exaltation they had heard that morning. One thing that did not change from one plane of existence to the other was the enthusiasm of children, all those around the table devoured their breakfast with youthful abandon. Cael found the familiarity rather comforting.

"So Cael, any ideas where you'll start on your hunt?" Ferdinand asked scraping the last few morsels of griddlecake from his plate.

"I'm not sure I thought I'd try asking around town to see if anyone has seen something that could lead me in the right direction," Cael answered around a mouthful.

Ferdinand nodded, "I have a few things that need to be done today but, I could ask a friend of mine to help with that if you would like."

"That would be helpful, we don't really know the area very well," Darius responded.

The large minotaur drained his tumbler and set it down soundly, "good, let's get started." They excused themselves from the table, and Cael followed the bull out the front door. "I'll introduce you to my friend Moloch; he'll be able to help you find the answers you're looking for."

"Moloch, huh? I was afraid you might have been talking about Mavis," Cael commented half-jokingly

Ferdinand chuckled, "you shouldn't be too hard on her, there's a reason she's so cynical. She's been through a lot."

They made their way through the middle of town and down a number of winding streets until they finally came to the storefront of a place that seemed to sell leather armor. The large bull man had to hunker down to squeeze through the doorway. Cael and Darius sidled through behind him. Inside, stood a man with a slight build with long hair pulled back into a ponytail much like the way Max wore his hair. The man, whom Cael assumed was Moloch carried a sword on one hip, and a hammer on the other, one hand casually rested on the pommel of the sword, and the other leaned against the counter.

Moloch smiled warmly at Ferdinand in greeting, "how are you, old friend? What brings you here?"

Ferdinand smiled in return, "Moloch! I was hoping I could ask a favor of you, my friend here, Cael, needs some information. I wondered if you could help him get it."

Moloch laughed and leaned against the counter with arms crossed, "As I recall, Ferdinand, you've always been more streetwise than I."

"Maybe, but the council has need of me this morning," Ferdinand replied.

"Ah, now it makes sense." Moloch stood away from the counter, "alright then, Cael, what are you looking for?"

Cael told him everything about his hunt for Dartain as succinctly as possible. He ended by explaining that whoever ran Sablewater had directed him to the area around crossroads. Ferdinand slipped out in the middle of his story to do whatever it was that he had to do today. By the time Cael had finished, Moloch was nodding. One hand went up to stroke the goatee on his chin thoughtfully.

"It's not a bad idea to ask around to see if anyone has seen your demon. I can take you down to the marketplace; the traveling merchants there would be our best bet." With that Moloch swept past Cael and out the door, he and Darius followed close behind. The marketplace was loud and busy. Booths and tables fought each other for the limited space on either side of the street. People filled the area in-between, crowding around each booth and competing for the attention of the vendors.

Moloch wove his way through the crowd with practiced ease and stopped before one woman selling pewter tankards and goblets.

He leaned casually against one of the wooden posts that held up the canvas canopy with his arms folded across his chest. "Hey, Tara, do you have a minute?"

The woman spared him a quick glance before turning her attention back to her customers. "Does it really look like I have a minute?" she responded wryly.

Moloch eyed the masses crowding around the booth, "you may have..." but what Tara had exactly was never voiced. A small, reptilian creature came running up and grabbed hold of Moloch's arm. The thing only came up to the man's waist. It was dressed in loose black clothing and had sheathed daggers tucked away everywhere.

"Moloch! I'm glad I found someone quickly! There's danger coming, an entire army of hobgoblins are heading this way. I didn't see who was leading them, but there must be at least a thousand of them out there!" the creature spoke quickly and insistently.

"What? Kardak are you sure? How far away are they?" Moloch demanded.

The small reptilian creature thought a moment, "about a day and a half's march away."

"Good that gives us some time to gather everyone together. I'm sure Shallahai would be able to pick up most of the old group in the Juggernaut quickly enough.

Kardak nodded a strange gleam in his eye, "it does have Gnomish afterburners."

Moloch started off back towards the town square. He paused, ever so briefly, to look back, apologetically, at Cael. "I'm sorry it looks like finding your answers is going to have to wait a little while." He then turned back to Kardak and said, "Let's find Counselor Ferdinand, he'll want to know about this immediately."

Cael was jogging to keep up with the man's long stride. Darius padded next to him with ease. "Hey don't worry about it. I can even help against this army. It sounds like you're going to need everyone you can get."

Moloch smiled at him appreciatively, "you don't have to, this really isn't your problem."

Cael shrugged, "you were willing to help me when it wasn't your problem, how can I do any less?"

They made their way back through the crowd and toward the town square where the statue of Ferdinand stood. Moloch moved passed the square and into a long rectangular building. They followed a path only he seemed to know, turning down one corridor after another until they reached a set of double doors. Moloch didn't hesitate before pushing the doors open; he strode into the room and barked, "we've got trouble! There's an army of hobgoblins marching on the town!"

Ferdinand surged to his hooves, "are you sure?"

Kardak spoke up, "yes, I was scouting on the north side, and I saw them coming."

The bull-man nodded once, "alright then, I want this city in lock-down! All warriors who are ready to fight, need to report to the town square. Moloch! Kardak! Cael! Darius! Come with me! Let's see if we can't get the Rediron Avengers back together." He began to march out of the room, through town hall and into the square.

"Do you still have your communing stone?" Kardak asked.

In answer, Ferdinand reached into the pouch at his belt and pulled out a very ordinary looking rock. "Who is available? Do we know?"

"Sheldara is still in Riverway," Moloch began, "Delsinor is probably still in the Celestial Archipelago. Nobody's heard from Korak in months."

"Okay, how about Takal? Did he return to Horndock? I suppose we can see if we can recruit the other mercenaries there as well," Ferdinand mused, spinning the stone between a thumb and forefinger.

"What about the Scion Primordia? Perky and Dalliahn would be really useful in this fight." Kardak asked.

"Certainly worth asking, who does that leave? Shield? He's got a whole Kingdom to revive; I doubt he could help, Gromin, I think is likewise preoccupied. Shallahai will be the first we contact of course." Ferdinand walked a short distance away and began speaking into the stone.

Cael was at a loss, half of what was said in the short exchange, he was sure had been translated by his medallion but it still meant nothing to him. He reached behind him and took hold of the handle in one of his bladed gauntlets, taking comfort in the secure feel of it in his hand. Moloch was right, the army that was descending on Crossroads had absolutely nothing to do with his task. Still, he certainly couldn't stand by and do nothing while these people were attacked. He would do everything he could to help defend them.

* * *

It took a whole day for Ferdinand's reinforcements to arrive. The Rediron Juggernaut, as it turned out was a giant metal airship that landed just outside of town. From it poured a slew of strange looking individuals; one was a woman with literal steam rising up from the top of her head, one was what Cael would have sworn was a dwarf with green hair and a matching braided beard. Another minotaur also stepped forth from the ship, for some reason this minotaur decided to wear his horned helmet sideways. The most ordinary of the lot was a young man just a little older than Cael himself, a bow and quiver bristling with deadly looking arrows strapped to his back. Next came a woman who would have seemed normal if it wasn't for the lithe, almost savage way she moved like she was more of an animal than a person.

The last to step from the airship was what looked like a tree given a vaguely feminine shape with an almost contemporary looking tool-belt around her waist, a baldric of pouches across her chest and a pair of goggles rested on her forehead ready for use. The entire band of misfits marched down the gangplank and stopped in front of Ferdinand. The green bearded dwarf grinned, "It's been forever, Ferdinand! Shallahai tells us you need someone to pull your tail out of the fire."

Ferdinand's own grin in answer was somewhat rueful, "something like that, Perky."

The steam headed woman spoke up then, "how long do we have before this army gets here?"
In answer, the bull-man looked to Kardak. The reptilian creature pondered a moment before he spoke, "ten hours, maybe more that should give us time to prepare."

Wasting no time, they got straight to work. Crossroads had three main streets branching out from its central square. They blockaded the two lanes on the sides and began fortifications on the front central road. Cael and Darius were put to work digging trenches fifty yards out from the first buildings and on either side of the road. Darius was particularly suited to the task. He scoured away at the ground with almost puppy-like enthusiasm. Cael had a hard time not laughing at his familiar's exuberance, for some reason he had the feeling that such levity would be out of place.

When the trench was about shoulder high a thought occurred to the young alchemist. He felt rather foolish for not realizing it earlier. Setting aside his shovel, he knelt down and placed one hand on the ground beneath him all he had to do was transform the dirt into the air for several more feet. Cael was prepared for when the earth vanished from under him, and he landed more or less gracefully on his feet. Darius had no such warning and fell flat on his stomach with a rather irritated look at Cael.

"What?" Cael asked with a grin as he scrambled up over the top of the trench, "I just assumed your legendary animal grace would save you from well such an embarrassing landing. I guess I was wrong."

In answer to his partner's teasing Darius leaped out of the trench in one smooth motion, his back legs bunching like a coiled spring before launching him into the air.

The sight that met the pair when they stopped to pay attention was a much-transformed landscape from when they had first arrived in the city. The field between the town and their trenches was swarming with warriors with varying qualities of gear. They were equipped with everything from pitchforks and blacksmith's hammers to elaborately forged armor and weapons. Several different siege engines had also been assembled, Cael counted five catapults, one trebuchet, and three ballistas.

Just on the other side of the trenches, a vicious looking tangle of thorny vines swarmed on either side of the road. As Cael understood it, they were hoping to bottle-neck their adversaries negating the number advantage that the approaching army clearly had on them. Cael just hoped it would work.

Ferdinand walked through the battlefield side by side with the steaming headed woman, "it looks like preparations are nearly complete, Sheldara. We should let the troops use what time we have left to rest and prepare themselves. Kardak went back out scouting with Takal they say we have maybe an hour left." their conversation continued, going over battle plans but by then they had moved too far for Cael to really hear them.

That hour seemed to be the longest in Cael's life. He knew one on one combat, but warfare was something completely different, or so he assumed. He kept wishing that the army would just get there already if only so it would end his nervous waiting.

When the first ranks of the hobgoblin army appeared in the distance, it took all of Cael's will to hold his position and not charge out to meet them. The advance was slow and methodical. The warriors marched out to the town of Crossroads with a tireless, mile-eating pace.

The people of Crossroads tightened up their formation, standing shoulder to shoulder as they faced down the hobgoblin hoard. The man next to Cael anxiously shuffled his feet, and he noticed nervous sweat beading on his forehead. Cael could only imagine how he looked, probably a bit like Darius who had his ears flat against his skull, and a snarl on his lips.

The invading hobgoblin forces reached their blockade soon enough. Once they did, Cael lost all sense of the broader picture. He did not see the hobgoblins trying to jump the blockade and either falling into the trenches or being impaled on the spiky thorns before them. He did not even hear the twang of the strings on the balistas as they launched bolt after bolt into the masses as fast as their siege engineers could fire. All Cael could spare attention for was his blade flashing as he blocked and slashed at enemy after enemy, and he tried to ignore the bodies that had begun to pile up.

At one point Cael found that the fighters on either side of him had been struck down, leaving gaps in the defenders' formation. Before more of Cael's compatriots could rush in to fill these gaps, Cael found himself and Darius surrounded by five angry, snarling hobgoblins. Cael quickly sheathed Howling Wolf and pulled out his claw gauntlets. Darius lunged for two hobgoblins, spring-boarding off one to pounce on the other going for its throat.

Cael whirled around, slashing across the face of one opponent and driving his claws into the gut of the one standing next to it. Lastly, he came up behind a hobgoblin that was turned toward Darius's back with its rusty sword blade poised to strike. Fearing more for his friend than what he was about to do, Cael drove the blades of his claw gauntlet into the monster's kidneys, and it went down in a heap.

Cael could not be sure how long the battle raged, after what seemed like forever and no time at all, the hobgoblins fell back, and Cael heard Ferdinand's clear, forceful bellow to press their advantage and drive the invaders out. The townsfolk of Crossroads poured out of every available pathway to hound the army as they fled.

* * *

After several days later, clean-up of the battlefield was wrapping up while scouts and guards continued to keep watch at the fringes to ensure the hobgoblins did not return. Cael and Darius stood near a line of trees guarding the townsfolk as the filled in the trenches and cleared away siege engines. So far the wooded area around the town had been quiet. The birdsong, buzzing insects, and sound of squirrels in the underbrush were even rather cheerful.

Cael found the atmosphere incongruous with his current demeanor, no matter what his eye looked upon all he saw humanoid figures falling to his blade. Darius sensed Cael's dark mood; he whined slightly breaking Cael's reverie.

He sighed, "This was very different from fist fights on the street." He wanted to say more but found he couldn't find the words, so he just turned his gaze back to the battlefield. He watched as a small child ran across the space and stopped in front of a woman who was filling in a trench with a shovel. The woman paused in her work and smiled down at the boy. The child brought a package forward from behind his back with a triumphant grin.

Inside the parcel was what looked like lunch, the pair settled down on the ground for an impromptu picnic.

In the middle of an old battlefield, a mother and son could sit and eat lunch in peace. Cael's breath caught at the sight, to see the two laughing and enjoying a meal together. He knew then, with a depth that he had never understood before that such moments were worth protecting. The hobgoblins that had attacked yesterday had known the risk they were taking, they had to have. Yet they took the risk to take everything from these people who had done nothing wrong.

If they were willing to take the lives of innocent people, then Cael could be willing to do whatever it took to defend them.

"Um... Cael! Snap out of it! I could use some help here!" Darius barked his voice near panic.

Cael whipped around with Howling Wolf in his hand instantly. What he saw was a vision almost exactly like his nightmares. A massive red furred mountain lion was grappling with Darius, and the wolf was not doing well. Cael rushed forward, his motions almost on auto-pilot, he stepped in-between the two combatants and slammed his metal arm into the mountain lion's mouth and shoved it backward. The big cat fell on its back and fought to find its feet.

Cael did not give it that chance; he drove his sword through the monster's stomach. When he pulled his blade free, instead of blood, flames erupted from the cat's wound and coated the edge of Howling Wolf. It took Cael a second to recover from the shock of seeing the fire. The red mountain lion took advantage of his distraction to claw his foot.

Darius came to Cael's rescue then. He leaped on the cat and clamped his jaws around the monster's neck to hold it in place. Cael, balancing on one foot, sliced the beast from chest to tail. The fire that spat from the wound began to eat away at the cat itself, and soon the creature was entirely consumed. Darius had quickly leaped back from the mountain lion as soon as he realized that the monster was done for.

Shocked and off balance, Cael fell hard on his butt, his arms limp in front of him, "what was that?"

Darius shook himself, "I'm not entirely certain, truth be told. That creature had Dartain's energy signature, but obviously, that was not Dartain. I think, however, that this creature was the very source of the energy signature we were chasing. Honestly, I think we're going to need more in-depth answers of how to go about accomplishing our task. I think we need to travel to this Sablewater and demand an explanation; because this doesn't make any sense."

Cael nodded and climbed to his feet. He found that his ankle was not too severely damaged and that it would bear his weight. "I think you're right. We need to know what's going on and how to make our attack. Let's finish our guard shift, then go find Ferdinand and let him know before we go; I'd hate to leave him wondering where we went after all the help he's given us."

Once Cael's relief came, they took off toward the section that Ferdinand was guarding. He greeted them with a warm smile and a wave of his hand. "Didn't you just get off guard duty? You should head over to the Golden Hound to relax."

"I actually think we should get going. We think we may have found a clue to what we were looking for, and there is another place where we can get some concrete answers," Cael replied.
The large bull man gave an understanding nod, "if you have a lead you should definitely follow it. I'll hate to see you go, though, you helped us out a lot."

"It was my pleasure, you helped me out a lot too, more than you know," Cael responded with a dismissive wave of his hand.

Ferdinand laughed, "just the same I'd like to reward you for your service to Crossroads. I noticed your bag is rather sorry looking," he gestured toward Cael's backpack that was more duct tape than canvas and pulled a small green leather belt pouch from a satchel at his side and handed it to Cael, "reach your hand into there."

The young alchemist took the offered pouch and gingerly felt inside, and his hand kept going. He had reached in up to his armpit before he found the bottom. "Wow, that's incredible!"

"It'll cut down a good deal of your bulk and weight too," Ferdinand laughed.

"Thank you, I don't know what more to say," Cael began, at a loss for words.

"Say you'll be safe on the rest of your journey," the counselor supplied.

Cael chuckled, "I was in a war this week I think safe is out the window but I promise I will be careful."

"That will certainly have to do," Ferdinand offered his hand, "take care."

"Thank you, again," Cael said taking the offered hand in his own. He then turned to Darius who had been waiting off to the side, "ready?"

"Ready," the wolf confirmed and opened a portal with the characteristic clang of metal. They both stepped through toward what Cael hoped would be a solid plan of attack.

Chapter VII:
Sablewater

The Illuminated Mists seemed, if possible, brighter than Cael remembered. "ugh, this place again," he grumbled.

"Yep!" Darius responded brightly, "and this time you are going to practice sensing your surroundings."

Cael scowled at his lupine companion, but he knew the wolf was right. He closed his eyes against the glaring light of his surroundings and tried to ignore his physical senses. He summoned up his magical energy and tried to reach out with it. There was a tree right next to him, he could feel it. Delighted, Cael reached out and touched the bark. But as soon as he did, he lost all sense of it but the feel of it under his hand. "Okay, that didn't work," he muttered to himself.

"Try again, that was good," Darius encouraged.

Cael let his hand drop and once more summoned his energy. He found the tree and tried to extend his awareness further; the ground started to slope a bit downward to his right. He couldn't seem to push it much further, but he thought he could travel with as much as he had. "Where to?"

The wolf padded off, and Cael slowly followed with unsure footing, his wounded ankle only making matters worse. The going was slow, and several times Cael had to stop and gain his bearings. By the time Darius stopped and opened a portal, Cael was exhausted. The walk itself had not been too strenuous, but mentally he was drained.

Cael stepped through the portal and was buffeted by the roaring of a massive waterfall. The behemoth water feature cascaded from the top of a cliff face fifty yards above Cael's head and another hundred yards below the ledge he now stood on to pool in a small lake. Cael was so impressed with the waterfall that he did not notice the ornate door the was nestled slightly behind it until Darius trotted up to the entrance and sat in front of it with wolfish panting laughter at his human companion's wonderment.

"Do we knock?" he tried to ask, but the cacophony of the waterfall drowned out his words. Darius seemed to understand though and put his front paws on the door as if to push it open. Cael followed suit and pressed hard on the great portal. With effort, it swung open and once closed the deafening roar of the waterfall outside was only a distant murmur.

Just as Cael was turning from the door, there was a high pitched squeal, and he found himself being tackled to the ground. With a yell, Cael pushed back at the assailant.

"Cael! Cael, calm down it's just me!" a familiar voice exclaimed from next to him.

The young alchemist looked up to see Abby laughing at him. "We're rather jumpy today," she commented.

"Abby! What are you doing here?" Cael asked with a laugh of his own.

"I finally decided it was time to get control of my abilities, so Dorothy suggested I spend the summer going to each of the creation temples and learning what they can teach me." Abby explained, "Come on there is somebody you are going to have to meet." She grabbed his arm and Cael could have sworn there was a measure of wickedness in her grin. He could only wonder what she had in mind as she dragged him down one corridor after another. They reached a staircase and Abby finally let go of Cael's arm before descending the steps. Apparently, she was now confident that Cael and Darius would, in fact, follow behind her.

They passed several people dressed in black jerkins with a blue waterfall design appliqued on the back and blue linen trousers with black leather boots. These people smiled warmly at the trio as they passed but largely they just went on about their business. Cael was beginning to feel entirely lost after the twelfth corridor they turned down. Abby finally led him to a door that was a replica of the massive one outside. When Abby knocked, they were commanded to enter.

The three of them entered the chamber, inside was a spacious vaulted ceiling and a huge bay window on the opposite wall that looked out to where the waterfall outside pooled into the lake and the jungle stretched out to the horizon. On the floor of the chamber, several large fur rugs where laid out and in the middle, there was a pedestal where a large stone basin was displayed.

Then there was the woman who stood behind the pedestal. She had her back to the group, looking out at the jungle below. Her black hair was so silky it was almost luminous. It spilled over her shoulders like the very waterfall upon which she gazed. She was wearing the same simple blue linen pants, black leather boots, and a black leather jerkin.

She turned around to greet them. Her face was lit up with a welcoming, warm smile; her full lips stretched upwards at the corners. Her sparkling ice blue eyes crinkled as well, lighting up her whole face. She looked young; she couldn't be much older than Cael himself. Her complexion was a soft, light brown. "Ah good, you have finally made your way here, my..." at this she cleared her throat, a slight blush rising in her cheeks. She recovered quickly, "you have made it here, Champion Cael." She spoke with a slight Brazilian accent.

Abby elbowed Cael in the ribs when he did not immediately respond. "Yes! We ... uh, that is Darius and I... we, um."

Darius padded forward to save him, "we have some questions for you madam, and we hope you might be able to provide us some information about our adversary."

The woman nodded her demeanor becoming serious though she never quite lost the touch of warmth to her expression. "I will be glad to help you in every way I can on your journey. First though allow me to introduce myself; I am Marina, master of the creation temple Sablewater."

"I'm Cael, but it sounds like you knew that already, and I think I already said that this was Darius, he's my familiar, which you probably already guessed cause he talks and normal wolves don't do that. Something tells me you already know Abby, she's my sister, well kind of." Cael babbled.

At this Marina let out a light chuckle, "Yes I have known of you, Cael, for quite a long time. I have tracked your progress through your training, and ... the first steps of your quest." Here it seemed to Cael as though she was going to say something else then hurried on to finish her sentence.

"You've been tracking me?" Cael asked, puzzled.

Marina's face went a dark shade of red, "I wasn't spying on you or anything. I had to ensure that you would be ready to complete the task put to you. I had to know that you could survive the fight against Dartain."

"And can he?" Darius demanded.

"I have every faith that he will be victorious," Marina answered.

Abby came up and ruffled Cael's hair, "yeah we're pretty proud of him."

The glare Cael shot his sister did not hold much malice, and it only caused her to stick her tongue out at him. Darius took the opportunity to sneak up behind her. All the wolf did was lean against her legs, but the force of his sheer mass was enough to knock her off balance. She stumbled forward and scowled at the familiar. "I feel distinctly out-numbered at the moment."

Cael shrugged, "I can't help it if I have the advantage."

Abby turned to the temple master who had been watching the exchange with a bemused expression, "come on, and back me up here Marina."

Marina's smile grew a slight mischievous hint to it, "oh do not worry; we'll have plenty of time to get them back."

Somehow, Cael did not like the sound of that.

"But for now," Marina continued, "Cael, Darius, you must be tired from your journey. Let me show you to your chamber here in the temple where you can wash and rest. Once you are better recuperated, we can go over the more detailed aspects of your task."

With a nod, Cael followed the temple master through the door, down a hallway or two, up some stairs, and down another hall. By the time the dark-haired woman stopped Cael felt very lost. "This place is massive, how do you keep it all straight?" he asked.

"I have lived in this temple my whole life; I know it as well as you know the streets of your city. In time you will learn your way around... that is if you stay with us for a while. You are welcome to stay as long or as short as you like, of course. I have many things I could teach you that would help you on your journey. Anyway, this will be your chamber for your stay however long it might be." She spoke in a rushed manner as if to cover up embarrassment.

Cael grinned, "thank you, that's very kind."

Abby bounced forward a few steps, "my chamber is right next door if you need a guide anywhere, I've been here for about a week, so I mostly know my way around."

Marina nodded, "dinner should actually be starting relatively soon, why don't you freshen up and meet me in the banquet hall in an hour? You'll find fresh clothes in the chest at the foot of the bed" with that she turned and started back down the hallway.

"Sounds good, thank you," Cael opened the door to the chamber and stepped inside. He turned to Darius who had slipped in behind him, "that was twice she mentioned cleaning up, was that a hint?" he sniffed himself, "do I stink?"

"Well to be fair, I don't think either of us has had a bath since leaving Purple House and we did fight in a war and dug trenches in the dirt," Darius responded.

"Ah, you have a point. Not exactly the best first impression was it?"

The wolf grunted noncommittally.

"Let's do something about that then shall we?" He began the rather involved process of removing his gear and armor. He set his backpack down on one of the beds; he had yet to transfer its contents to the belt pouch that Ferdinand had given him. He would get to that later. He found a clean set of clothing right where Marina said they would be, before stepping into the bathroom.

The shower was tiled with rounded river stones, and it took Cael a second to realize the stone outcropping at the top was a cleverly disguised shower head. The room was fairly spacious, Cael noted, as he stepped up to the sink. It was a simple trough of cast bronze; the spout was crafted in the likeness of a tree branch.

Closer inspection led Cael to discover that the trough was being held by more intertwining bronze branches and the mirror in front of the sink was likewise framed in artful bronze. The overall effect made it look like the sink was nestled in the branches of a great tree.

As Cael began to disrobe in front of the mirror, he noticed several bruises and scratches. He had been aching from his recent battles but it was a little shocking to see the full effect of the damage they had left, even if they were only minor wounds. Even his ankle was only slightly swollen with some light cuts; it looked more sprained than anything. Cael hoped the hot water from the shower would help to ease his aches and pains. When he stepped into the shower, though, it took him a full minute of staring at the wall before he figured out how to get the water started.

When Cael stepped back out, after he'd finished his shower, he felt refreshed and relaxed. The clothes he had been provided turned out to be the blue linen trousers and black leather jerkin that the acolytes and Marina wore. He went to show Darius who panted his laughter, "you look like you belong here."

"I kind of feel like I belong here, in all honesty," Cael replied, then he ran his hand through his short brown hair, "well, let's not keep Marina waiting."

Cael got as far as out of his door before he realized he had no idea where he was going. He was momentarily at a loss for how to proceed until he remembered the video communicator watch around his wrist. "Hey, Abby are you free?" he asked holding down a button on the side marked "talk."

Abby's voice came through the small device as her face appeared on the screen, "yeah, what's up?"

"Have you gone to dinner yet? I have no idea how to get to the banquet hall," he admitted.

"Not a problem, I'm still in my room we can walk down together," the image pulled away from his sister's face, and showed a random section of her chamber as if she had let her arm drop. Then a door to Cael's right opened up and Abby herself appeared before the screen went black altogether. Abby bounded forward, grabbed Cael's arm and dragged him off down the hallway, leaving Darius to follow behind after them.

Once they had gone down a hallway or two, Cael shook himself free. He folded his arms in mock offense and stomped off in the direction they were heading. Abby rolled her eyes and dashed forward. As she passed Cael, she smacked the back of his head and ran harder. Cael gave chase and they ran through the temple at a volume that was just this side of irreverent. They burst through the doors of the banquet hall laughing at their game.

When Cael caught sight of the temple master, he sobered immediately. He gathered up all the dignity he could muster as he strode along the length of the banquet table to take a seat at Marina's left side. Darius sat at Cael's left and Abby sat next down the line. The table was already heaped with all manner of exotic dishes Cael had never even imagined.

There was a smirk on Marina's face as she took in Cael's appearance, "As cores da Águapreto terno você, Campeão."

Cael tilted his head to one side in bewilderment, "what?"

A flash of confusion briefly passed over Marina's face, before transforming into realization. She stood up and leaned in close to the young alchemist. Cael could feel the heat of a blush rising in his cheeks at her familiar proximity. She reached out to touch something near his chest. It was his translation medallion; she lifted it up and tucked it under the lacing that fastened his jerkin. Cael remembered then what Dorothy had said about skin contact with the amulet. He could also not help but notice that her hands lingered on his chest longer than was necessary for the simple action.

"I was saying that the colors of Sablewater suit you," the temple master explained, as she resumed her seat.

Cael looked down at himself, and smoothed the jerkin over his chest, "yeah, I kinda like it. I bet with this over my chain-mail, I'd be armored pretty well."

Marina looked thoughtful, "if you are in need of it, I would be happy to help protect you; you should take the jerkin with you when you go."

Cael graciously nodded his head, "thank you, my lady."

At this last, Abby snorted into her mug but did not comment further.

Marina raised an eyebrow at Abby before gesturing at the table, "help yourselves I don't know how familiar you are with Brazilian cuisine but I am sure you will find something you like."

Abby elbowed Cael and pointed to a dish that appeared to be some kind of roasted pork, "that one is my favorite so far. And you have to try the cane broth!"

"Cane broth?" Cael asked incredulously.

"Made from sugar cane, it's tastier than it sounds," Marina said with a bemused smile. She poured a greenish yellow liquid into a ceramic tumbler from a pewter pitcher and set it in front of Cael. It turned out to be incredibly sweet and actually quite good.

As dinner progressed, Cael had sampled all number of exotic foods. Most of it was delicious though he found he had no taste for the roasted chicken hearts. He was enjoying himself so much that the young champion had nearly forgotten the question he wanted to ask the temple master and, in fact, the whole reason he had come to Sablewater in the first place. That is until Darius brought it up again.

"Marina, while we were in crossroads we came upon some kind of fire cat, or rather, it came upon us. I could tell that it carried Dartain's energy signature, but I would like to know more about it."

Marina nodded the smile on her lips at the joke Cael had just told fading into a more somber expression. "You are right; you need to be informed of the new development in Dartain's tactics. I would prefer to speak of this more privately though; perhaps we should go back to the Viewing Chamber, the room we first met in."

When they had finished the meal, they navigated back through the corridors to the Viewing Chamber. Marina crossed to the basin in the middle of the room, "you want to know what that fire cat really was. It seems Dartain has fractured his very spiritual essence and created incarnations of himself to serve him."

"His spiritual essence? You mean like his soul?" Cael asked.

"Well, demons don't have souls as such, no, but you've got the right idea. If you intend on tracking the demon king by sensing his energy signature, these incarnations will likely throw you off," the temple master strolled to the bay window and perched on the edge of the bench underneath.

"That is going to make hunting him down infinitely harder then," Darius commented.

"Yes, it does make things quite a bit more difficult doesn't it?" Marina said sympathetically.

"Do you have any suggestions on how to find him?" Cael asked, concerned.

Her brow furrowed in concentration, "for now I can keep track of him in the Sablewater," she indicated the basin in the middle of the room, "perhaps I can learn more of his plans and find him in a weak position."

Cael frowned, "that seems like a lot of work for you just to complete a task expected of me."

Marina shrugged, "it's actually not far from my usual duties to keep an eye out for threats and work with Greenwood to send out Runners to help. Though," she paused as if a thought just occurred to her, "if you were to hunt down the fire cats one by one you may be able to learn something of their master's plans."

Cael nodded, "it might not be a bad idea to do both."

Marina smiled, "my thoughts exactly. I would recommend, however, that you don't rush off immediately, I can teach you how to communicate with me mentally so that I can keep you informed of Dartain's movements as I discover them."

This surprised Cael. He had never even heard that what Marina suggested was even possible. He had eaten slept and breathed magical training for the better part of the last eighteen years, but it seemed he still had much to learn. "Wow really? That would be incredibly useful."

Marina nodded and clapped her hands together once. "Excellent, we can get to work on that tomorrow. You'll need your mind as sharp as it can be."

Cael sat down at the edge of the bench, next to the temple master. "I appreciate the reprieve, I haven't done too much today but I am exhausted." He spoke in a huff as if he could expel his tiredness from his lungs forcefully.

Marina looked out the window to the waterfall and jungle beyond, "yes, you have been through a lot in a very brief amount of time. How are you feeling?"

The question caught him off guard. He looked at the woman beside him and studied her face; he only found concern there. Cael didn't want to seem weak to her, but he somehow felt it would be okay. "Unsettled," he admitted at last. "I had to do things in Crossroads that I wasn't really prepared for. I understand now that it may be something that has to be done on occasion, but I'm still not comfortable with it."

"Killing," Marina said bluntly. He nodded his confirmation. "I think, Cael, you should only be concerned when you do become comfortable with it."

"I guess you're right, have...," Cael began, suddenly uncomfortable, "have you ever been in that position?"

"Oh my, no, I have spent most of my time in this temple, first as an acolyte and then later climbing to the ranks of temple master. I have spent my whole life studying the arts of a seer."

"Your whole life? Even when you were a kid? What did you do for fun?" Cael asked bewildered.

Marina looked a touch sad for a moment. Cael regretted pressing the point and was about to apologize when she spoke again. "Growing up, the other acolytes and I found our fun when we could but yes it was rather somber childhood. My talent as a seer was powerful even when I was young, the temple master before me who was my teacher told me that my power only meant that more was expected of me and that I should work even harder. It was a great honor when he made me his apprentice; several years ago he retired and left the post to me."

"That sounds pretty rough," Darius commented.

"I was not without consolation," here the black-haired woman's soft brown complexion grew red in an inexplicable blush, "once I became temple master I gained access to the Sablewater. It is a powerful scrying tool. With it, I have been able to see the multiverse, experience through others a hundred different things."

Cael got the feeling there was something she was not saying, "what kind of things?"

Marina cleared her throat and carefully avoided looking at Cael, "things like patrolling a big city to keep its common people safe from harm."

Whatever he had been expecting her to say, this wasn't it, "the Wolf Pack? Were you watching us? I know you said you'd kept an eye on my training but our patrols too?" He wasn't mad, just surprised; surprised that anyone would bother paying attention to him, but his reaction may have given the impression that he was upset because Marina gave him a scared look with glistening eyes.

"I'm so sorry Cael I meant no harm by it. I really did need to be certain you were ready to face Dartain. I couldn't forgive myself if you weren't ready and got hurt." the pain in her voice broke Cael's heart.

"Hey whoa, it's okay. I'm not angry it just caught me off guard, please don't cry," he was close to panic at this point.

She didn't cry but she said again, "I am sorry, and you should know that when I did have to check on you, it was the highlight of my day it was like I was part of the group, like I had friends outside of the temple."

Cael gave a small laugh, "well maybe sometime later you can come up and hang out with us in person."

"I would like that though I fear I may not be able to until my calling releases me," in response to Cael's confused look she clarified, "my talent, my ability as a seer has called me to this position, this duty. I will serve until I am released."

Bewildered, Cael asked, "and you chose this life?"

Marina laughed, "I promise you it's not as bad as it sounds. It is a simple, quiet life, and I get to help so many people." She glanced outside at the moon hanging high in the sky, "It is getting late I suggest we both retire to our chambers for the night."

Cael checked his watch and realized she was right, at some point during their conversation Darius had curled up and gone to sleep. He nudged the wolf awake and they marched out of the room. Marina walked him to his room and they shared a companionable silence. When she took her leave at his door, he was rather sad to see her go.

He strolled into his chamber and took a seat in the armchair in the corner. Darius jumped up on one of the beds and went straight back to sleep. Cael, in contrast, picked up a book from the shelf next to his chair and cracked it open. The words on the pages were pure gibberish to him. He guessed the translation medallion did not work on text. With a sigh, he snapped the book shut and set it back down on the shelf.

He wasn't quite ready to surrender to sleep just yet, however, so he slipped out of his room and quietly shut the door. He then skipped over to the next door and burst through it much to the surprise of its tenant.

Abby looked up from the notebook she'd been scrawling in with consternation, "what the vulgarity happened to knocking?"

"Come on, tell me you're not happy to see me," Cael prodded bouncing down on the edge of the bed. He gestured to the notebook, "they giving you homework?"

"What, this? No, I'm brainstorming ideas on how to extend the range of the video communicator watches. I tried several times to reach you this last week but it just wouldn't work. Not much point to it with you running around all across the multiverse if the signal can't reach you."

"That does present a problem doesn't it?" Cael agreed. "Marina just mentioned mentally communicating across planes of existence; I wonder if there is a way to use magical energy to carry the signal."

"Say, now there's an idea. Though, I can't even begin to think of how to contain that kind of energy. I bet I could find a way at Redearth; I'm told they have extensive libraries there I'm sure that magically infusing an artifact has been done before." Abby spoke with such unconstrained enthusiasm that all Cael could do was grin in response. She became lost in a flurry of ideas, writing in her notebook a mile a minute.

With a chuckle, Cael left her to it and returned to his room. He found slumber a distant hope that he could not seem to achieve.

126

When sleep did finally claim him, his dreams took the form of shining black hair and a warm, smiling face.

* * *

Cael followed Darius down the corridor to the banquet hall, half asleep. It had been late the previous night that he had finally gotten to sleep. In the morning Darius had leaped from his bed to pounce on Cael's chest. It had made for a rather rude awakening and Cael was still rather grumpy about it.

The banquet hall was still slowly filling up when they arrived, though, the tables were already populated with platters of fruits and cheeses and warm, fragrant bread that had clearly come fresh from the ovens. Marina was already sitting down at her usual place at the head of the table.

Cael found his grumpy mood had mysteriously disappeared and he approached the temple master with a warm smile. "Good morning my lady, did you sleep well?"

"I'm afraid I had a bit of difficulty getting to sleep. I'm a bit groggy this morning. It is good that we have such strong coffee here at the temple," Marina answered.

Feeling his own latent lethargy, Cael let out a sigh of relief, "you have coffee here? Oh, thank goodness I could really use a cup."

Marina chuckled a bit at his enthusiasm and began to pour him a cup while refilling her own, "Coffee is one of, if not the biggest export of Brazil. We drink it quite regularly." She handed him a small mug as he took his seat. "Here is your little coffee."

Cael gratefully accepted the mug and took a drink. He was rather unprepared for the sheer intensity of the flavor. He choked down the first sip and had to recover from a short coughing fit. "I was not expecting it to be quite that potent," he confessed in a strained voice.

Marina regarded him with a bemused expression, "I do believe I did say it was strong."

"Apparently American strong is not the same as Brazilian strong," Cael noted and took another sip. This one did not send him into a fit of coughing but it did not go down easy either, "that's going to take some getting used to."

"Nothing like your morning brew at home I take it?" Marina probed teasingly.

"That is an understatement," Cael laughed. "Back home Dorothy and I would sit down to a morning cup; it was a long, quiet, contemplative sort of thing. She would always take hers with like a pound of sugar and milk. I don't know how she could stand to drink it with all that stuff in it."

"That sounds nice," Marina commented.

"Yeah it was, didn't realize how much I miss those moment's until now," Cael frowned.

Before the conversation could turn down that somber road, Abby came bounding up, "good morning!" she exclaimed. She paused at seeing Cael's serious face and Marina's concerned one, "what's with the long faces?"

"I think Cael is feeling a little homesick," Marina answered.

"Really? It's only been a week how can he possibly feel homesick," Abby questioned.

Marina shrugged, "sometimes the slightest hint of the familiar in a strange place can make one yearn for the comforts of home."

Cael looked back and forth between the two during the exchange, "does no one see me sitting here suddenly?" he turned to Darius, "Did I become invisible?"

Marina colored upon hearing this, "I'm sorry I did not mean to exclude you."

Darius panted his laughter, "felt compelled to defend him eh?"

At this Marina had no answer, her coloring only became a faint shade of red; Cael felt an unusual pang in his chest at the sight. Before he could contemplate the implications of his reaction, or hers, he reached across the table to claim a piece of bread, a slice of cheese, and an orange. He began eating rather more enthusiastically than he normally would have.

Abby snickered and gathered her own breakfast before taking her seat. While she was chewing on a banana, she looked down the table, "not eating Marina?"

"Oh I finished my meal a little while ago, but I'm enjoying sitting here with you. I'm reluctant to leave for the Viewing Chamber, besides I do need to teach Cael mental communication, so there's no need to leave without him." She took another sip from her coffee cup and sat back in her chair.

They finished the rest of their meal in relative silence. Cael was suddenly very eager to have a course of action to follow. He wolfed down his bread and cheese. He nearly choked on the juices from the orange he'd grabbed from the speed that he tried to consume it. Abby snorted into her drink at his plight but Marina, concern awash on her features, rubbed his back until the coughing stopped.

The close proximity with the blue-eyed, dark-haired woman caused Cael to nervously jump up from his seat. "H...hey! I'm fine, really. We should get going shouldn't we?"

He hurried down the hall toward the exit. Marina stared after him, for a moment of stunned confusion, before following behind him. Abby and Darius looked at one another, Abby was the first to crack a smile and the wolf let out a snort of laughter. The chortles from the two followed Cael and Marina out the door. Abby seemed to find it infinitely amusing to see them dance around each other so delicately.

Cael did not speak until they had reached their destination, he could not seem to find the words for what he wanted to say, so he stopped trying. "So, how does one go about communicating mentally?" he asked with the briskness of one seeking to change the subject.

A voice spoke from the back of the room near the bay window, "it is quite simple once you make a connection with the person you're trying to reach." A light blue otter jumped down from one of the window's benches.

"Very true, it's really not that much different from talking," Marina said with a smile, "Cael, allow me to introduce my familiar, Lyris, the water otter."

"A pleasure to meet you," Cael said with a slight bow, "shall we get started?"

Marina nodded and assumed the air of a teacher and gestured to the fur rug adorning the stone floor, where she herself took a seat. Cael took a deep breath; he sought to quiet his spirit. He attempted to prepare himself for a different kind of training, a type he found rather difficult. He took his seat in front of the Temple Master and looked at her expectantly.

"Okay, now close your eyes and try to keep an open mind. For the first few times, I shall attempt to forge the connection between us."

Obediently Cael closed his eyes and tried to open his mind, "alright I think I'm ready."

"Can you hear me?" Marina's light accented voice came through to Cael's mind like his own thoughts.

Surprised, Cael let out a highly undignified, "whaugh!" and fell backward into the fur rug behind   him.

Marina's laughter was loud and exuberant and Cael could feel the warmth of a blush rising in his cheeks, "okay, so I wasn't expecting it to be quite like that."

The laughter died down to quiet giggles, "I'm sorry, I've never seen so big a reaction before." She let out an amused sigh, "let's try that again, shall we?"

Cael nodded and closed his eyes once more and tried to prepare himself. Now that he knew what to expect, he was at least partly sure that he would not jump again.

"*Boo!*" Marina's voice came quick and sudden.

"*Very funny,*" Cael thought back wryly, unsure if she would be able to hear him.

"*Sorry, I couldn't resist.*" the woman's reply was tinged with a hint of laughter.

"*Well, I'm glad that I'm such a great source of amusement for you,*" the comment was thought in a dry tone but the truth was that Cael was just enjoying hearing Marina laugh, the sound was almost musical.

Marina gasped and Cael could actually feel the connection drop. "That's never happened before," she commented distantly, and then in a much quieter voice, "I wonder..."

"What is it? Is everything alright?" Cael opened his eyes and leaned forward. For a moment he had the impulse to reach out to her but uncertainty stilled his hand.

"Um... yes everything is fine," she closed her eyes and touched one delicate hand to her temple as if to stem a headache blooming just beneath the surface of her skull.

Cael's brows knitted together in concern, "are you sure?"

A blush rose in Marina's cheeks, "Yes, I just, um... I need to step out for a bit." She rose to her feet in a single lithe motion and hastened across the room and out the door.

As the door clicked softly shut, Cael shared an astonished look with Lyris, "What was that all about?" He asked.

The familiar simply gave a shrug that looked terribly out of place coming from an otter.

Chapter VIII:
Language Barrier

By dinnertime Marina had still not returned, whatever had called her away had proven to be far more time consuming than Cael had imagined. He just hoped that she wasn't avoiding him. The young alchemist had waited for a considerable length of time for the temple master's return in the Viewing Chamber. After many minutes had passed, he had drawn Howling Wolf forth from its sheath and had run through several drills. Even that could not distract the champion forever, though.

Cael's slow footsteps echoed in the halls, providing steady accompaniment to his troubled heartbeat. He passed corridor after corridor on his way back to the banquet hall in the hopes that he would find the temple master taking her meal there. When he arrived he found Abby with her nose buried deep in a leather-bound book, but no one else he recognized.

The young alchemist dropped heavily into the chair next to his sister with a frustrated growl. It took Abby a moment to withdraw from her reading before she regarded Cael with questioning eyes. In answer, Cael described the exchange between Marina and himself.

"And now I can't find her or even Darius for that matter." As if summoned by his name the iron-hued wolf came padding in from a door at the back of the hall looking quite pleased with himself.

"Guess what I was doing today!" Darius exclaimed the moment he was in earshot.

Cael only raised an eyebrow in answer, but Abby spoke up, "what were you doing Darius?"

The wolf nearly pranced his way over to where they were seated, "I," he began proudly, "went out hunting in the jungle for tonight's dinner."

"Really? What did you catch?" Abby asked, impressed.

"A wild pig," Darius answered, "I figured with you both off bettering yourselves I would go and do something useful."
Abby grinned, "And you were probably no little bit hungry yourself, I don't imagine cheese and fruit are to your tastes."

Cael frowned thoughtfully, "come to think of it Darius; I don't think I have ever seen you eat at all."   Darius panted his laughter, "That would be because I don't eat. Were you not paying attention when I told you I am not exactly corporeal? My body does not need to be sustained with food."

"I guess that makes sense. When you were out, did you happen to see Marina?" Cael asked.

"Was she not with you?" the iron-hued wolf tilted his head inquiringly.

For a second time, Cael told the story of those morning's events, not bothering to hide his worry at the temple master's strange behavior.

Dinner was brought to the table then, and the acolytes of Sablewater did not wait upon their master's arrival to partake in the feast. Darius's wild pig came out roasted and spiced. Throughout the whole meal, Marina still did not appear. Cael found himself bolting down the food put before him. A plan was forming in his head. As soon as he was finished, he jumped up to carry it out.

Alarmed Cael's companions moved to follow him, but he waved them back to their own plates. He then rushed out of the banquet hall. Once outside that great chamber with all its noise, Cael closed his eyes, opened his mind and tried to reach out to Marina mentally. To his surprise, he found her almost immediately out on the cliff above the entrance to the temple. When he tried to hear her thoughts, all he got was a confused impression of sadness and hope.

Cael hastened toward the giant heavy doors at the temple's entrance. With an effort, he shouldered them open and on the other side pushed them closed again. There was a path to his left that led to the cliff above. It was a steeper climb than he would have liked to tackle right after wolfing down so much food so quickly but he managed to make the ascent.

At the top Marina stood, looking out at the lake formed by the massive waterfall. She seemed to be saying something over the ambient roar. Cael moved in closer to better hear her. To his surprise and mild bemusement, he discovered she was singing;
I have seen his face
A hundred times or more
For years I've longed for his embrace
But seeing him standing there
Smiling o'er at me

I fear it might have been
Nothing but a dream

Cael was stunned. He was reasonably sure that Marina was singing about him. At least, he hoped she was singing about him. But he couldn't quite make sense of her meaning, why would she think that her hopes were in vain? He felt the need to reassure her, but how? With a sudden rush of inspiration, he took a deep breath and began to sing himself;

Perhaps it really is
Only just a dream
But who says that it is
Something to be feared?
A dream is to be searched for
To cherish and to hold

He felt like an idiot, and his rhythm wasn't quite as fluid as Maria's had been. By the time he had finished Marina had turned around. Her surprise was written all over her features. She obviously had not been expecting any kind of company let alone Cael's. He wondered how often she came up to this spot to think. The area seemed perfect for it.

"What are you doing here?" Marina had stepped away from the edge of the cliff to stand in front of Cael.

"Looking for you, to be perfectly honest," Cael answered with a grin.

"And what do you plan to do now that you have found me?" she asked timidly.

What was with this girl? "Well, why don't we start with discussing our little duet?" Cael suggested.

Even in the fading light of the sunset, he could see her complexion turning a darker shade of red. She looked down at her boots, "oh, you heard that did you?"

Cael laughed good naturally, "I think it's safe to say that I did." He stepped closer to her, "did it mean what I think it meant?"

"Well that depends, what do you think it meant?" Marina evaded.

"That maybe you... are interested me?"

The temple master continued to look down bashfully at her shoes, "and how would you feel if that were the truth?"

Cael stepped even closer and reached out to lift her chin up with a finger so he could look her in those crystalline blue eyes. "Relieved," he said, "it would be a shame for my attraction to you to be so one-sided."

Her face lit up at that, "really?"

Cael chuckled, "what? You couldn't tell that I'm struck dumb any time I see you?"

"I was afraid I just saw what I wanted to see," Marina commented. "In case you hadn't noticed I don't have a lot of social experience."

Cael shrugged, "the way I see it, it's never too late to start." He walked over to the edge of the cliff and sat down with his feet dangling over the cliff edge he patted the ground beside him and looked at Marina expectantly. When she joined him at the edge of the cliff, her manner was still bashful; she sat down a little distance away from him. It was starting to affect Cael too. He rubbed the smooth titanium of his arm nervously. He had never dated much back in Charnley, so he was just going by instinct, and with the way she was acting, he was afraid to be too forward. He didn't want to scare her off.

"So... what do you think of the view?" the dark haired woman made a sweeping gesture at the valley below. "This is my favorite spot in the whole temple; it reminds me that there is a whole world out there just waiting to be explored. That, and there is nothing quite like jumping off the waterfall."

"Wait, what? That waterfall? Are you crazy? It's huge!" Cael exclaimed.

Marina laughed, "and because it's so huge the lake below is more than deep enough to cushion the fall, it's perfectly safe."

Cael stared at Marina for a few moments in stunned silence, seeing her now in a slightly different light. This glimpse of her adventurous spirit made him like her even more. "Do you jump off the waterfall often?"

Marina gave him a mischievous grin and jumped to her feet, "often enough, Champion. Care to give it a try?"

Cael gave her a grin of his own "I'd follow you anywhere."

She led him over to where the river cascaded over the cliff. She smiled back at him one last time before running towards the precipice and leaping over with an exclamation of the purest joy. Cael took a brief moment to wonder why he thought it was a good idea to agree to throw himself over a 150 yard or so drop, but he certainly wasn't going to back out. He pelted toward the edge and flung himself forward.

The wind rushed up to meet him, and his stomach leaped up into his throat. He felt completely out of control and, after he had a moment to let the fear fade, he felt completely free. All too soon it ended, and he found himself plunging into the warm waters below.

It took a little while to resurface; he gasped in air to refill his lungs. Marina had come up a little before he had; she was flinging her hair back out of her face with a flick of her head. Her wet hair clung to her neck. She tread water and turned in a slow circle to find him. They locked eyes, and he greeted her with a wide smile.

"That was amazing! And terrifying, and exhilarating, and..." Cael laughed, "and I don't even have any more words to describe it."

Marina joined him in his laughter, "I'm glad you enjoyed it. Now, how about we head inside and get dry?"

"Oh you need to get dry, huh?" he asked and playfully splashed her, "how about now?"

She gave him a mock incredulous look, "oh you do not want to start a water fight with me, sir. I am the queen of water." She punctuated the end of her sentence with a huge splash of her own. Cael sensed that she had even used some of her magical abilities to guide more of the water into his face.

Now it was war, he manipulated the lake around him with his magic and sent a wave crashing down on Marina, when the water settled, though she wasn't there. Panicked, Cael twisted around looking for her. What he saw was a wall of water twice as tall as the one he's just thrown. It pushed him down deeper into the lake when he once again broke the surface of the water he put his hands up in surrender.

"I give up, you win."

Marina grinned at him, "well that is mighty gallant of you. I told you that you didn't want to start anything with me."

Cael was smiling too, "touché, how exactly did you do that anyway?"

She was swimming to the shore now with Cael close behind, "it was just simple levitation."

The conversation was put on pause as they hiked up the cliff to the temple door. The only sounds punctuating their trek was the squelching of their sodden shoes and rustling foliage as Marina knocked away the vegetation that had begun to swallow the trail.

Once inside, Cael noted that the interior was now lit with what looked like glowing branches set into regular sconces on the walls. When he mentioned this to the temple master, she explained that they were raw cuttings harvested directly from the Illuminated Mists.

"Well, at least the blasted brightness of that place is good for something," he grumbled. This comment was met with a bemused look of confusion from the dark-haired woman. "Seriously, have you ever been in the Illuminated Mists?"

Marina laughed slightly before answering, "I have, the other creation temples are located in other planes of existence. Though, we do usually wear eye protection when traveling through the Mists."

Cael nodded, thoughtfully as he headed for his chamber, "that must make it much more bearable."

The temple master once again walked him to his room. They stood outside his door for some time. Cael was reluctant to say goodnight, but before he could direct the conversation to any new topic, Marina bid him to sleep well. Seemingly without thinking, the blue-eyed woman reached out a hand and caressed his forearm. She must have caught sight of the grin on Cael's face at this and realized what she'd done for she rushed down the hall after that with embarrassed haste.

* * *

The next morning found Cael and Marina sitting on the fur rug facing each other in the Viewing Chamber. Lyris sat curled up in Marina's lap, and Darius was laying down behind Cael. Sunlight slanted from the bay window and stretched across the polished stone floor, illuminating the voluminous but rather bare room. Cael breathed in deep the smell of wet stone.

"I really must apologize for running out on you yesterday," Marina began, "I must say I became a little flustered when the depth of our connection became clear. When mentally communicating with another magic user, you usually only have access to each other's surface thoughts, not to memories or emotions."

"Really? But when I was trying to find you I did so by forging a connection, but all I got was emotions," Cael interrupted.

"Yes, that is my point. Our connections seem to be stronger than normal. Yesterday when we were practicing I could feel the way you... shall we say, admired my laugh."

"Well it is quite lovely," Cael commented. "I can't say I'm surprised, honestly, that our connection is stronger than usual. I mean... um... I certainly feel a connection to you without even trying."

Marina smiled warmly at him and reached out to place a hand on his, "I know what you mean. I feel it too." She cleared her throat, "we should probably get started on practicing though." Cael felt her establish a connection between their minds, *"so what should we talk about?"*

"I'd like to know more about your childhood here at the temple. What did you do for fun?" Cael asked.

"A lot of swimming, and hiking and dancing, after lessons each day we would go down to the lake and swim much like you, and I did last night. The temple also hosts a modest library as well as a collection of books in each room," Marina explained.

"I did notice some books in my room. I couldn't read any of them though." Cael commented.

There came the impression across their link of sorrowful realization, *"oh that's right, you don't actually speak Portuguese."*

That was right, Cael's hand involuntarily went to where his translation medallion hung from his neck, beneath his jerkin. Without it, he and Marina wouldn't even be able to talk to one another. It certainly didn't seem right to Cael for them to have such a handicap. What would they do if the medallion was taken away from him or destroyed?

"Maybe we can do something about that," he thought slowly.

"What would you suggest?"

"Do you think you could teach me Portuguese? I could also teach you English," Cael offered, sending a sense of eager hopefulness through their connection.

"What a wonderful idea!" Marina exclaimed, *"shall we start right away?"*

They spent the rest of the afternoon in language lessons. Cael had to alternate between touching the translation medallion and letting it sit outside of his jerkin so that he could hear both Marina's instruction and her pronunciation. It was an awkward, cumbersome task at first, but eventually, Cael got the hang of it.

For the next several weeks, Cael and Marina closed themselves away in the Viewing Chamber. Cael brought some of the books from his room, and the temple master guided him through the stories inside. Cael, in turn, borrowed a notebook and a pen and wrote simple notes for Marina to practice reading. And of course, nearly all of their conversations were conducted mentally. A fact that provided Abby with endless irritation as Cael would burst out laughing at something Marina told him through their connection that Abby couldn't hear.

A week and a half after Cael arrived at Sablewater Abby had decided to move on to the next Creation Temple to continue her instruction. Cael was sad to see his sister go but he knew she had a lot to do at Redearth. It did not hurt that he was a bit distracted himself.

In between language lessons, Marina scoured the multiverse in the Sablewaters to find some hint of Dartain's movements. Either the demon king was expertly hiding his actions, or he was taking a vacation because the Sablewaters revealed nothing. Every morning the temple master would search and yield no results.

One morning Cael watched over Marina's shoulder as she gazed into the water. The surface seemed to glow for a moment before an image materialized. It looked like a throne room constructed entirely of mahogany obsidian. The only movement was the firelight that flickered against the walls. The rest of the scene was deserted, only an empty throne populated the image.

Marina gave a frustrated sigh, and the image shifted to a courtyard also made of mahogany obsidian. In one corner of the yard, a burly man was standing at a forge hammering a glowing hot piece of metal into shape on an anvil. "He's not there either," Marina whispered in Portuguese and the scene changed again. Location after location, Marina was unable to locate Dartain, until finally in the middle of a desert dotted sparsely with dead mesquite bushes stood a figure.

Cael felt the blue-eyed woman tense, and the image drew in closer on the figure. It stood like a man but had the head and tail of a lion straight out of Cael's nightmares, its face was a dark red, and the mane was a deep orange. He was wearing full plate armor of black metal with a massive ax strapped to his back. The lion man did not appear to be doing anything other than standing still, however.

The image faded and Marina stepped back, bumping into Cael. He placed his hands on her waist to steady her and turned her to face him. "Who was that?"

She looked up at him. The fear in her eyes was infectious; he could feel it begin to grip his heart. "Cael... that was Dartain."

"But that's not the man that attacked me."

"It looks like he has fused with his familiar, Gerik, the fire lion."

Cael glanced down at his own familiar who was lying in the bay window with his head between his paws. "Dorothy mentioned fusing once; she said it was pretty dangerous though."

"There are inherent risks, yes. If the magic user and familiar do not separate afterward within the time limit of four hours, they will remain fused permanently. In exchange, the magic user experiences an extreme boost in power." Marina explained.

"So, he's stronger now," Cael said softly, "is fusing something I'd be able to learn to do as well?"

"If you are serious about it, yes, your best bet to learn how would be at Redearth. The temple master, Afran, and his familiar Everard the granite hyena are masters of the technique." Lyris offered from her place next to Darius on the bay window.

Cael nodded, his eyes distant, "I should probably go then."

"Do you have to go right now?" Marina blurted, panic coloring her words. She then paused, a blush coloring her cheeks, "oh but of course I can't ask you to stay."

A smile slowly spread across Cael's face. He moved closer to where Marina had stepped back and gathered her up in his arms. "I can't see how one more night could hurt."

She laid her hands lightly on his chest, "we will prepare a grand banquet to send you off. I will let the kitchens know immediately." She closed her eyes and mentally contacted the temple cooks with her request.

"You know that hardly seems fair, Abby didn't get a banquet," Cael pointed out.

"Abby is not a champion." The temple master defended, "nor is she nearly as handsome."

"Ah! So it is favoritism," Cael teased, "you should be ashamed."

"With some counseling, I think I'll be able to live with myself."

Cael's imminent departure cast something of a somber light on the rest of the afternoon. They went out for a hike in the jungle, each lost in their own thoughts. Their sullen silence provided a counterpoint to the cheerful birdsong that flooded the wilds around them. All along the trail, Cael looked down at his shoes, blind to the vibrant palette of colors that surrounded him.

They stopped to rest in a small clearing where a large fallen tree provided a suitable bench for the pair to sit. In the middle of the clearing, young new saplings sprouted up from the charred remains of their predecessors. Cael indicated the ashes with a flick of his hand, *"I wonder what happened here."*

"Well," Marina began sheepishly over their mental connection, *"a few years back I and some of the other acolytes may have sneaked out of the temple to start a bonfire, and that bonfire might have just possibly gotten a tiny bit out of our control."* She pointed to one massive tree that to its credit was still standing but showed signs of being singed.

Cael raised an eyebrow at her and waited for her to further explain herself.

Marina graced him with an embarrassed smile, *"it was just after I had been promoted to temple master. I wanted to show my friends who were still acolytes that nothing had changed between us. So, after the rest of the temple went quiet, we crept out of our beds and slipped quietly outside. We came here and piled together the driest wood we could find, which was not easy let me tell you. Looking back, I may have gotten a little overconfident with just how high we made the pile, though, because some of the vines hanging from these trees here dried up from the heat of the blaze and eventually caught fire themselves before we really knew there was even a danger.*

"The flames spread quickly from the vines to the trees they covered, and after a few moments of panic, Gabriela calmed down enough to remember her druid training and summoned rain to kill the fire. To this day we still laugh and talk about that night."

Cael burst out laughing, *"You know, there is a spot on Dorothy's property; mind you it's a lot smaller, that bears the scars of a similar incident. The Wolf Pack and I sneaked out at midnight on a Friday, and we* had gathered up a big pile of old pallets and plywood boards. We started the whole fire with a glob of homemade napalm that Jim had figured out how to make that afternoon. When Dorothy found us, we thought she would go ballistic, but instead, she went and dragged over more scrap wood that had been sitting around for a while and joined us at the fireside. The bonfire got a little too high at that point and charred some of the lower hanging branches in the area, but it was nothing too severe."

Marina giggled at the conclusion of Cael's story. "I've heard a great deal about Dorothy from my master, that is, the temple master before me. She kept coming back here to Sablewater and to Redearth searching for a secret that would help her with her task, but I have never heard of this side of her before."

Cael grinned, "yeah, she's pretty great."

They stayed in the glade awhile longer before reluctantly heading back to the temple and the banquet that marked the end of Cael's stay. When they entered the hall, a near supernaturally delicious smell greeted Cael's senses. As soon as he reached his customary seat at the table, a surprising dish met his gaze.

"You got them to cook deep dish pizza?" he asked turning to the side to look at Marina and Lyris who sat on her shoulder. For the entire course of his stay at Sablewater, all the food had been decidedly Brazilian.

"I remembered you said it was your favorite," the temple master grinned.

Cael placed a hand over his heart, "I'm touched, thank you."

The meal was heavenly, all the more so because of Marina's gesture to make Cael feel at home. As he ate, he quietly regarded the woman. He had not known her for more than two months, but it already felt natural to be in her company. He wondered how he would deal with her being so far away. He really did not want to leave, but if he was honest with himself, he had already stayed longer than he should have.

He wanted to tell her how much their time together had meant to him. For so long he had only focused on the task that was expected of him, but Marina had shown him that there could be more to his future than demon slaying, that he could actually have a life after his task was completed.

Marina caught him staring at her and shot him a bemused grin, "something on your mind?"
Flustered, Cael fought to find his voice and the words that had suddenly left his mind, leaving it blank. "Uh... well... I...," he sighed, defeated, "I was just thinking about how much I'm going to miss this place, to miss you."

Marina's expression grew sad, "I am going to miss you too, and the temple will not be the same without you."

All too soon dinner was over. Cael and Darius walked back to their room side by side with Marina and Lyris. Cael looked down at his shoes, at a loss for what to say. Their footsteps echoing in the empty, cavernous halls of the temple were the only sounds of their passage.

Outside Cael's door, they stopped and looked at each other. Marina looked away first, "well you have a long journey ahead of you tomorrow. You should get your rest."

"Yeah, I guess you're right," Cael agreed sheepishly, "I will see you in the morning." He stepped inside and softly closed the door once Darius slipped inside.

Before settling in for bed, he double checked that all his equipment was safely in the pouch Ferdinand had given him. Even his old backpack was rolled up at the bottom of the pouch. He couldn't quite bring himself to throw it away.
Cael checked to make sure that his Sablewater jerkin would fit comfortably over his chainmaille. There was some slight stretching of the leather across his chest, but it did not hinder his movement any, and he figured he'd just have to break in the garment a bit. His

other clothing had also been laundered, so he kept his t-shirt under the chainmaille and wore his jeans. Marina, upon seeing the worn-out state of his sneakers, had insisted he take a pair of boots as well.

Everything seemed in order, but just to be sure he triple checked his weapons. They were all razor sharp and well oiled, just like they had been the first two times he'd checked them.

"Do you expect anything to suddenly disappear?" Darius asked.

"No," Cael admitted, "but if I don't do something I'm just going to sit here and think about how much I don't want to leave her... I mean here."

Darius snorted, "I think you were more right the first time."

Cael raised an eyebrow at his familiar, then his shoulders slumped, and he sat down on the edge of his bed. "Fine, yes I admit it. I just don't want to leave Marina."

"It's not like it's forever, we can come back. Apparently, Dorothy did," the iron hued wolf pointed out.

"True... still," Cael struggled to find words for the idea only half formed in his head, "maybe I should do something for her. Give her a gift of some sort, something to remember me by."

Darius laughed, "I doubt she could forget you."

Cael scowled at his partner, "you know what I mean."

He rolled his wolfish eyes, "so what kind of gift do you have in mind?"

Cael considered the question; he wanted it to be something she could wear, some kind of jewelry, perhaps. The problem was he had next to no artistic ability so it would have to be simple, a cuff bracelet perhaps... made of iron? He thought about the dark-haired woman leaping off the giant waterfall outside, no, not iron. He rubbed the smooth surface of his left arm, titanium then.

He began to conjure the metal and shaped it into an elegant cuff, more or less. He regarded it for a moment and thought it was rather plain. He got up and rushed to the bathroom where he had access to a proper mirror that he could get a good look at his Wolf Pack tattoo. She had said that she often felt like part of the gang so why not make it official?

Cael did his best to transfer the rampant wolf design of the tattoo onto the bracelet. Only when he was reasonably pleased with the results did he set the cuff aside and settle in for sleep.

The morning brought mixed emotions to the young alchemist, he wanted to see the look on Marina's face when he gave her the bracelet, but he dreaded the occasion for which he was giving it to her.

He began to get his gear ready for the journey to Redearth. He donned the now familiar black leather jerkin over the chainmaille that Jim had given him. Next, he strapped on his weapons and the pouch holding the rest of his gear.

Cael and Darius then sought out the master of the temple to say his goodbyes. He did not find her in the dining hall as he had expected. He wasn't too disappointed; he really had no appetite. His first thought was to try the Viewing Chamber next, but he realized she would not be there. Cael made his way out of the temple and up above to the top of the waterfall.

Sure enough, the temple master stood at the edge of the cliff, gazing out at the horizon. "So you're off to continue your adventure out there in the great big world." Her voice had a distant, wistful quality to it tinged with no little sadness. "Oh, how I wish I could go with you..."

The lump that had suddenly formed in Cael's throat made it difficult to speak. With effort, he said, "There is nothing I would like more."

Marina shook her head, "but I can't. My place is here at the temple. You still need me to keep an eye on Dartain's movements, not to mention the rest of the multiverse is counting on my vigilance."

"It suddenly doesn't seem fair, all this responsibility heaped on our shoulders. You know I never once questioned the task expected of me, until this moment."

"Perhaps it's not fair, but it is right. We have the ability to help, so it is our obligation to do so," Marina asserted, "and it isn't forever. One day I will be able to see the world, and we can be together, there are just a few things that must be done first."

Cael grinned ruefully, "You're right of course. Until that day I have something for you, to remember me by." He withdrew the cuff he had made from the pouch at his belt and held it out to her.

"Oh Cael, it's perfect," she gingerly lifted the slightly misshapen bracelet from his palm and fastened it to her wrist, "thank you so much... I don't know what to say. I didn't think to make you anything, though perhaps..." she spoke the last softly and reached into a pocket. She brought out a smooth black rock a little smaller than her palm.

"It's quartz, I found it one day at the bottom of the lake there," she gestured to the water below. "I have kept it with me for years. I want you to have it, to remember me by."

"It will be my greatest treasure," Cael swore, accepting the gift and gingerly placing it in his bag. "I suppose I should be on my way now."

He reluctantly looked to Darius to open a portal to the illuminated mists. The clang of metal sounded, and the patch of air before him gave off a slight glow.

"Promise you'll come back now and then," Marina blurted before she could stop herself.

Cael grinned and stepped closer to her, "ha! You'll be begging to get rid of me I'll visit so often."

"I can't see such protests coming from me," Marina said softly. She bit her lip briefly as though deciding something, then stepped up next to him and grabbed hold of the baldric strapped across his chest to pull him closer. She lifted her face up to meet his and pressed her lips against his mouth. "Until next time, safe travels." With that, she pushed him through the open portal.

Chapter IX:
Wild Heart

Cael was climbing up a particularly rickety ladder constructed of well-worn tree branches. They had traveled rather uneventfully through the Illuminated Mists, though Cael was rather proud of himself in that he achieved some measure of success with navigating the frustrating plane. It turns out all he needed to do was close his eyes, and perhaps all the practicing on communicating with Marina had helped him with using other forms of non-material forms of magic.

At the top of the stairs was a gigantic pueblo complex set into a gap in the cliff face. The air in the shadow of the cliff was cool and dry. Cael started up the path toward the largest door in the widest building.

"So, are we going to talk about it?" Darius asked teasingly for the twentieth time, panting out his wolfish laughter.

"No, I don't see how it's anything to talk about," Cael scowled.

"But she kiiiiissed yoooouuuu," Darius persisted.

"And?"

"And you liked it," the wolf continued.

"So what if I did?" Cael demanded.

Darius huffed, "you're no fun."

Their conversation took them all the way to what appeared to be the main building in the complex. Cael pushed the door open and stepped inside to a room dimly lit with cuttings from trees of the Illuminated Mists. The ceiling was relatively low, Cael's hair brushed up against the stone ceiling. Most of the room was furnished with rough-cut wooden benches and chairs.

A man stood at the back of the room. He wore gray linen pants and a red leather jerkin with a gray mesa insignia on the back, on his feet were red leather sandals. His hair was white and fell to his shoulders, and his chin was graced with a neatly trimmed goatee. His skin was dark and heavily wrinkled, and his nose, lip, and left ear were pierced, sporting small silver rings. This man looked up as Cael and Darius entered the room.

"Greetings traveler. I am Afran, master of Redearth, to whom am I addressing?"

"I am the champion, Cael Ivywood."

The old man smiled, "ah, the champion of the Creation Temples, I have wondered when you would come through my door."

Cael looked grim, "well the time has come, I need to learn how to fuse with my familiar here." he gestured to Darius who was sitting at his side.

Afran mirrored Cael's expression and nodded, "understandable; we will begin first thing in the morning."

Afran then escorted the duo to another small building that served as a private room. A rustic wooden bed sat in a corner with a cedar chest at the foot, and a nightstand on one side, a fireplace spanned the majority of one wall with two wooden stools placed in front of it. "This will be where you stay for the duration of your visit, Cael." He turned to leave but before he could Cael spoke up.

"Has my sister, Abby Brooks been here yet?"

A grin flashed across the old man's features, "miss Brooks did stay here for a time, ransacking my libraries, but she left not long ago."

"That's a shame it would have been good to see her again," Cael lamented.

* * *

The next morning found Cael and Darius in a large stone chamber with a low ceiling. Afran stood before them next to his familiar, Everard. Cael had been given both dinner and breakfast in their room. Apparently, that was just how they did things in Redearth. It seemed like a lonely contrast to the familial feeling of meals at Sablewater.

They were going to start their training with a demonstration. Afran shook out his limbs in preparation. Everard shook and stretched his forelimbs in a facsimile of a bow before leaping into Afran's chest. The change was sudden, Cael wasn't even sure he had seen the whole thing. The grizzled temple master now had gray fur on every visible inch of his body, his ears stood at attention at the top of his head, and his face had lengthened into a snout with the hyena's features.

Cael couldn't help but gape at the spectacle. Though he supposed it wasn't much stranger then meeting Ferdinand, but the sight was still bizarre.

Afran's laugh when he caught sight of Cael's expression fit his new countenance perfectly. It was the barking laugh of a hyena. "If you can manage to pick your jaw up off the floor, you two can try it next."

Cael closed his mouth and gulped, but nodded after a quick glance at Darius. They moved to the middle of the room. Cael stretched a bit and looked to Afran, "so I saw what you did, but how exactly did you do it?"

"Your familiar is already a part of you, all you have to do is be open and accepting of that part," came the temple master's reply.

With that cryptic thought in mind, Cael nodded to the iron hued wolf. Darius loped full tilt at him, and the alchemist tried to remain open. The wolf then jumped forward and into Cael, but no fusion occurred. He tackled the young man to the ground with a solid thud.

Afran laughed again, "that didn't quite work. You might want to try again."

Cael gave a frustrated growl and struggled to untangle himself from Darius and get to his feet. He had to be open to the part of him that was Darius, but what did that mean? Cael liked to think that he was pretty open about the kind of person he was already, so what was he missing? He looked down at his familiar who gave a shake as if he was dislodging water from his fur.

Cael still got that feeling that he was looking into a mirror. Darius was a part of him, he could feel it, but what part? Then he looked at the wolf's sharp fangs, the powerful muscles around his shoulders, and the goofy panting grin. It was then that Cael realized that Darius was all of it; he was every part of him, the savage power and the wild playfulness.

He nodded to his familiar to go again. With just a moment's hesitation, Darius charged forward once more. A split second before the wolf reached him; Cael had a moment of feeling like he was in two places at once. Then the iron familiar leaped up and into Cael's chest.

The whole world seemed to expand and shrink all at once. Cael could feel his bones shifting, starting with his skull. His face became longer ending in a snout, and his ears shifted upward, his tongue also stretched to greater length. Fur sprouted all over his body, and a tail grew from his backside.

As Cael was trying to adjust to these changes, his nose was assaulted with the musty smell of the stonework around him. His ears caught the sounds of Afran shuffling his feet. All of his senses seemed to have been magnified tenfold, and it was overwhelming.

Cael fell to his knees and clamped now mismatched hands over his lupine ears and shut his eyes tight. "Make it stop!" he whimpered rather pathetically, or at least that's what he tried to say, it came out in a pronounced lisp as he struggled to control a tongue that was too long.

It seemed however that Cael's negative reaction was all that was required to break the connection. Cael fell back on the floor in relief and stayed that way for several minutes until Afran came to stand over him. The temple master's hyena face swam before Cael's vision for a moment. "Are you alive?"
In answer, Cael sat up with a loud groan.

Afran gave a soft chuckle, "I take it you weren't quite expecting it to be that intense."

"Not even remotely," Cael replied.

Darius came to sit next to his human counterpart and looked to the elderly temple master, "why on earth would it be that intense? I know my senses are acuter than a human's senses usually are, but that was exponentially more than even I am used to."

Before answering, Afran and Everard chose that moment to separate, and they joined Cael and Darius on the floor. "Well, you know that you are the physical manifestation of Cael's magical energy. What that amounts to is that you house Cael's excess energy. When it becomes reunited, it is frequently more than the magic-user can handle. This can manifest in a variety of ways, in this case giving you both senses heightened to an almost unbearable level."

"You're saying this may be something I can't handle?" Cael asked.

Afran looked the young champion straight in the eye and held the gaze for a moment to ensure that he had the teen's full attention, "that depends entirely on you, my boy."

"I think perhaps, however, you should take a short break to catch your breath before you try again," Everard suggested.

Cael nodded and climbed to his feet, "good idea."

The rattled duo walked out of the room on shaking legs and stepped out into the arid climate outside. Cael found a rough wooden railing that protected passerby from tumbling over the steep cliff face and leaned his forearms against it. He let out a long sigh and clenched his jaw and stared out at the pine forest below. Afran's last words rang in his head. If there was anyway, he could make this fusing thing work he would do it. If Dartain had made himself more powerful with the technique, then Cael had no choice but to master it as well. He had seen how scared Marina had looked when she first saw the demon king in his new form. It was all too likely that Cael would not succeed if he failed to get stronger.

With a huff, Cael turned from the railing and its panoramic view. He returned to the company of the aged temple master with renewed determination. He found the old man and the hyena sitting in a pair of chairs at a table that had not been there before. Afran was sipping tea from a small steaming teacup. There was a teapot resting on the table.

When Cael approached Afran gestured to a second teacup, "I find a hot cup of tea to be exquisitely relaxing. Perhaps, it will help to calm your nerves before you try again." The gray-haired man gave a flick of his wrist and muttered a phrase too low for Cael to quite catch it, and two more chairs appeared.

Cael and Darius took their seats. "What class of magic was that?" Cael looked at the temple master curiously.

Afran smirked at Cael over the rim of his teacup, "I am a Sage if that is what you're asking. My abilities require years of research and study to fully master. It is, incidentally, one of only two classes that require incantation to shape the energy. Though, the other class, wizards, is something of a gray area in that unlike the other benevolent magic classes a wizard's magic will manifest regardless of whether or not they live a life of virtue." While he spoke, Afran picked up the teapot and poured a clear red liquid into the second teacup and slid it over to Cael.

"But they're technically considered sorcerers if they don't" Cael supplied to show that he understood. He picked up the cup and took a small sip; the drink was hot and had a tartness to it. "What kind of tea is this?"

"Rooibos, it's one of my favorites," Afran answered taking a long sip from his own cup.

"Huh, never had it before but it's good," Cael commented. They sat in silence as they sipped their tea. Cael focused on his next attempt at fusing with his familiar. He tried to mentally prepare himself for the resulting sensory overload. He found that the warm beverage went a long way to calm his nerves.

He drained the last of his cup and rose to his feet. With a deep breath, he looked over to Darius, "ready?"

The wolf nodded and hopped down from his seat and crossed the room with Cael to a clear space. They faced one another, and Darius once again rushed toward his partner. This time Cael knew what to expect which lessened somewhat the discomfort of the transformation. Once it was over He was again assaulted by his own senses. He grits his teeth as the smell of the musty earth bombarded his wet black nose. His long lupine ears held flat against his skull in an effort to dampen the cacophony of his own shallow breathing.

An angry growl tore its way from his throat and the claws on his right fist bit into his palm. The consequent agony that laced his arm was enough to bring him to his knees. He snarled in frustration, and he could feel his gut clench. He had been in pain before, and it had not broken him then and it would not now, he refused to allow it.

Despite this notion, the overwhelming waves of senses soon became too much for Cael to bear. He and Darius broke apart. Cael found himself on his hands and knees staring at the stone floor. He squeezed his eyes shut and asked in between gasps, "how long was that?"

"About five minutes," came Afran's reply.

Cael shook his head, "that will never be enough."

Afran's measured footsteps grew louder as he approached Cael and knelt down beside him, "if I might offer an observation?" To Cael's grunted assent the temple master continued, "you're too tense. You're fighting the onslaught of your senses when you should be accepting them and giving your body time to adjust to accommodate the input."

At these words, Cael thought back to the first time he had ever gotten into a fistfight. He remembered the tenseness in his shoulders and how he had stiffly tried to block his opponent's onslaught. He had nearly been knocked out right there on the playground of his elementary school, and Gavin had been forced to drag him all the way to the nurse's office. The next day Dorothy had shown him how to loosen up his shoulders and how that made it much easier and quicker to react to attacks. Perhaps he could apply the same principle here.

"I think I know what you mean," Cael had shifted to a sitting position on the ground, and now with Afran's assistance, he climbed back to his feet. He looked over to Darius, "you think you've got one more go left in you?"

Darius scratched behind an ear with a back paw, "I'm not in any hurry to try again, but I'm game if you are."

Cael stretched his neck side to side and shook out his limbs. He gave Darius a nod, and the wolf rushed at him once more. Cael couldn't help but tense up during the transformation, but once it was over, he did his best to relax his muscles over again. He focused solely on loosening his limbs in an effort to ignore the rest of his surroundings. His body kept tensing up of its own accord, and Cael had to fight with himself to decompress.

Eventually, the tightness of his shoulders built up despite his best efforts and Cael was forced to again sever the connection. When he once more became aware of his surroundings, Cael found Afran beaming down at him.

"That was a huge improvement you doubled your time! And you're still standing for once!"
Cael scowled in annoyance, "I still won't be able to defeat Dartain in ten minutes. Not to mention I can't do a single thing while fused."

The rebuke did not seem to faze Afran, "it will take practice to get proficient with the technique, yes, but you are on the right track, and that was only your third time. You really are doing well. I think it would be best if you did not over-do it today, though. I would recommend you retire to your room. Fusing can be a terribly draining experience."
Cael was about to protest, but the weariness in his joints and shoulders demanded that he take the temple master's advice. With an exhausted nod, Cael made for the door with Darius right behind. Cael shuffled along the pathways while staring at his shoes. He had

no real awareness of his surroundings. it was fortunate that the paths themselves seemed deserted. He would later marvel at the solitary nature of the acolytes of Redearth, but at the moment the only thing he had attention for was how worn out he was. When they made it back to the room, Cael fell face first onto the bed and promptly fell asleep.

He woke up a short time later to another consciousness on the edge of his awareness, *"Are you free to talk?"* Marina mentally asked.

Cael rubbed his face to clear away his grogginess, *"sure, what's up?"* He was really just surprised that their connection actually did reach to another plane of existence.

Marina's embarrassed smile flashed briefly in Cael's mind; he could practically see her brush a lock of ebony hair behind one ear. *"I just wanted to know how things were going at Redearth."*

Cael sat up with a sorrowful sigh his eyes fell on a plate of food that had been left on the nightstand, *"not as good as I would have hoped. I'm having difficulty adjusting to the effects of fusing."* Cael didn't like admitting it, especially not to Marina.

The raven-haired seer seemed to understand, *"it is a challenging technique. Lyris and I have never even attempted it."*

Cael's laugh had a slightly bitter edge to it as he picked up the flatbread sandwich and took a bite, *"I would not suggest you do if you can avoid it. It hurts like nothing else I have ever endured."*

"I'm so sorry you have to deal with that," came Marina's empathetic reply.

A thought occurred to Cael as he watched Darius sleeping in front of the fire, *"couldn't you have just watched my progress in the sable water?"*

"I thought it would be more polite to simply ask," she conveyed over their connection with just a hint of bemusement.

Cael grinned, *"well it does give me the excuse to talk with you, so I'm certainly not complaining."*

He could all but feel Marina's returning smile, *"I must confess; it is not the same here without you."*

Cael nodded and then remembered that she would not be able to see it, *"I know what you mean, Redearth does not have nearly as good company as Sablewater."*

"The acolytes there do focus on their studies above all else. Socializing is not really among their skill set," Marina laughed.

Cael chuckled as well, *"I had noticed that."*

* * *

It was several grueling weeks before Cael started to get the hang of fusing with Darius. He was slowly learning to adjust to his heightened senses, though talking was still something of a challenge; everything came out with a severe lisp. All things considered though, Cael was quite pleased with his progress. He could almost forget his frustration with himself when he first started.

Cael was beginning to notice something else that he hadn't had the time to experience before. As Cael and Darius combined stood in the middle of the stone room; Cael felt more savage and wild than he ever had before. He and the Wolf Pack had their wild moments, but this was entirely different. This flooded Cael's system with adrenaline, it made him want to run out into the forest and hunt, to take apart his prey with bare hands.

When he said as much to Afran, the aged temple master gave a wry, lopsided grin, "you may want to curb that impulse," he told the young wolf-man.

Cael gave an answering grin, "unless Dartain is in the area." He growled dangerously.

"Be careful not to let your confidence cloud your judgment; it could be a lethal mistake."

Cael sobered at the warning. He checked his watch, the numbers quickly counting up to nearly four hours. "that's time." He willingly severed the connection between Darius and himself. He had a brief sensation of his bones shrinking as his form returned to normal.

Afran clapped a hand on Cael's shoulder, "come walk with me, won't you?" temple master and familiar strolled out of the room and down one of the pathways with Cael close behind.

They climbed down the rough ladder and hiked along a game trail. Cael was watching his feet to prevent himself from tripping when he noticed that Afran walked barefoot over the stones and twigs that littered the path, but he seemed utterly unhindered by it.

"You're doing very well," Afran began, "in fact, I'd almost say there is nothing left for me to teach you. At this point, I think all you need is a bit more practice, and I would like to observe just a few more sessions but you..."

The rest of Afran's sentence was drowned out by the desperate scream of another temple master, *"CAEL! HELP ME!"* Marina's cry came through panicked and afraid.

Cael stopped dead in his tracks causing Afran to pause in turn, "what is it? What's wrong?" panic threatened to overwhelm Cael as well.

Marina sounded close to tears, and Cael's heart shattered, *"I don't know how he got in, but Dartain infiltrated Sablewater. He over-powered our acolytes, grabbed me and left. I think he's taking me to the fire desert, his home plane of existence."*

"Are you injured? Where's Lyris?" Cael felt numb with shock; he wasn't sure what to ask.

"Cael, are you alright?" Afran asked. Cael held up a hand to forestall any more questions.

"I'm not seriously hurt. Honestly, I'm sure I'm just the bait. Lyris is here as well, but I think he just wants to draw you out."

"Well if he wants me, that's exactly what he's going to get," Cael thought back darkly, to Afran he said, "I'm afraid practice is going to have to wait, Marina is in danger."

With no further explanation, he nodded to Darius to open a portal to the Illuminated Mists and took off through the portal at a sprint.

Chapter X:
The Fire Desert

"Where the obscenity are we going?" Darius demanded as he loped after Cael's desperately racing form.

Cael leaped off of what he was pretty sure was a boulder as he barked, "wherever he's taking Marina! That's where we're going!"

The iron-gray wolf rolled his eyes in an almost human gesture, "that's not terribly specific."

"Well, I don't know the specifics! I'm just following my connection to her. It's not like I have a ready-made road map to the fire desert she mentioned," Cael retorted.

"Fine," Darius rejoined, "but can we talk about how this is quite obviously a trap?"

Cael was silent for several moments as he crashed through the landscape of the Illuminated Mists. He knew very well that they were walking right into a trap, at reckless speeds no less. Cael found it very difficult to care that his own well-being, even his life, might be forfeit. All that mattered to him was Marina's safety. In answer, Cael snarled, "I don't care! If he has hurt her in any way, I will tear him apart with my teeth! I will rend the flesh from his bones if I must, but she will be freed if it is the last thing I do!"

"Promise me that when we get there, we'll at least stop and assess the situation instead of charging blindly in and getting both you and Marina killed?" Darius pressed.

Cael gave a surly grunt in the affirmative and continued running. The longer they traveled, the more Cael began to notice something, the first thing to make him slow down since Marina had contacted him, The light of the Illuminated Mists started to take on a different quality, almost like the light cast from a flickering fire. The environment around him seemed to waver occasionally casting sinister shadows haphazardly across the landscape. This quality only became more pronounced the further in they ran.

Eventually, they came to a jagged cliff jutting up high above Cael's head. He couldn't even sense the top of it. Cael turned to Darius in an irritated huff, "Great, how do we get past this?"

Darius looked terrified, his ears lying flat against his skull and his tail between his legs, "we don't," he whined, "this is the end of the Illuminated Mists. This is the entrance of very lowest plane of existence."

"It appears then, that we have reached our destination," in answer to Darius's look of alarm, Cael gave a dark grin, "we always knew we would have to come here at some point. This is where Dartain is crossing the boundaries of what the creation temples will allow. This is his seat of power, and we're here to dethrone him."

Reluctantly, Darius opened a portal, and the two stepped through to the blisteringly hot desert on the other side. Cael's feet sunk in slightly as he stepped onto the soft sand the heat from that sand could be felt even through Cael's boots. Everywhere around them, spurts of fire shot out of the ground sporadically. The landscape before Cael had none of the sparse vegetation that he and Marina had seen in the Sablewater. Dunes of sand stretched out desolately to the horizon.

Cael could feel the pull of his connection with Marina tugging at his heartstrings, drawing him deeper into the unforgiving desert. He and Darius marched doggedly onward. Their pace was slowed slightly by their surroundings. Sweat dripped down from Cael's nose as he traveled, even the area where his titanium arm joined with his shoulder was becoming uncomfortably warm.

Cael paid little attention to his discomfort, however. His sole focus was on moving as fast as he could across the dunes. His diligence was soon rewarded. Cael and Darius reached the crest of a particularly tall sand dune and caught sight of their adversary. Cael quickly fell flat and carefully inched forward hoping that he had not been seen. He whispered to Darius, "we're going to need to fuse together for this." Darius nodded his understanding, and they turned their attention to the scene below them.

Dartain stood in front of Marina in the valley between three dunes, a small, crude cage stood off to the side. Cael's eyes widened in shock and outrage when he saw Marina's hands, they were bound in front of her by ropes of fire. Closer inspection revealed that her feet were hobbled with similar bindings and worst of all, fire ropes were fastened around her neck as well.

That sight was the last straw for Cael. Blood pounded in his ears, and his vision hazed over with red as he surged to his feet with a roar of fury. Despite the warnings of Darius and his own common sense, Cael charged forward.

Darius gave a snarl of exasperation and leaped forward into Cael's back to spark their fusion. Cael stumbled for a step or two as the transformation took place, but he quickly regained his footing.

He barreled down the dune with sand flying haphazardly behind him.

"Let her go! You deplorable bag of filth!" Cael bellowed as soon as he was in earshot.

Dartain's lion features broke into an arrogant smile, "so you've finally come to save your wench." he had the other end of Marina's fiery bindings in one hand, and he yanked on them now causing the temple master to stagger forward. "You're going to have to make me release her."

"Cael! Be careful!" Marina shouted before another tug on the ropes made her cry out in pain.

Cael growled and drew out his sword, "you will release her. Now!" He charged forward, sword at the ready. He swung with all his might at the demon king's head, but Dartain stepped to one side and dragged Marina into Cael's path instead. Cael skidded to a halt, sending a spray of loose sand flying. He saw her face twisted in pain, dirt caked into the tracks on her cheeks left by her tears and asked with no small amount of desperation in his voice, "are you okay?"

She started to nod, then her eyes widened in shock, "look out!"

Cael turned his head just in time to see Dartain's boot coming right at him. The next thing he knew; he was lying flat on his back, and Dartain was flying at him. Cael had just enough time to get his feet up and right into Dartain's mid-section. The lion man rolled off to one side with a groan of misery. When he recovered, he pulled the giant, double-bladed ax from its place on his back and swung it down, hard.

Cael hastily scrambled out of the way as the ax crashed down behind him. He glanced back at Marina to see her inching toward the cage, which he noted, imprisoned Lyris. Cael turned his attention back to his opponent. Dartain swung his weapon at Cael's stomach. Cael battered it down with his own blade. Then he stepped in close to his adversary and bashed the lion's muzzle with the pommel of Howling Wolf.

Dartain lurched forward, holding his face with one hand. Then he stumbled back toward the cage as Marina was struggling with its lock. He grabbed hold of her bindings once again and pulled her to him. He held her firmly with one massive arm and pressed one blade of his ax against her throat.

"Drop the sword, or she dies, Champion!" he snarled passed a bloody nose.

The breath was knocked out of Cael by the sheer force of his fear for the woman he had come to care so deeply about. His mind was a complete blank of a way out of the situation. Cael stood there, unable to move.

Dartain's eyes narrowed, "you try my patience, boy, drop your weapon."
Almost of its own volition, Cael's hand loosened its grip, and his sword plummeted to the hot sand at his feet.

Dartain took full advantage of Cael's shocked and newly disarmed state. He flung Marina to the ground and in turn grabbed hold of Cael. He then swiftly conjured more ropes of pure flame and bound the champion in an identical fashion to the temple master. The demon king wasted no time in dragging Cael away, leaving behind the still bound Marina and her incarcerated familiar.

This snapped Cael out of his daze, "wait one vulgar minute! You have me. Let them go!"

"I just did," came Dartain's flat reply.

"But they'll die out here tied up like that!" Cael protested.

"I don't care."

Cael snarled, angry and ferocious. Dartain's only response was to yank on Cael's ropes causing him to pitch forward into the sand. A second tug on the fiery tethers forced Cael painfully back to his feet. Dartain marched onward across the blazing dunes, heedless of Cael's suffering.

Time wore on, and still, Cael trudged on behind his captor, the searing heat of his bindings bit into his throat, wrists, and ankles. It was all he could do to remember how to even walk. He had no attention to spare for anything but the pain that was even amplified by his fusion with Darius. Early on in their trek, Cael tried to break the connection between him and his familiar in the hope that the wolf might be able to help him escape or go back and help Marina alone. To his utter dismay, he found that they could not separate, nor could he use any of his magic for that matter. Something about the ropes must have inhibited his abilities.

So it was that Cael downheartedly stumbled dejectedly after his adversary. The love of his life was most likely dying in the dirt. He could not use his magic. He didn't even have his sword anymore. He had his bladed gauntlets and his throwing knives but with his hands bound he could not reach them.

Cael's whole world shrunk to the confines of his own body, the rest of his surroundings melted away. He no longer saw the endless expanse of umber dunes or the fire that erupted from the sands. He only felt the ground's heat beneath his boots and the excruciating burn of his bonds. The pain had spread up his arms and legs and down to his chest to the point where he wasn't sure if there had ever been a time when he hadn't been in agony.

Eventually, they came to a stone platform surrounded by arches, in the center stood an altar of mahogany obsidian. Dartain slammed Cael onto the altar and lashed the other end of his bindings to it. Cael lay there with his arms up above his head

"Do you remember what I told you when we first met, champion?" Dartain asked as he slowly circled the altar. When Cael did not respond, Dartain paused to frown down at him. "No? Well, let me refresh your memory. I told you that I would find a way around that annoying champion's protection of yours; the protection that prevents your soul from being separated from your body by any magical means. The protection that enables you to still use the arm I destroyed." he flicked Cael's titanium arm with one claw before continuing.

"While I could simply take my ax to your head, at this point, I'm not sure even that would do the job, and I cannot afford to take any risks with you. You are the only one who stands any chance of defeating me. So I'm going to take this knife," from a sheath at his waist the lion man pulled out a dagger with a crooked blade that glinted in the firelight, "and I'm going to use it to graft a piece of my essence to your soul. You must be corrupted. With any luck, it will taint you enough to make you lose your benevolent status, and you'll lose your magic altogether."

Cael snarled through gritted fangs "fat chance!"
Dartain chuckled darkly, "you say that now." Dartain approached the altar and slowly lowered the dagger's blade to the center of Cael's chest.

Cael experienced an awful tearing sensation in his torso followed immediately by more intense burning, as if he hadn't endured enough of that already. Through the haze of pain, Cael noticed that Dartain's efforts were taking their toll on him as well. The demon king was hunched over Cael's prone form, his fangs clenched and a look of desperate focus across his features, as if he were just barely in control of the procedure.

Just as Cael was hoping in vain that Dartain would lose control entirely, he felt the fiery ropes holding him sputter and die.

Wasting no time, Cael bolted up to a sitting position. As he came up, the dagger cut a path across his left cheek. He cleared the altar and began sprinting in a random direction; all that mattered was putting as much distance between him and Dartain as possible.

Cael expected the demon king to give chase at any moment, but when he glanced over his shoulder, the lion man was laughing.

Cael dreaded the implications of this. He put his focus on making his legs move as fast as they were able. After several moments, with no pursuit in sight, Cael slowed to a stop. He needed a plan, first thing was first; he had to get out of this plane of existence. The only problem being he had no idea how to open a portal, Darius was the one who did that.

Darius. Oh no, how long had it been? It felt like an eternity but for all he knew it could have been fifteen minutes. Cael looked down at his watch only to find a twisted, melted mass of plastic on his metal arm. Only one way to find out then, Cael attempted to sever the connection between Darius and himself. He felt something part but not completely. He and Darius separated, but after the split, the iron hued wolf lay motionless in the sand before dissipating like fog in the sunlight.

Cael couldn't believe what he was seeing. The hands he looked down at were now entirely human, but Darius was gone. Darius was gone. He did his best to force his panic down and tried to think. Even if Darius was gone, the magical energy had to still be there, right? Unless Dartain's plan had worked. Unless he had lost his magic.

Cael conjured a piece of iron. He stared at it sitting in his palm. Okay, so he still had his magic, just not his familiar anymore. He wasn't sure what that meant. He stood there in the middle of the fire desert trying to calm his frantic heart. He breathed in the suffocatingly hot air slowly. He could hear the sound of his breath much louder than it should have been. In fact, his senses had not diminished when he and Darius had separated.

Maybe he had the ability to open the portal. Working on pure instinct, Cael raised one hand and summoned his energy. When he swiped down to tear the hole into the Illuminated Mists his arm briefly shifted to look like the wolf claw he had when fused with his familiar. Cael blinked and moved his hand again, but it now appeared normal.

To Cael's infinite relief, however, the now routine sound of clashing metal had echoed across the desert as the portal flared into existence. He stepped through the tear and into the blinding light. His usual animosity for the over bright plane between planes gave way to fatigued alleviation. The portal snapped closed as soon as he passed through but Cael did not notice.

The strain of the day was quickly catching up to him. He sank to the ground and leaned against a fallen log and put his head in his hands. He was now safe but, he had left Marina in the Fire Desert, anything could have happened or could be happening to her while he was sitting on his butt. He attempted to rise, to re-enter enemy territory from a better position to rescue her. He could figure out his Darius problem once they were both safe. But he couldn't seem to stand; he couldn't even keep his eyes open. Before he knew what was happening, Cael slipped into unconsciousness.

* * *

The first thing that Cael became aware of when he awoke was that he was wet from neck to toe, which was a welcome change from the dry heat that had been his world a short time previously. The next was that he was no longer in the Mists. Sunlight filtered emerald through vibrant trees that flanked the creek he was laying in. the ambient sounds of insects and birds filled the otherwise silent air.

Cael stared up at the sky, unwilling to move for the moment. He took stock of himself slowly and deliberately starting with his head which throbbed painfully. His neck, wrists, and ankles where he had been bound were strangely numb, as did his cheek where Dartain's dagger had cut him. Everything else ached to some degree or another. Cael was afraid to, but finally looked deeper inside himself, he found something dark and sinister lurking there, and right next to that shadow was a wild spark of ferocity.

Cael did his best to push down those feelings and pretend he didn't see them in the first place. He sat up seeking to distract himself with movement. As he clambered out of the shallow creek and up the bank, footsteps sounded somewhere beyond the trees. Cael tensed and reached for his sword only to find empty air where it should have been. That's right, he'd left Howling Wolf back in the fire desert. Cael reached down for his bladed half-gauntlets but before he could draw them a man came into view. He wore a green leather jerkin very similar to Cael's own black one. He also had brown linen pants and brown leather boots. He had wild short red hair and a 5 o'clock shadow. In one hand he lightly held a sturdy wooden staff.

"Ah, you're finally awake. Good, I was beginning to worry," the stranger nonchalantly made his way down the path to the bank.

Cael's hand hovered behind him, near his weapon, "who are you? How did I get here?"
The man gave a boisterous laugh, "oh sorry! I should have started with that! I'm Seren Greenwood, temple master at your service." He gave a short bow, "After your... shall we say, ordeal..."

"Failure more like," Cael interrupted bitterly.

Seren gave a scowl but there was a measure of concern in the expression, "like I said your ordeal, we were worried about you, so I had Argentcloud transport you here to Greenwood. I treated your wounds with a poultice; you may find them a bit numb from the mixture still and did my best to bring down your temperature here in the creek, it also has some measure of restorative properties of its own."

Cael flexed his right hand as he drew it away from his bladed gauntlet, "I had wondered about that. Thank you for helping me, but I have to go back, I have to save Marina."

Seren waved the comment away, "There's nothing more that can be done on that front. Come on, let's get you into some dry clothes and then there is someone you might want to see."

Cael frowned, it felt like a rock had settled into the bottom of his stomach. Nothing more to be done? What did that mean? Was she dead? Had she already been rescued? What? But he had come to trust the temple masters, so he followed Seren along a path to a glen populated with rough log cabins arranged in a circle around a central fire pit. They entered one of the first cabins, and Seren handed him a bundle of clothing in this temple's colors and left him to change.

Cael carefully set aside his Sablewater jerkin, logically he knew that the one from Greenwood would protect him just as well, but he could not help preferring the one from Sablewater. He made a mental note to retrieve the article of clothing once it had dried. He pulled on the green leather jerkin, these ones had a dark green pine tree insignia stitched onto the back of it. Cael made a check of all his gear as he carefully laid it all out to dry, everything was in working order, but the absence of both Howling Wolf and his communicator watch from Abby made him feel strangely bereft.

When he stepped back out into the sunlight Seren stood by to greet him and standing next to the muscular redhead was Marina.

Cael surged forward, tears threatening to overwhelm his vision. He slammed into Marina and wrapped his arms around her, "I was so afraid you were dead," he choked out before burying his face in the crook of her neck. He was overwhelmed by a sense of relief opening like a floodgate washing over him. He felt every muscle in his body uncoil from a tension that had threatened to snap from the moment Marina had reached out to him for help.

"Me?" she asked, incredulous, tears apparent in her voice as well, "when Dartain took you away I was sure that was the last I had seen of you, and it would have been all my fault!" She broke down into relieved sobs, and they both sank to the ground in a weeping heap.

Several minutes stretched on, and neither of them moved until Seren cleared his throat awkwardly. The pair untangled themselves from one another and rose looking away, embarrassed. Cael glanced back at Marina with a smile, he was so glad she was okay. Marina locked eyes with him and smiled back.

"I thought you might be happy to see her here," Seren interjected a hint of laughter in his tone. "You must be hungry there is lunch ready on the fire." He pointed to the fire pit where a giant cast iron cauldron was suspended above the flames.

As Cael drew nearer to the fire pit he could feel his gut clench, and his pulse quickened, and all he could think about was ropes of fire around his throat. He could not make himself get any closer than the ring of chairs positioned around the campfire. Seren ladled some of the thick stew into a wooden bowl and handed one to Cael and Marina each and lastly one for himself. He eyed the uneasy looks on his companions' faces and briefly looked to the flames.

"Why don't we sit over on that bench there?" they sat down on a fallen log overlooking a training yard where several acolytes supervised sparring matches between a diverse collection of magic users.

Cael balanced on the edge of the log and turned to Marina, "so, how did you manage to get out of the Fire Desert?"

The look in Marina's eyes grew distant and haunted, "after Dartain dragged you away, I used your sword to cut Lyris free. We came straight here after that, and Seren was able to disable my bonds. Greenwood has the best healers in the multiverse, my limbs are on their way to a speedy recovery," she laid one hand delicately over one bandaged wrist.

"Which reminds me, after lunch we need to have our healers take a look at your wounds Cael. That poultice is probably wearing off right about now," Seren interjected around a mouthful of stew.

Cael absently nodded, but his words were for Marina, "I'm so sorry you had to go through that."

Marina shrugged, a small smile on her lips, "it was no worse than what you had to go through. Truth be told, the worst part of the ordeal was knowing I played right into Dartain's hands by asking you for help and luring you into that trap. It was a stupid thing to do."

Cael shook his head, "I'd do it again in a heartbeat." Cael paused, a part of Marina's story finally registering in his brain, "wait a minute, you have my sword?"

"Oh. Yes, it is in the cabin I stayed in last night." Marina answered.

They soon after finished their food, and Seren led them to the medic cabin. Utilitarian cots lined the walls down the entire length of the building. Most of these cots were empty with the exception of one halfway down. A man wearing a cowboy hat and boots was standing over a young woman lying in the cot. He seemed incredibly worried, she just seemed exasperated.

"Beau, Brenda have you seen Courtney?" Seren asked as he strode through the room.

The man, Beau, answered in a Cajun accent, "well sure she's just in that room there." He pointed to a door at the back of the hall.

Seren turned to Cael and gestured to the bed next to the other couple, "stay here I'll be back in a moment." He then disappeared behind the aforementioned door.

Once Cael had perched on the edge of the bed, the woman in the bed smiled and said, "Hey there! I'm Brenda Rogers, and this is Beau Francoeur, what brings you guys here?"

In answer, Cael held up his right wrist to reveal the blistering flesh. Brenda gave a sharp inhale of breath, "ooh that looks pretty nasty, it must hurt something fierce."

Cael gave a sardonic grin, "well it certainly isn't comfortable."

This earned a chuckle from Brenda, she sat up and leaned forward which caused her companion to lurch forward in concern. She impatiently waved him away, "I'm fine! You stabbed my shoulder it's not like you punctured a lung or anything!"

"You stabbed her shoulder?" Marina asked disbelievingly.

Flustered, Beau attempted to defend himself, "we were just sparring and, mais, I don't know, I guess I lost control of my knife, or she dodged in a direction I didn't expect. It happened so fast. Have I mentioned how sorry I am, chère?"

Brenda rolled her eyes, "yes, about twenty times now and I assure you I will be fine. This isn't even the worst I've been hurt, do you remember when Lightning Strike kicked me and cracked four of my ribs?"

"Lightning Strike?" Cael asked.

"My horse," Brenda clarified.

Seren returned, followed by a blonde woman in a white frock. The woman, whom Cael assumed was Courtney, knelt down next to him at the edge of the bed to better inspect his injuries. Wordlessly she applied more poultice to the burns and wrapped them in clean linen bandages quickly and efficiently. Then she checked the cut along his right cheekbone and applied the poultice to that as well. She then, just as quietly, turned and left the room.

"Downright chatterbox, that one," Cael commented.

Seren shrugged, "Maybe, but she's a great healer, and that's what I need her for."

"Why do you need a healer in a creation temple anyway?" Cael inquired.

Seren tossed his head toward Brenda and Beau, "didn't you hear what happened to her? We get beat up a lot around here, so we need somebody to patch us up after our training sessions."

"Greenwood trains Runners, magic users who go to various planes of existence to assist with a variety of small conflicts and threats that may arise," Marina supplied.

"Mais, not all of us are magic users," Beau interjected.

"True," Seren conceded, "mundanes are allowed to serve as Runners if they are teamed up with a magic user."

"So I take you're the magic user in the team then," Cael asked Brenda.

"Yep! I'm a druid; I can communicate on a basic level with animals and control various aspects of nature."

Seren grinned, "Just like me. I like to take a special interest in training other druids and this one's as tough as nails."

"I was beginning to get that impression," Marina commented.

Brenda blushed and looked down at her lap, "Y'all are embarrassing me."

"Then you should stop being so impressive," Seren replied making Brenda's blush grow to a deeper shade of red, he then turned to Cael and Marina, "so what is the next step for each of you? Where do you go from here?"

Marina's sigh held a hint of weariness to it, "I need to get back to my temple as soon as is reasonable and help it recover from Dartain's invasion. And this experience has shown me that it is time to take on an apprentice, someone who can look after things if anything happens to me. I cannot leave the Temple entirely bereft of guidance."

"And for you?" Seren leveled an inquiring stare at Cael.

"I honestly don't know." it was the only reply he could come up with. After everything that happened in the Fire Desert, he wasn't sure he was ready to go after the demon king again. And without Darius to help and guide him, he was at something of a loss.

"Well, you are welcome to stay here at Greenwood until you figure it out," Seren offered

The trio said their farewells to Brenda and Beau and left the medic cabin. Once outside they were met with the sight of a large mahogany colored elk, sitting on its back was Lyris. The two familiars ambled through the dense foliage surrounding them. They casually made their way to the group to come to a stop right in front of them.

"Cael, where is Darius? I thought he had gone on patrol with Lyris and Baledin," Marina turned to Cael with concern washing over her features.

Cael looked away, an embarrassed scowl darkening his face. "I'm not sure exactly; when Dartain dragged me away, I couldn't separate from Darius. When I escaped, our physical forms separated and he just sort of... disappeared. I don't know, it's like our energies remained fused though, it still feels like we're united."

"How long were you fused?" Seren asked after laying a hand on the elk, Baledin's, back in greeting.

"I have no way of really knowing," Cael answered.

Marina gave Seren a skeptical look, "you don't think they separated right at the time limit? That's an incredibly rare occurrence, it's nearly unheard of."

Seren shrugged, "there's only one way to find out. Hey, Cael, you up for some sparring?"

Cael laid a hand on his bandaged wrist, "if it gives you the answer I need, then yeah, I'm game."

"You'll need your sword first," Marina commented before dashing off to where the cabins sat with Lyris right on her heels.

Seren gestured for Cael to follow him and Baledin and went back to the training ring that they had observed during lunch. They marched right past several runners training with their own weapons and the acolytes that watched over them. Cael felt a little self-conscious about trying this kind of experiment in front of a crowd of people he'd never met. Seren waved to the acolytes to clear the ring, and runners and acolytes alike scurried out of the way to make room for the two combatants with no few excited whispers. It was a rare treat at Greenwood to see the temple master fight.

Marina, with Lyris curled around her shoulders, returned with Howling Wolf in her hand. Even with everything going on Cael had to pause and admire how good she looked with a weapon in her grip. He gave her a smile as he took the sword from her. Marina smiled back warmly before finding a place in the crowd to stand.

"I'm sure you know of the technique to reinforce your weapon with raw magical energy, yes?" Seren began and continued after Cael's nodded confirmation, "good, I want you to use it for the entirety of this fight."

Cael readied himself and faced Seren and raised Howling Wolf up in front of him, an iron-gray light enveloping the blade. Seren twirled his wooden staff between his hands. Cael ignored the gesture as a mere flourish, but then Seren stepped in close and used the momentum to bring the staff down hard at Cael's head. Cael swiftly batted the blow aside with the flat of his blade.

"Impressive misdirection!" Cael complimented with a grin.

Seren raised an eyebrow at him, "this is a fight! You're not supposed to be having fun!"

With a laugh, Cael spun and slashed at the temple master, "Oh please, my pack and I spar all the time just for fun."

Seren snorted in frustration and blocked Cael's attack when the magic-infused steel sword made contact with the wooden staff the wood glowed with the rich brown light of Seren's own magical energy. The staff held its own against the blade, much to Cael's surprise. "Is this how you plan to fight Dartain?" Seren roared.

Cael scoffed, "no, but then I don't want to actually hurt you. Dartain is another matter entirely."

"Then take this seriously, Champion! Your fighting means nothing if you don't intend to inflict harm!" Seren jabbed the butt of his staff into Cael's gut. He doubled over momentarily and worked to catch his breath. He had brought up some magical energy to help shield the blow, but it hadn't been enough.

Cael growled low in his throat, it rumbled in his chest and sang in his blood. He swung upward with his sword, cutting into the temple master's jerkin. If Seren wanted a serious fight, then fine, that's exactly what he would get. He circled around his adversary he could smell the sweat of his prey. Cael leaped forward with Howling Wolf held high, ready to bring it crashing down on Seren's head.

The burly temple master answered the attack by side-stepping the swing and ramming his shoulder into Cael's chest, "is that really the best you can do? If that's the case, then we're all in trouble."

Aggravated, Cael charged forward calling up more magical energy ready to throw it like a grenade at his opponent. As he ran, he could feel his face lengthening and fur sprouting all over his body. He snapped at Seren with now sharp teeth in his newly formed snout. Before Cael could fling the ball of energy, Seren leaped backward with a triumphant grin.

"I'd say that confirms it," he announced.

Shocked, Cael looked down at his now mismatched hands; one metal but human shaped and the other covered in fur and ending in sharp claws. The hair slowly receded from his right hand as he watched leaving it exactly the same as it had been before. He looked up at Seren, "I don't understand."

Seren stepped forward, opening his mouth to explain, but he suddenly frowned and looked down at his stomach. He pushed aside the edges of the gash in the leather of his jerkin and pressed a hand into the hole. The fingers he pulled away had blood on them. In response to Cael's horrified expression Seren said, "it doesn't look bad, I'm confident that I will live, but I should still go see Courtney. Come along I can explain while she patches me up."

Seren led Cael, Marina, Baledin, and Lyris back to the medic cabin where he shed his jerkin and moved to fetch Courtney. Marina stopped him and made him sit down on the edge of one bed. "you helped both Cael and me when we were hurt. Now allow a fellow temple master to help you."

She disappeared into a back room that might have been Courtney's office, and both women returned shortly after. The healer's sharp eyes took in the blood stain slowly spreading across Seren's white linen under tunic. Concern washed the woman's features, and her jawline twitched. "I need you to remove that tunic," She ordered.

Seren stood up and lifted the ruined fabric up over his head, and a blush inexplicably blossomed on Courtney's cheeks as he did so. Seeing this, Cael tilted his head in confusion, a medical professional shouldn't typically be embarrassed to see the bare chest of someone of the opposite gender.

Courtney muttered a few incantations and conjured clean bandages and hot water and began working on Seren's wound. "How did this happen, Seren? Were you boxing with Baledin again?"

Seren laughed and gestured to Cael, "no, I was sparring with a wolf. That's basically what your transformation meant. It seems that when you and Darius ended your fusion, it must have been right at the four hour limit, so your bodies separated, but your energy remained combined. That technically makes you what we call a magi animalia or animal magic user. Usually, that term describes magic users and their descendants who are more traditionally fused, but it certainly fits your situation as well.

"Our little fight seems to confirm that you only take on Darius's form when you use a certain amount of your magical energy because you look perfectly normal right now."

Cael scowled, thinking, "so everything that Darius was is just gone?"

Marina put a comforting hand on his arm, "not really, it's just that he is fully apart of your consciousness now."

Cael nodded, but his scowl remained, he was just really getting to know Darius, and now he wouldn't be able to, but then again maybe the wolf had always only been a reflection of himself, though that answer didn't seem particularly satisfying.

Courtney interrupted Cael's reverie, "if it is just the use of his magic that sparks the transformation then why was it necessary to fight him?"

Before Seren could answer she threw a clean under tunic at his face, "there, you're all patched up," she turned from Seren who's chest was now tightly bandaged, and rounded on Cael, "try not to hack up our temple master in the future please." Then she moved to leave the room without another word.

Seren grinned at her retreating back, "before the sword wound happened, it was a lot of fun." This comment earned him a scowl from Courtney before she disappeared into her office.

Cael turned to leave as well but paused to look at Seren as he pulled on the fresh tunic, "by the way, you surprised me in our match. You're the first magic user besides Dorothy that I've met who reinforces their attacks with magical energy."

Seren laughed, "It is purely a combat technique. I don't imagine anyone from the other temples has much of a use for it."

For the rest of the day, Cael wandered around the woods surrounding Greenwood. Marina walked at his side, with Lyris once more curled around her neck but she refrained from speaking. She let him mull over what he had learned in silence. Cael was glad of her company; her presence was a quiet comfort.

He was unsure how to feel about the loss of Darius, but aside from that, he was different. He could feel it lurking at the edges of his consciousness. Magi animalia is what Seren had called it. Did that mean he was an animal now? And what about that dark, sinister shadow within him? Did that mean Dartain had succeeded in grafting a portion of his essence to Cael's soul? If he had, Dartain's plan must not have worked, Cael still had his magic, and he didn't feel corrupted in any way. Did he?

Cael's thoughts ran in this circular pattern until the early autumn sun began to darken and Marina turned them around to head back to the temple. Supper consisted of roasted chicken and vegetables. This time they ate at picnic tables under a wooden roof supported by rough-hewn logs. It seemed the whole temple was there and the night air rang with the boisterous songs and laughter of the Runners.

The cheerful atmosphere went a long way to bringing up Cael's spirits. He, Lyris and Marina even joined in a raucous rendition of "the rattlin' bog" at the end on the night. Soon after, they returned to their separate cabins to sleep.

Cael lay awake, staring up at the rafters and wondered what his next move should be. Truth be told, he felt a little lost. He felt like he needed counsel and as helpful as the temple masters had been there was one person in his life that had always given him the best advice; Dorothy. The more Cael thought about it, the better a trip home sounded. Not only would Cael be able to speak with his mother and mentor but hopefully, he could catch most of the Wolf Pack even though they must have already dispersed for college. Maybe he could even get Abby to replace his communicator watch, he thought ruefully as he picked off a piece of melted plastic from his metal wrist.

Cael drifted off to sleep wondering what his pack had been up to while he had been away.

Chapter XI:
Home Again

The next morning found Cael checking his gear and making sure he had everything he needed. He was now dressed once again in his Sablewater jerkin; he had left the Greenwood one laid out on the bed. Once he was confident that he was all set, he made his way back to the picnic tables where they had eaten dinner the previous night. He was not disappointed to find everyone with their faces in plates of egg and sausage.

Marina looked up from her breakfast and frowned, "leaving so soon?"

Cael nodded somberly, "I think it's time I make a trip back home. I need to get my head back together, but that begs the question; how are you holding up from all this?"

Marina smiled and pushed a plate of food at him, "I'm holding up just fine. I don't think I'll be curling up by any bonfires again anytime soon, but I can put it behind me."

Cael sat down and took one of Marina's hands in his own, "I just want you to know that if you ever need anything, I'm here for you."

"I appreciate that," Marina smiled, "the same goes for you, it's not like I am hard to reach."

Cael laughed, "no, I suppose you're not."

The morning passed more quickly than Cael would have liked. Before he knew it, he was stepping through a portal and back into the Illuminated Mists, equipped with a large circular tin of Courtney's poultice and instructions to change his bandages once a day. Cael didn't think he would have to use it too much. As bad as his burns had been, whatever was in the poultice had just about healed it with only two applications.

Cael barely noticed his passage through the over-bright surroundings of the Mists this time. It was only when he was almost in the area that would open up to the outside of Purple House that he realized how comfortable he had suddenly become with previously hated plane of existence. Presumably, this was another side effect of his fusion with Darius.

Perturbed, he tore a portal open. He noted this time that, yes, his hand did in fact briefly shift to a clawed appendage covered in iron hued fur.

Purple House looked mostly unchanged this morning. Cael supposed it hadn't really been all that long since he left. Had it only been a few months? It felt like a lot longer. He went to push open the gate, but the doors held firm.

"Of course it's locked," Cael laughed and shook his head. Without hesitating, Cael hopped up on the stone wall off to the side and vaulted over the iron poles jutting out. His landing, however, has not as smooth and he had to roll into it to regain his feet. He had to admit that he was glad no one was around to see his misstep.

Cael sprinted across the lawn to the front porch and paused at the front door. Should he knock? Or should he just walk right in?

He laid a hand on the brass doorknob, better to just walk in, Cael decided. He knew he was always welcome at Purple house even if it wasn't technically his home anymore. As soon as he stepped over the threshold, Cael was met with the familiar noise of screaming children. Joey was chasing Jessica around the parlor with a lizard he had found outside.

They stopped abruptly when they noticed Cael in the doorway. "Uncle Cael!" the two children rushed forward with hugs and smiling faces, and Cael found himself immeasurably comforted by such a warm greeting. The pair then began tugging him, one child at each arm, toward Dorothy's office.

"Miss O'Donnell will be so happy to see you!" Joey exclaimed. "She set up a boring old dummy in the practice ring. It's no fun to watch her fight anymore."

Cael chuckled, "well maybe we can spar a bit while I'm here."

"You mean you're not staying?" Joey asked looking back.

Cael shook his head, "I'm afraid I can only stay a little while."

The young boy looked disappointed at this news, but brightened after a moment, "that just means we'll have to have as much fun as we can before you leave again!"

"Joey who are you..." Dorothy's question dropped off abruptly when she emerged from her office to find Cael standing in the hallway with the two kids. Her gaze roved over his neatly bandaged wounds, and the cut at his cheek and her eyes welled up with unshed tears. "Oh, my poor dear! Look at you! What have you been doing?"

The next thing Cael knew he was being captured in a crushing hug. She only let him go when he let out a grunt of discomfort as he felt his ribs compress. "Funny how your first reaction to seeing me all busted up is to try and collapse my lungs," Cael complained rubbing his side.

"Sorry," Dorothy smiled sheepishly, "I've just been so worried about you." She led Cael through the house to the kitchen and sat him down at the table. Joey and Jessica, sensing a good story pulled up chairs as well. Dorothy paused to make coffee for her and Cael and get milk for the two kids and shooed them out of the room with much grumbling on their part before she took her own seat. "Tell me everything."

Cael took a grateful sip of the dark, warm liquid before he began, starting with meeting Ferdinand. ("You would have really liked him, he kinda reminded me of you!") He tried to downplay the danger he was in during the attack on Crossroads and his encounter with the fire cat, he didn't want his mother to worry too much. As he told her all about his stay at Sablewater, Dorothy smiled knowingly at him, and he felt his cheeks warm up as he spoke.

He had trouble finding the right words to accurately describe the sensation of fusing, but in the end, he felt as though he got the point across. When Cael got to the part about the Fire Desert, he had difficulty keeping his voice level and his temper even, and Dorothy's face only became more and more concerned, an expression that was alleviated only slightly when he told her about being taken care of at Greenwood.

"It sounds like you have been through quite a lot," Dorothy commented, "worse than what I went through."

Cael nodded absentmindedly, "truth be told, I don't really know where to go from here."

Dorothy was silent for a moment as she contemplated his problem, "and Seren called you magi animalia?"

"That's right."

"Hmmm well, firstly I would recommend you take a few days to just recharge your batteries so to speak. And then, there is a plane of existence that is entirely populated with Magi Animalia. It might do you some good to spend time with them. They may be able to help you make more sense of your new state of being."

"Maybe," Cael conceded, "but I think you're definitely right about the first part, I need to spend some time with the Wolf Pack."

"Absolutely," Dorothy nodded, "before you go running off, however, I expect you to eat some lunch."

"Well I didn't mean today, I just got home," Cael remarked.

"Oh!" she laughed, "right, my mistake."

Cael spent the rest of the day out on the lawn with the other kids of Purple House. They were playing a cross between hide and seek and tag. At one point Cael hoisted himself up onto the roof of the porch. He was only discovered when Tommy got far enough away from the house that he could see the whole roof. Cael had to jump down and roll into a run but before he could really get going Tommy tackled him around the knees. Once he was on Tommy's team the two of them rather quickly round up the rest of the kids.

They played round after round of the game until the storm clouds covered sky which darkened beyond the point of usefulness and Dorothy called them all in for dinner. After being sustained with a variety of exotic foods for the last few months, Cael could really appreciate the comfort of enjoying his mother's cooking. There was something special in its familiarity.

There was no other room for Cael to sleep that night other than his old bed in the boy's dormitory. So Cael folded up his things and laid them out neatly in the cedar chest at the foot of his bed. He made sure to put his weapons at the very bottom. He knew that because of the mage sheaths the children would not be able to touch them, but he didn't want to risk it.

Cael laid down on his old familiar bed and let the sound of the soft rain that had begun to patter against the windows lull him to sleep.

Cael ran toward a building that was remarkably similar to the manor at Purple House and yet nothing like it. He heard a scream and leaped onto the front porch. The light from within flickered and danced with a chaos that could only mean one thing.

The house was on fire.

Cael pressed his hands and face to one of the front windows to look inside and discover who had screamed. The heat from the glass forced him to pull away with a sharp intake of breath, but he had seen that is was Marina who was trapped inside. He faced the door and backed up a few paces and threw his shoulder at it with all his might. Cael did this again and again, but even after the sixth time, the door would not budge. The seventh time he slammed into the door the window to his right blew outward, tongues of flame hungrily licking out in all directions seeking the oxygen of the outside air.

He couldn't see Marina anymore, but he heard her scream again with a panic that threatened to claim his own heart along with hers. Cael would not allow this; he couldn't take her being in danger, not again, once was way more than enough.

Cael awoke in a cold sweat; he pressed his fingers to his eyes in an attempt to rid himself of the images from the dream and waited for his heart to return to its normal rhythm. When he removed his fingers he noticed a faint light flickering under his left eye. It was coming from the vicinity of the scar that had formed from where Dartain's dagger had cut him in his escape from the Fire Desert. It seemed so weak that it was only in pure darkness that it could even be noticed.

A light flashed just outside the window, and Cael's heart jumped up into his throat. He bolted out of bed to investigate, but he saw nothing outside. A moment later, a boom of thunder shook the walls of the house. The storm had grown in ferocity during the night. Nothing was on fire.

Cael turned to get back into bed, still rather unsettled by his nightmare. An exclamation of fear came through the darkness, and a small voice asked, "what was that?"

"It's just the storm, Tommy," Cael reassured.

"That thunder sounded really close though," Tommy whimpered, "I'm scared."

"Whoa hey," Cael sat down at the foot of Tommy's bed, "there's nothing to be afraid of."

"Are you sure? What if lightning hits the house?" the question came from Peter's bed deeper in the darkness. At this point, all the boys in the dorm had woken up and were looking about fearfully. Ben, whose bed was right under the window, flinched as another bolt of lightning lit up the room. When the following thunder shook the window pane, Jason, Zack, and Joey jumped up from their beds simultaneously and rushed to where Cael was sitting.

"If anything happens I will keep you safe," Cael said. He pulled the covers back up to Tommy's chin and sat Zack down on his knee before he began to sing a soft lullaby;

worry not, though the storm rages on
and bombards our walls, I will keep you safe
I will let no harm come to you
no matter what threat knocks on the door
worry not, though the lightning will flash
and thunder shakes up the sky, I will keep you safe
and the rain will soon fade
and the sun will chase all the clouds away
worry not, tomorrow there will be blue skies again
and I will keep you safe

By the time he had finished the boys had looked calmer, and Cael found that by calming their fears, his own had quieted as well. He stood up and ushered everyone back to their beds before climbing into his and drifting off to sleep himself.

* * *

Cael came down to breakfast the next morning feeling more lighthearted than he had since setting out on his mission. In the kitchen, Dorothy was making pancakes. Half the chairs at the kitchen table where occupied by children giggling with excitement. Cael slipped into his seat and picked up his knife and fork and started a chant of, "Pancakes! Pancakes!" The rest of the table promptly picked up the chant, and soon the whole kitchen was full of the sound.

"Okay, okay, here they are," Dorothy set two plates that were heaped high with the fluffy breakfast bread down on either side of the table.

The kitchen quieted down almost immediately while everyone's mouth was too full to speak. The volume went right back up as soon as breakfast was over and the children tore out of the mansion like a pack of shrieking beasts to play out in the yard. Cael watched them go with a slight smile on his face.

"They're good kids, incredibly energetic, but certainly good," he commented to his mother as they began to clean up.

Dorothy laughed, "do you not remember when you and the Wolf Pack were the ones screaming at the top of your lungs as you stomped through this house?"

"I'm sure I don't know what you're talking about," Cael sniffed in a dignified manner.

"Of course not," Dorothy grinned.

Cael put the last dish away and headed out to the base of operations for the Pack. It had only been a few months since he had left the city, but for some reason, he had expected it to somehow look different. Nothing was, of course, everything was exactly how he had left it, even the door to the base had not changed in any way.

Once inside the dilapidated building, Cael announced himself with a wolfish howl; the sound of it reverberated in his chest. Five howls answered him, Cael had managed to catch the whole pack. Up the stairs, Cael marched and into their usual room.

"Cael!" Brock exclaimed as soon as Cael came into view. The redhead leaped over the back of the couch he'd been sitting on and bounded over to his friend. "You're back! Did you win already?"

Cael ran a hand through his hair, "not exactly, I kinda got my butt handed to me, actually," he admitted, "I'm here to regroup."

"What happened?" Gavin asked, sitting forward.

Cael related the story as succinctly as possible. He tried to downplay the dangerous parts as much as possible, but when he got to the part in the fire desert, Max grabbed his right hand to look closer at the bandages on his wrist. The look of concern Max gave him nearly broke his heart. "I'm sorry, I know it puts you guys in a horrible position but if I can protect innocent people that need it; this," he held up his wounded wrist, "is worth it."

At this, a scowl slowly etched itself into Max's features. He flicked Cael's titanium arm, "and is this worth it?" he demanded, "what about that cut across your cheek? These battles are tearing you up, and I can't stand seeing it. What's worse is you don't even seem to care about what happens to you! It's almost like you enjoy walking around all torn up."

Everyone in the room sat for a minute in stunned silence, even Max himself seemed a little surprised at his own outburst.

Cael eventually found his voice, "it isn't that I enjoy getting hurt, it's just that I'm strong enough to take it. Even after getting dragged through the Fire Desert I'm still standing. Someone else might not come out of an encounter with Dartain so well."

Max's anger seemed to have died down a bit. "I still don't like it," he muttered.

Cael placed a hand on his friend's shoulder, "I know, I'm sorry. I really am being as careful as I can... most of the time. But enough about me, what have you all been up to?" Cael moved to sit down with the rest of the group, Brock and Max resumed their seats as well.

"Same old stuff mostly, man, except Abby," Gavin gestured to the girl sitting across from him, "she disappeared shortly after you did and came back a few days ago, we were just trying to get her to tell us where she's been."

Cael looked at Abby questioningly, she was still trying to keep her magic secret? Cael had figured that since she had taken the trip to train at the temples, she had also let the secret out, but that was apparently not the case.

As they stared at each other, Abby seemed to be coming to a decision. Eventually, she hung her head in defeat with an exasperated sigh, "Alright fine," she said, "but before I tell you where I went this summer, there's something you should know first." Here she paused as if she was gathering the strength to continue. "Cael isn't the only magic user in the group, I'm a seer. I went to learn how to use my magic. That's why I sometimes get a faraway look, I get these visions of little stuff that's about to happen." she fell silent as if afraid to continue.

Jim leaned forward, "why didn't you say so before?"

"I... I was afraid of what you would think. I know it sounds dumb because we are all so used to Cael, but that's just it; Cael had his magic under such firm control, and mine just seemed to happen so randomly without any push from me." Her voice cracked with emotion, but she swallowed it down and continued, "so when the opportunity came to change all that I seized it as quickly as I could. I have it under control now."

After a moment she brightened considerably, "oh! And I figured out an upgrade for the communication watches, I just have to make a few tweaks, and we'll be able to talk to Cael no matter what plane of existence he goes to."

At this Cael cleared his throat uncomfortably, "well, about that. Um... when Dartain tied me up, the fire rope kind of... melted my watch."

"He melted your watch?!" Abby shouted.

"That's extra harsh," Gavin commented.

"Yikes," Brock sputtered.

"Yeah," Cael rubbed the back of his neck, he didn't know what else to say.

"I guess it's kind of a good thing that wrist isn't made of flesh in this instance. Could you imagine how much melted rubber would hurt on bare skin?" Jim said.

Cael shuttered, "I don't want to."

Abby shook her head, "Well you are in luck I have a prototype of the new design you can have, I was going to give it to Marina, but it would probably be better to give her one after she's met the rest of the Pack."

"Who's Marina?" Max asked interestedly with a smirk.

Cael could feel his face heat up in a blush, "she, uh... she's this woman."

"Just a woman?" Brock teased.

"He loooooooves her," Abby taunted.

"Wait, Cael is actually interested in a girl? That hasn't happened since Tiffany at the beginning of freshman year." Gavin said.

"This is different," Cael responded in a slightly wistful tone, "she's beautiful and caring and adventurous and playful. She can turn around the worst of situations just by being there. Even after

197

having my rear end handed to me by Dartain, everything seemed better just because she was near me."

Gavin grinned, "sounds like you've fallen hard there, buddy."

Cael ran a hand through his hair, "I guess I have." He then looked around the room at each member of his pack in turn, "but, seriously, enough about me what have you guys been up to?"

"I switched to full time at Silversmith's, I'm currently working on a rather elaborate set of wedding rings," Jim offered.

"Wow, that sounds fancy," Cael commented.

"Yeah, it's been a bit of a challenge," Jim replied.

"And I've just started at Rockfield, that's the culinary institute I got accepted into, this is the first weekend I've been able to come down, so you have good timing," Gavin said.

"Ugh, don't remind me," Brock whined, "I have three essays to finish this weekend."

Max shook his head, "that's what you get for putting it off till the last minute. We've known about those essays for two weeks."

"Didn't classes only start two weeks ago? You were assigned essays on the first day?" Abby asked.

"Yes," came Max's prompt response.

"Well I suppose they want to give us our tuition's worth by cramming in as much work as possible," Brock reasoned.

Cael nodded, "Makes sense, are you guys roommates in the dorms?"

"Naturally," Max answered.

"Even though you still live here in town?" Abby asked.

"I was not staying at my dad's house," Max asserted.

"For me, it's not a need as such, no, but I feel living in the dorms would be not only more convenient, but it would allow us to have a more full college experience," Brock explained.

The Wolf Pack spent the rest of the afternoon catching up. Apparently, Brock's little sister, Janet, had joined a roller derby team and two weeks into practicing took a hit and cracked a bone in her forearm and had to be rushed to the hospital. Now the only thing she was still complaining about is that the team wouldn't let her skate until it was healed. Cael was impressed, Janet had always been a little firecracker. It seemed like Brock couldn't decide if he was more proud or exasperated with his little sister.

Jim's Abuela had taken to bragging to anyone who made the mistake of sitting still long enough in her presence about how proud she was that her grandson had acquired such a respectable profession right out of high school. This caused Jim no end of embarrassment.

At the end of the day when the pack got up to leave, the strangest feeling came over Cael, like something was wrong. He paused to listen but couldn't hear anything. He was reminded of Dartain, but nothing around him seemed to be amiss. Maybe it was just shadows of the nightmare he'd had last night.

Gavin looked back from the door to see Cael standing in the middle of the room looking around, "everything okay, brother?"

"Hmm? Oh, it's nothing, just stress I guess. I just need to relax," Cael rubbed the back of his neck and gave the rest of the pack a smile.

The Pack got no more than halfway down the hall before the feeling overcame Cael again, stronger this time. He could not brush this off as an overreaction, something was wrong. He was about to speak up when a crash sounded from one of the unused apartments. Cael pushed forward to stand in between the pack and whatever was coming.

For a moment, nothing happened, and Cael had the time to second guess his instincts. Maybe he was wrong? Maybe Dartain hadn't come to attack him and his pack? The answer came a second later as a fire cat exploded through the half-broken door that closed off 5D.

With a gasp, Cael threw out his left arm to block Jim's way to keep him out of danger. With his other hand, he drew one of his bladed half-gauntlets. The halls were too enclosed to use his sword. "Stay back, let me handle this," Cael warned, stepping forward.

With a growl, the fire cat prowled forward. Cael stepped into a defensive stance and waited. The fire cat leaped forward with claws extended. Cael darted to the right and plunged his blades into the fire cat's side; he then used the beast's momentum to slam it into the floor with a thunderous crash. Cael immediately understood the full danger he was in as fire clung to his half-gauntlet and dripped onto the carpeted floor from the demon's ribs. He had to finish this thing off as efficiently as possible.

Halfway through this thought process, the animal had quickly turned around to pounce on Cael. Together they tumbled to the ground. Cael's weapon was knocked from his hand, and it slid across the floor out of reach. He tried to make a grab for it but the fire cat bore down on him, and he was forced to contend with the demon's sharp fangs. He smashed the palm of his left hand against the monster's snout and drew one of his throwing knives from its place at his chest and slit the fire cat's throat.

Jim rushed forward to pull the monster off of Cael seconds before the beast burst into flames that burnt savagely and quickly died out leaving only minor scorch marks on the carpet. Cael sat up with a huff, "you just really saved my bacon there, thank you."

Jim offered a hand to help Cael to his feet, "well you did just fight a demon for us so we'll call it even."

"Deal," Cael agreed.

Chapter XII:
Athanor

A few weeks later, the fading light of the setting sun found Cael, Dorothy, Althea and the whole rest of the Wolf Pack in the woods on the Purple House grounds. Since his return, Althea had shown him the proper way to open portals into the Illuminated Mists. He had just done so before turning to look at his family. He once again had all his gear packed away in the pouch at his belt and his weapons secured on his back.

"Well, this is it. I should get back out there," Cael offered Dorothy a warm embrace and each of the Wolf Pack in turn.

"The next time I see you, I want to hear all about your victory over this demon," Gavin said as he let go of Cael's hug. Then he reached up and ruffled Cael's hair, "because I know you can beat him."

Cael gave a lopsided grin and tilted his head to one side, "thanks for the vote of confidence."

With one last grin and a wave, Cael stepped through the portal. Dorothy had told him that his best bet was to travel to the city of Athanor to make contact with the Knights of the Silver Tree, so that's where he was headed. Navigating through the Mists seemed more natural now, it also seemed to take less time, but Cael was sure that was all in his head.

Cael came out of the Mists in front of a cinder block castle whose courtyard was illuminated by stadium lights. An asphalt road led up to a lowered drawbridge where two guards stood watch one was a scowling jackrabbit-man, and the other was a bored looking alligator-lady.

As Cael approached, the jackrabbit's scowl only deepened but the alligator's gaze alighted with interest as she regarded him, "Well well, what do we have here?"

The jackrabbit rolled his eyes, "name, rank, and purpose?" he demanded.

Cael was taken aback, "Um... Cael Ivywood, and uh champion of the creation temples, and well... information... I guess?"

"What kind of information does a pink-skinned champion need from the Knights of the Silver Tree?" the jackrabbit shifted his grip on the halberd he was holding.

At this point, the alligator waved off her partner, "oh don't mind Jared he's been a stick in the mud since the day he was born. What can we help you with sugar?"

Jared looked rather offended at this, "a stick in the mud am I, Oretha? Better a stick in the mud than a cross on the ground which is all too likely these days with the Blackfire legion on the prowl again."

Oretha brushed him off flippantly, "that doesn't change our main purpose to protect and serve."

"Um, to answer your question," Cael interjected, "the temple master of Greenwood told me that I had become an unusual example of magi animalia after my most recent encounter with the demon king Dartain. I suppose I need information on being a magi animalia."

"You sure don't look like one of us," Jared grumbled

"I only gain my familiar's aspect when I use my magic excessively," Cael retorted.

Oretha turned to the interior of the castle and shouted, "hey Zander! Can you come here?"

For a few seconds, nothing happened, but then a white wolf-man appeared. This one seemed younger than the first two. He jogged up to Oretha eagerly. "Yeah, what's up?"

"Zander, hun, could you be a doll and take Cael here to Sir Alexander?"

The wolf seemed to puff out his chest in pride, "it would be an honor. Though could you cool it with the 'huns' and the 'sweeties' I was already knighted last week."

Oretha smiled, "my mistake."

"Thank you," Zander beckoned for Cael to follow, "this way."

They passed under the portcullis and took a side corridor that skirted the courtyard. Zander gave Cael an open, friendly smile, "got some business with the Patriarch huh?"

"Patriarch?" Cael asked.

"Yeah, Sir Alexander, he's our leader," came Zander's reply.

"Ah. Then yeah. I just need some guidance on what to expect now that I am a magi animalia."

Zander paused and studied Cael's face a moment, "what was your familiar? Some kind of monkey? Even then you don't look like a monkey."

"Nope, he was a wolf," under normal circumstances Cael might have been offended by the young knight's words, but his demeanor was so congenial Cael knew he meant no offense.

"Get outta town!" Zander exclaimed.

"No it's true, something weird just happened when we tried to separate," Cael explained yet again.

"Well color me purple! Anyways Alexander will know just what to do with you!" Zander pushed open an impressively large iron-banded door and led the way through. Inside there was what could only be described as a war table that took up the center of the chamber around this several heavy wooden chairs were situated. On one wall there was a row of floor to ceiling windows and on the opposite hung a row of heavy tapestries. On the back was an enormous portrait of a regal looking lion-man with golden fur and rich brown mane, beside him was painted an equally regal looking lioness with amber fur. On the ceiling and currently lighting the room was several strips of fluorescent lights.

Sitting at the head of the table was the lion-man from the painting. To his left was a woman with the features of a raven and to his right was a sapphire colored panther-man. They seemed to be in deep conversation and for a moment did not notice when Cael and Zander entered. Then the panther nudged the lion and gestured to the newcomers. Zander stepped forward, placed his right fist over his heart and bowed at the waist. The other two around the table stood and copied the gesture before the lion-man spoke, "Sir Zander, what matter do you bring before us?"

"Ah yes Sir Alexander, this is Cael, a new magi animalia who comes seeking guidance," Zander said after straightening from his own bow.

The sapphire panther seemed to regard Cael with great care, but the lion man approached him congenially, arms wide open. He moved out from behind the table and came to stand before Cael.

"Welcome to the ranks. Sometimes the transition can be a bit much to deal with, though you seem to be dealing with it quite... okay are you sure you're a magi animalia? You don't look like one."

Cael sighed, exasperated, "my familiar and I separated right at the time limit. I only look like a magi animalia when I use a great deal of magical energy." Cael practically snarled the sentence. He was getting tired of explaining his situation to every single person he met.

Sir Alexander's frown turned into a wry grin, "ah yes there it is."

The panther spoke from his place at the table, "separating exactly at the time limit is nearly impossible to do. What? Did you watch the clock and split then on purpose to gain your familiar's power?"

Now Cael did snarl; a growl that started low and built up in his throat. Without thinking he nearly tore his sword from its sheath. Halfway through, he remembered himself and slid the weapon back home. "Something... prevented me from splitting with Darius until it was too late. He vanished before my eyes."

Alexander placed a comforting hand on Cael's shoulder, "Take it easy my friend, and pay no mind to Jasper he has spent the last month breaking up a racket of Shifters; benevolent magic users that slay their familiars to get stronger and shift to the side of malevolence. I fear the time spent has darkened his viewpoint somewhat." the lion casts a glance over his shoulder to give Jasper a displeased look.

The raven woman cackled, "I don't know about that, sir, he's always been a cynical son of a..."

"Rona," Jasper interrupted warningly.

"Enough," Alexander commanded. He then turned to Zander, "I wonder if you could do me a favor Sir Zander, take Cael with you on your duties, for the next few weeks at least. Let him pick up on what it means to be an animal magic user naturally. I would do it myself, but I fear with the Blackfire legion on the move I have my claws full directing our forces."

Zander stood at attention, "yes sir! No problem sir!"

The lion-man grinned at the young wolf's enthusiasm, "very well then you two are dismissed."

Zander turned around and beckoned Cael back out of the room and down another set of hallways. He looked over his shoulder at his new charge, "I had just been on my way to the barracks actually. So, let's see if we can't grab you a bunk."

The bunks as it turned out were all on the other side of the castle. Zander brought him to a large room lined with beds, not unlike the boy's dormitory at Purple House. All the bunks were empty except for one near the door. A black jackal sat on the bunk's edge looking up at an impala woman with a look of pure annoyance on his canine features. "Look, Cindy, I'm not his keeper I don't know where he went. I'm sure he has a lot of responsibilities now with being a knight and still working to get his pilot's license."

"Ugh, just tell him that..." her head turned at the sound of Zander and Cael's approach. "There you are! You left this at Mom and Dad's house the other day." Cindy abandoned her place in front of the jackal to shove a sheathed long sword into Zander's arms.

The white wolf quietly sighed, "you came all this way for that? There are a million of these lying around. This castle has twelve armories."

"Whatever, our parents just didn't want you to get in trouble, and I like a good sister took the time to bring it to you, but if you're going to be a butt about it, I won't bother next time." the impala waved one hand dismissively and walked out of the room.

"Was that seriously all she came here to say? She pestered me for a quarter hour about where you were!" the jackal exclaimed, standing up.

Zander scratched at one ear sheepishly, "sorry, Dane, you know how persistent my big sister can be."

"Sister?" Cael asked, "but you're a wolf, and she's... not."
For a moment, Zander seemed confused then he brightened, "I guess that's one of the things you need to learn about our kind. My dad is an impala, and my mom is a wolf. Their kids," he gestured to himself, "can be one or the other."

Cael shrugged agreeably, "I guess that makes sense."

"Yep, anyway," he slung an arm companionably around the jackal's shoulders, "this is my best friend, Dane. And this," he gestured to Cael with his other arm, "is Cael; he's a wolf magi animalia. He just doesn't look like it."

Dane looked momentarily skeptical before Zander hastened to explain. Cael was grateful that for once since arriving he did not have to relive losing Darius. It was draining having to explain to every new person he met why he didn't look like an actual wolf. Dane gave Cael a sympathetic look at the end of Zander's explanation but offered no further comment.

"So what were you doing just hanging around the barracks anyway?" Zander asked.

"Waiting for you actually, are you off patrol yet?" Dane inquired.

Zander merely nodded, "where are you going with this?"

At this Dane gave a smirk and shrugged off the white wolf's arm before companionably punching his arm. "Revels tonight!" he exclaimed. "several in town actually. I figured it would do you some good to cut loose, you've been so busy lately. Not to mention we never properly celebrated our elevation to knighthood."

Zander waved him off, "you know I never let a heavy workload get to me."

"Fine, but the occasion should be marked with some fanfare at least regardless," Dane protested.

Zander laughed, "I never did say that I didn't want to go. What kind of revel did you have in mind?"

In answer, Dane gave the pair of wolves a wide grin and left the room. He led them out of the Barracks and to a large garage. Their footsteps echoed against the corrugated steel walls and bare concrete floor. Inside there where countless vehicles that looked a lot like ATVs that were designed for street travel as well as for the wilderness. Dane hopped onto one of these vehicles and fired it up.

Zander paused and turned to Cael, thrusting a thumb in the vehicle's direction, "have you ever ridden a steed before?"

"Never in my life," Cael answered apprehensively. He had never driven before back home there hadn't been much point when he could just take the subway everywhere he needed to go, and when that wasn't an option, Abby had always enthusiastically offered up her driving talents.

"Better ride with me tonight then. Maybe while you're here, we can teach you it's a good skill to have." Zander swung his leg over another steed as he'd called it and patted the seat directly behind him indicating that Cael should mount up as well.

They tore out of the garage with a deafening mechanical roar. The headlamps on the front of their steeds lighted their way as they crossed the drawbridge and headed toward the city lights in the near distance. As they traveled, Cael's legs and hands began to go numb from the cold he was unable to move them much to warm them up, so he just grits his teeth and hoped they were almost to their destination.

Their destination, as it turned out was a club. Its name "The Courtyard" was emblazoned on the front in glowing neon; A long line of patrons, waiting to get in, stretched down the sidewalk. A large bison stood by guarding the door. An assortment of other Magi Animalia strolled up and down the street in and out of the other various shops and restaurants in the area.

The trio approached the bison at the door who raised an eyebrow at them. "What makes you think you can skip the line boys?" Then the bouncer took in the appearance of the two knights before him; the combat boots and the black cargo pants and lastly the dark silver sleeveless workout shirt with a white tree on the chest. "You're knights of the silver tree? That changes things. Thank you for your service, go on in." The bison opened the door and stood to the side and allowed the three of them to pass.

Cael breathed a little easier he didn't think he would have also been let in quite as easily as his companions, he mentioned as much to Zander.

"The knights command a lot of respect in Athanor, I'm sure he could tell you were with us, he might have even assumed you were a knight too. You carry yourself like one."

"Do I?" asked Cael, taken aback, "huh..."

They strolled deeper into the club. The room was largely dark with colorful spotlights dotting the area. A pounding baseline reverberated in Cael's ribcage and the music it accompanied sounded vaguely pop-y. There were several patrons of varying species seated on stools clustered around tall round tables. There was a dance floor in the middle of the room that, at the moment, was only populated by a single couple.

Dane led them to a slightly secluded area where a number of couches framed a rectangular coffee table. Sitting on one couch was a grizzled old mallard with a deep gouge carved across his bill and feathers that wouldn't quite lay flat on his head anymore. He wore the same black cargo pants and gray workout shirt that Cael's companions wore. He sat nursing his drink as he watched the crowd with sharp eyes.

"I don't believe it! You're Leopold the Mighty!" Dane exclaimed, "Could we sit with you?"

The mallard gave a rueful grin, "sure kid, so long as you just call me Pold. Have you seriously ever heard of a duck called Leo?"

Zander smiled as he settled on an adjacent couch, "just you."

Pold settled back into the couch, "yeah well I'd just as soon avoid it." he studied the two young knights closely, largely ignoring Cael. "Aren't you a couple of the pups that just got knighted?"

"Yes, sir! Just last week," Zander promptly answered.

Pold laughed, "well welcome to the club."

"Thanks! We're actually celebrating it tonight," Dane explained.

"You two have quite an adventure ahead of you." the mallard chuckled.

"I bet you've had more than your share of adventures huh?" Zander asked.

"Yeah! Tell us about the hedgehog burrow," Dane pleaded.

"Oh jeez that, well my squire at the time and I were out investigating this rash of killings miles outside of the city when this hedgehog archer appears out of nowhere up on a cliff ahead of us. We stop just outside of his range, and he warns us to turn around and leave. My squire, he was a bobcat, you might know him now as Sir Oswald. Anyway, he heard several other attackers moving around to surround us.

"So no lie there I was outnumbered and surrounded, so I take my hand ax and throw it, taking out the archer. Oswald had his sword out in a flash and leaped behind some bushes and comes outdueling two more hedgehogs with swords. I draw my own and meet the charge of still two more. They managed to push me to the edge of this shallow ravine so instead of fighting it I jumped down to the bottom of it. The whole thing was maybe five feet deep, so I still had a good shot of their feet.

"Well, what do you think I did? I cut those cowards down at the ankles! By the time I climbed out of the ravine Oswald had taken care of his opponents as well. When we searched the area, we managed to collect all the evidence we needed to prove they had been the ones doing the killing."

Dane let out a low, impressed, whistle, "wow you took out three hedgehogs just like that? No wonder you're a legend among the Knights!"

Pold shook his head amiably, "I've just been at this a long time. You two will get the chance to collect your own stories."

Cael leaned forward from his seat at the far end of the couch, "what was the hardest battle you ever fought?"

"Oh I don't know, they all had their difficulties," the mallard said dismissively. He then turned back to Zander and Dane and asked much more excitedly, "so what assignment are you pups on?"

Cael scowled, he got the distinct impression he was being ignored. He turned his attention away from the conversation and scanned the interior of the club. More patrons seemed to have trickled in; the dance floor now had a small crowd all moving to the music pounding out of the overhead speakers. The tables seemed to be more heavily populated.

One group at the tables caught Cael's eye; five animals sat in what appeared to be a deep conversation. Every minute or so a different member of the table would turn to scowl at Cael and his companions. This went on for a solid twenty minutes. In the intervening time, Pold was regaling Zander and Dane with another story.

With an angry shove away from the table, a goat-man approached the small group at the couches. "Hey mongrels!" he bleated, "you self-righteous curs have no business showing your ugly mugs here. This is Blackfire territory."

212

Dane scowled up at the goat in response while Zander jumped to his feet and started to bring his fists up before Pold placed a restraining hand on his arm. The mallard calmly rose to his feet as well to meet the goat eye to eye.

"Our presence here offends you I take it?" Pold asked with a measured tone.

"I should say so!" the rest of the group from the table filtered in and a woman with the features of a terrier sneered at the knights and poked an accusing finger into Pold's chest.

As soon as the terrier made contact, Pold reacted; he grabbed her wrist and twisted it around behind her back. Cael heard a sickening crunch, and the dog woman stayed crouched on the ground cradling her arm. All four of their remaining opponents jumped on the older knight and began their assault all at once. Zander pulled one of them off and landed a solid right hook against the fox's head. Cael reached out and grabbed the back of the shirt-collar of an ox. He heaved back and dragged him away from his assault on Pold, using his magic to assist in moving the monolithic figure.

The ox turned to face Cael with a furious huff and rushed in to strike Cael with one massive elbow. Cael ducked under the blow and gave a hard kick straight to his foe's gut. The Ox reeled back but rebounded with a headbutt. Cael leaned back and reduced it to only a glancing blow, but a measure of pain still bloomed in his forehead. More prominent, however, was the sensation of Cael shifting into Darius's aspect.

Snarling, Cael leaped forward, his claws tore into the ox's button-up shirt, ripping a path open from his shoulder to his stomach. Patches of red spread across the ox's chest but it seemed to only enrage the fighter more. He snorted angrily and grabbed the back of Cael's neck to pull him forward. Instead of resisting, Cael moved with the action and met his attacker's forearm with his now sharp canines.

The ox bellowed in agony and released his hold on Cael, who took the opportunity to kick his opponent in the side of the head. The ox looked like he was about to go down, and Cael relaxed his stance slightly. As the massive bovine tipped over, he threw one wild punch that caught Cael by surprise as it connected with his right eye. In retaliation, Cael threw one last punch of his own knocking the ox out cold.

When Cael turned around to check on his companions, he found Pold regarding him with his fists planted on his hips. The rest of their assailants were incapacitated on the floor. "It seems I misjudged you, wolf," the mallard said in an almost impressed tone, "you just took out their biggest guy in the same amount of time that three full-fledged knights dealt with their opponents."

Cael nodded to the terrier woman, "except for her. It took you no time to beat her."

Pold waved it off, "I just caught her flat-footed is all."

A nervous-looking mole man approached the group with his face in his hands, "a full-on brawl in my club!" he exclaimed loudly. "what am I supposed to do with this?" he gesticulated wildly at the pile of unconscious forms on the floor.

Pold turned and regarded their defeated adversaries, "I can get a carriage and get these five to lock up you three should stay and continue your celebration."

The club owner looked at the older knight like he had spontaneously grown a second head, "how can you be so calm about this? I should kick all of you out for disturbing the peace of this establishment!"

Dane let out a snarl, "they came and attacked us! We are knights of the Silver Tree; we were simply doing our duty by neutralizing these dangerous individuals. This establishment is safer because we were here."

"Fine," the mole-man huffed grudgingly and stalked away.
It wasn't long before Pold had set off with his charges leaving Zander, Dane, and Cael behind. Before the trio had a chance to sit back down, three giggling girls approached the group, asking to dance. Cael found himself being dragged off to the dance floor by an energetic cheetah. Cael was not much of a dancer, but he did his best to move along with the pounding baseline. His partner seemed pleased, and he found he was really quite enjoying himself. He made a mental note to someday take Marina to a place like this.
By the end of the night, Cael was exhausted, he and his companions rode back to the castle, and it was no time at all before Cael was asleep.

The next morning found Cael and his new friends out in the training yard. Zander held his longsword loosely in one hand, "so, a big part of what we do is keeping our fighting skills sharp."

Already very familiar with this concept, Cael merely nodded.

Dane interjected with a step forward, "if I may, I noticed last night that you seem to lose a bit of your control when you transform into the wolf."

"I do feel a lot less... precise," Cael agreed.

"Hmm," Zander mused tapping his shoulder with the flat of his blade, "I wonder if that has something to do with the fact that you're not in wolf form full time. No really, hear me out, you only gain your animal form when you use magic, yes? So it doesn't leave you with much time to get used to the feeling of being a wolf. So maybe you just need to connect with your inner animal even when you're not sporting the fangs and fur."

"I can see the logic behind that, but how do I do that?" Cael asked.

"Well first off," Zander began giving his sword a twirl and returning it to its sheath, "I doubt sword practice is the right way."

"Hey what about a hunting exercise?" Dane suggested.

The white wolf's face lit up with excitement, and he jumped up with a clap on Dane's shoulder, "that's perfect! Let's go!"

Zander led them to a gymnasium equipped with large padded structures scattered throughout the room. The pads on the floor squeaked a bit with every step, but all other sound was muted. Dane and Zander had sat down on a nearby bench to remove their combat boots, so Cael followed suit.

"So what am I hunting?" He asked.

Dane grinned and shook out his shoulders, "me." and with that, he bounded off, leaped on top of a pile of blocks stacked high towards the ceiling. "keep up!" He called, flipping off the stack and leaping on top of another one.

"Um..." Cael hesitated until Zander smacked him on the back urging him forward. Cael sprinted after the jackal and tried to jump up onto the padded blocks after him. He did manage to get to the top, albeit with far less grace than Dane. His target was already off like a rocket to a different part of the gym.

Cael chased Dane to a corner, and for a second the young champion thought he would catch his prey, but Dane jumped up, pushed off one wall with his foot then the other and spun passed a slightly dumfounded Cael. "Come on you're still holding back, pup!"

Why was he holding back? What was he trying to avoid? Cael did his best to let go of his reservations, giving in to his more feral impulses. He could feel it in his muscles, it was like untying a knot that released a previously unused length of rope. He pelted off after Dane and vaulted over three consecutive blocks.

Cael had almost reached him when Dane grabbed hold of a bar hanging overhead and spun around it to land behind Cael, who in response, had to spring off the wall to reverse his momentum. He swung from the same overhanging bar and launched himself forward. He poured on the speed in pursuit of the jackal and dove forward in a tackle that sent them both crashing to the ground.

Zander was laughing, he stepped forward giving a few short claps, "that was great! Are you sure you've never done that before?"

Grinning, Cael disentangled himself from Dane, "sort of, actually. That was just an amped up version of roughhousing with my pack back home."

They stayed for another hour or so, Zander and Dane taking turns letting Cael chase them. By the time they broke for lunch, Cael felt ready to sleep for a week. The roast beef sandwiches in the Mess Hall went a long way to revitalize him, however.

"I've got a flight lesson in five minutes," Zander said checking his watch.

"And I need to report for guard duty at the gate," Dane responded.

Zander nodded to his friend and offered him a bow with his fist over his heart, "we'll catch up with you later on then."

Dane returned the gesture and left them to make their way to the outskirts of the compound to the helipad. There was a vast stretch of asphalt surrounded by airplane hangars full of robust looking helicopters and several biplanes. Zander strode purposefully toward one such hangar. On a back wall hung a line of brown leather bomber jackets. Zander threw one to Cael and pulled another over his own shoulders.

"In the inside pocket you'll find a pair of goggles, you're gonna need those," he commented as he marched back out onto the helipad where a tiger in an identical bomber jacket was waiting he was also wearing a pair of green tinted goggles and carrying a clipboard.

"Who's this?" the tiger asked with a wave to Cael.

"He's a new magi animalia, Roman. Sir Alexander has him shadowing me for the next few days," came Zander's response.

"Ah, well get in the back and try to keep quiet," Roman ordered.

Obediently, Cael climbed in the back of the chopper and found a seat. The goggles were right where Zander had said they would be in his jacket and he pulled a pair much like Roman's over his eyes. As Roman ran Zander through the pre-flight checklist, Cael found his eyes drifting out the window. The compound was situated on the top of a cliff and Cael could see an endless expanse of verdant forest past its edge. Half a minute later, Cael got an even better view of the forest as Zander pulled the chopper up into the air. Cael seemed to have left his stomach behind on the ground as they rose higher and higher into the air.

"Alright open her up and let's see what you can do," Roman commented.

Wind whipped violently around the cockpit through the empty doorways when Zander started to go through his maneuvers. Cael felt his hair pulled in every direction, only partially held down by the straps of his goggles, and the noise of it drowned out everything else. He tried to speak, but the wind tore the sound of his voice from his throat before he could form the words.

Zander banked hard to the left, and Cael lurched to one side, nearly falling out of his seat. He instinctively reached up to a safety strap hanging above his head to regain his balance. His hand didn't stray from the strap the whole rest of the ride.

They finally touched back down on the helipad, and as the engine died down, a voice was calling out, "Cael! Hey, can you hear me yet? Cael!" He spun in a circle, confused there were really only two people in this plane of existence that knew him, who could be looking for him? "Hey, dork! Look down at your watch!"

That made way more sense Cael thought as he brought his wrist up to his face to find Brock's mildly agitated countenance. "Oh hey Brock," Cael answered sheepishly.

"What were you doing? It was super loud." Brock asked.

"Riding in a helicopter."

"Emphatic profanity! Did you have to go somewhere in a hurry?" Brock seemed impressed.

"Uh, no not exactly...."

"Naw I'm just training for my pilot's license, see? and I've got to practice," Zander leaned over Cael's shoulder to speak through his watch too. "So are you one of Cael's mundane friends? And how does this doohickey work?" Zander tugged on the communicator watch and Cael's wrist along with it causing him to stumble forward.

Cael paused and looked at Zander questioningly, "you can understand him?"

"Athanor was founded by magic users from all over the multiverse, speaking a variety of languages, we happen to use English here at the castle," Zander responded.

Cael paused for a minute, pondering, he hadn't even noticed that everyone's mouths had actually been moving in sync with their words. He had just gotten so accustomed to ignoring the rather unsettling effect of the translation medallion that he completely missed when it wasn't happening.

He shook himself, remembering he had been in the middle of a conversation. "Ah! Right, sorry! Zander, this is Brock and Brock this is Zander, he's teaching me how to be a wolf," Cael introduced.

Brock blew a dismissive raspberry with a wave of his hand, "oh please do you remember that time you growled at Gavin when he tried to take your sandwich? You're already the most wolfish person I know."

Zander nodded sagely, "that's really the secret, Brock, he's just gotta relax and stop thinking about it. Stop fighting against his own ferocity."

Cael ran a hand through his hair, "I mean, there's a place for ferocity, sure, but not all the time."

Zander chuckled and shook his head, "well sure, no one feels just one way all the time. Not even wild wolves are mean and snarl constantly. And look at me, do I look ferocious to you?"

Cael was taken aback by the question, he had been so wrapped up in what he was going through he didn't stop to look at what being a magi animalia must be like for anyone else, which, when he thought about it, was precisely what he had come to Athanor to do. "No," he responded at last, "you don't."

"See?" Zander smiled, "whoever said you have to be any one thing?"

* * *

Nightfall a month or so later found Cael, Zander and four other knights sitting around a large propane camp lantern. They had been swapping stories for a few hours. Cael sat forward on the edge of a bench, his wrist resting on one knee, listening to anecdotes about prank wars with friends and dangerous stunts nearly gone awry.

"So I'm standing there with this pillow that we completely covered in duct tape, and she kicks it square in the center. The force of it sends me flying into the wall behind me," the badger telling the story clapped her hands loudly once to illustrate the impact. "When I stood back up we saw the giant dent that I left in the plaster. We stopped sparring in the house after that."

They were technically on what Zander had called roving guard duty. It was an extra precaution in addition to the guards at the gate to keep watch over the castle at night. Every quarter hour or so one of their number would get up and make a circuit around the castle walls, and then come back to the circle and continue with their singing and story-telling.

Cael sat up straighter and cleared his throat, "okay, once I was at my brother, Gavin's, house, and the uncle he lives with was out of town, so we decided we were going to climb up to the roof and try to jump off with a hang glider that we had made with a bed sheet and two hockey sticks. As you can imagine our hang glider collapsed instantly and Gavin plummeted two stories down and hit the ground hard. Miraculously he managed only a slight fracture on his leg." The end of his tale was met with a sharp collective intake of breath.

A bobcat man sitting next to Cael looked around the lantern light, "Most of you look too young to have been around when this happened, but have any of you guys noticed the portrait in the war-room? It's a painting of Sir Alexander and his wife, Gwendolyn. Gwendolyn's fate is the enduring tragedy of Silvertree. She was a first generation magi animalia, and she followed a battalion of the Blackfire Legion to another plane of existence to stop them. Alexander begged her not to go, she was pregnant, and he didn't want her to endanger the baby, but she felt she was the only one who could go.

"No one knows for sure exactly what happened, but we do know that she tracked down Blackfire and engaged them in combat. Their numbers were too great for her, and she was overrun. The matriarch of the Knights of the Silvertree never came home."

The group was silent for a moment, the badger in the meantime got up to make her circuit around the perimeter of the fort.

Then the hedgehog man sitting on the other side of Cael looked at him with a grin, "speaking of old Knight traditions, this one is a fair bit more cheery mind you. You know what I just realized boys?" he asked the group, "our guest here hasn't heard our war song yet." this proclamation was met a murmur of agreement and then the hedgehog began to sing and was slowly joined by the others around the lantern.

five hundred years or more
there came a vicious, fearsome hoard
they growled and snarled at our door
calling for our patriarch's head

the wind whistles through the trees tonight
the wind whistles through the trees alright
and the wind howls on
but the silvertree stands

the call came up across the wall
and the knights charged forward to defend
they took up shields, and swords, and archer's bows
and stood ready to fight to bitter end

the wind whistles through the trees tonight
the wind whistles through the trees alright
and the wind howls on
but the silvertree stands

the air grew thick with crossbow bolts
as each side sought their victory
the sounds of clashing steel rose up
when the knights pushed back against advance
and ran those curs out of the land

the wind whistles through the trees tonight
the wind whistles through the trees alright
and the wind howls on

but the silvertree stands

the wind whistles through the trees tonight
the wind whistles through the trees alright
and the wind howls on
but the silvertree stands

and the wind howls on
but the silvertree stands
the silvertree stands

By the end every knight in the circle was joyfully stomping a foot in time with the ballad, a few were even pounding fists on their knees as well. But the moment of solidarity was abruptly interrupted by a raccoon woman rushing toward them with a young gorilla girl hurrying behind her.

The young girl spoke before the raccoon knight could even open her mouth, "someone has to come save my sister!"

Cael was on his feet without even a second of hesitation, "what's wrong?" he asked, running forward.

"The house collapsed!" she cried.

Cael felt his blood run cold, "where?"

"Just over the way," the gorilla girl tearfully responded pointing off into the forest. "I'll take you there."

"Okay, let's go," and he set off into the forest following the young girl. It was only after a few minutes that Cael even became aware of the three other knights following as well. He'd been so focused on the girl that he had not noticed or truthfully cared if anyone came to help the small gorilla with him. All that had mattered was acting as quickly as possible.

"Daddy! I got help!" the girl ran on ahead forcing Cael and the three knights to pick up their pace in turn. They came to a clearing; in the middle was the splintered wreckage of what had once been a large cabin. A hulking gorilla man was on his knees next to the rubble, desperately flinging broken pieces of his home behind him.

At his daughter's call the gorilla looked up at the approaching knights, evident panic on his face, "please, you have to save my baby girl," he pleaded as they came to a stop in front of him.

"Have you seen or heard any sign of her?" Cael asked looking for a place to start.

"Her... her room was about right here," he sobbed indicating the ground in front of him.

Zander stepped forward and placed a comforting hand on the man's shoulder, "it'll be okay, we'll get her out."

They began the grim task of systematically clearing away the wreckage, piece by piece. The gorilla started calling out what Cael assumed was the girl's name, "Melisandre! Sweetie are you there?" each time they could not hear any answering call, and each time the girls' father became more and more despairing. He frantically dug in the rubble next to Cael and the knights until he gashed his massive forearm on a shattered wooden beam and his other daughter dragged him off to the side.

"Daddy, let the knights do that you'll be no good to Melisandre if you get yourself killed trying to get to her." the girl said reasonably. The young gorilla could not have been more than six years old, and yet she seemed to be handling the crisis better than her much older father.

The father sighed in a defeated way, "you're right Lana."

The hedgehog paused in his work clearing the rubble and pulled a small first aid kit from one of the cargo pockets on his black pants. He began dressing the man's wound when Lana took the gauze from him. "I can do this if you keep trying to find my big sister. Deal?"

The hedgehog, Corbin, smiled, "deal."

They worked into the wee hours of the morning until at last the breaking light of sunrise fell upon the form of a young fox. A board had seemingly fallen across the small of her back. She wasn't moving.

"Please just be unconscious," Cael gasped as he leaped over the broken remains of a bookcase to the girl's side. "Over here!" he called out to the rest of the rescuers. He crouched down next to the fox's head. As the others rushed over Cael watched her form carefully, holding his own breath. He let out a huff of relief there were clear signs of breathing! She was alive!

Together, Cael, Zander and Dorian, the bobcat, lifted the beam up off Melisandre's back and Corbin was able to carefully slide her clear. The hedgehog looked around and found a wide, sturdy board, "okay now help me get her on this, so we don't have to move her much." They got her on the board and moved her clear of the rubble before Corbin began reviving her.

Cael stretched his aching back and looked around. It was like coming up from underwater, so focused had he been on his work. Cael regarded the knights as they too stretched and massaged overworked muscles and wiped at sweaty, dirt caked brows. These men had, without hesitation, worked tirelessly through the night to selflessly help a family in need. Cael smiled, he had been foolish to ever think, even unconsciously, that they were savage monsters.

Down the road they had taken to get to the cabin an ambulance was approaching. As soon as the ambulance stopped an adult vixen and the same raccoon knight from before jumped out. "My entire shift at the gate ended, and you guys still hadn't come back," she began, "I began to get worried, so I grabbed this from the stables and followed, picking Josephine here up along the way. She's the mother."

Josephine fell into step as Zander, and the others carried Melisandre on the board to the back of the ambulance. The young fox was awake now but very weak. "Mommy?" she murmured looking around.

"I'm here," the older fox reached out to grab her child's hand. The girl smiled and lay back on the board. They got her loaded up into the ambulance and Melisandre's family piled in and drove off, Cael assumed, to the nearest hospital.

Corbin clapped a hand on Cael's back, "you did well today kid. Now let's go get some breakfast, I know this great diner not too far from here."

The hedgehog steered Cael away from the wreckage and back down the lane. Cael trudged almost mindlessly behind Corbin and Zander with Dorian behind him, several times one of the knights stumbled from exhaustion, but they kept moving. Cael almost cried in relief when the diner came into view. Dirt caked, sweaty and bone tired they passed through the glass double doors into the blissfully air-conditioned interior. Several patrons, a good half of which were knights with maple leaf pommeled long-swords hanging from their hips, sat eating breakfast at a long bar that wrapped around the kitchen and still more occupied the booths that lined the walls.

A brown rabbit girl heavily laden with dirty plates called out to them on her way through the kitchen doors, "have a seat wherever you like, and I'll be with you in a minute!" She found them a minute later in a large corner booth and took their orders and hurried back off to the kitchen. Cael was nearly nodding off by the time she came back with a big pot of coffee in hand. "Wow, I guess you boys really need this, huh? I'll leave the pot for you."

Cael gratefully took a long drink of the dark liquid. He set down his mug and contemplated it's depths for a moment when next to him, Zander half stood and raised a hand in greeting to Dane who had just entered. "There you are," the jackal began, "when I woke up, and you guys still hadn't come back from guard duty, I must admit I was a little concerned. I had planned to ask around after breakfast."

Zander grinned, "looks like we saved you the trouble."

Dorian raised an eyebrow at Dane, "are you planning to stand there all day or are you gonna sit down?" he gestured to the empty space across the table.

With a sheepish smile, Dane slid into the booth next to Corbin and looked from one face to the next, "so what happened to you guys? You look like you've been crawling around in a ditch."

They began recounting the night's adventures, pausing only when their waitress brought all their food and took Dane's order. When they had finished, the jackal sat back with a huff and scratched behind one ear. "Wow that sounds like a rough night. I imagine you guys are pretty tired, you certainly look it. Let me shuttle you all back to the castle so you can get some sleep."

Corbin gave a relieved huff, "that would be great."

It took a few trips, but they finally made it all the way back to the barracks. They each hit the showers to clean off the grime of the night's events before collapsing onto their cots. Cael was asleep long before his head hit the pillow. And he rested comfortably knowing he had made a difference that day.

Chapter XIII:
Preparation for War

Late in the afternoon, Cael woke up feeling stronger and more at peace with himself than he had in a very long time. He lay still, afraid to move lest the feeling go away. As he was about to pull his blanket up higher to his chin, he felt a nudge in his mind. *"Do you have a minute?"* Marina mentally asked.

"I'm free, what's going on?" Cael answered.

"I have news. I have been continuing to track Dartain's movement for the last few months, and I have finally discovered the location of his palace. He does not go there frequently, so it took a while but from the look of things he is there for an extended stay now."

"So now is my best opportunity to strike," Cael concluded.

"Yes, I have arranged with Argentcloud to drop you in that plane of existence as close to the palace as possible so you can avoid contending with most of Dartain's forces," Marina explained.

"That will actually help a lot," Cael agreed.

"But be careful, his most powerful lieutenants will be the ones closest to him," Marina warned, and he could feel her worry.

Cael nodded habitually even though Marina couldn't see it, *"it will be okay, Dartain can't catch me by surprise this time. Now I'll be ready for him."*

"I know, good luck, I believe in you." and with that their connection dropped.

He lay still for a moment, thinking. As supportive as Athanor and the Knights of the Silvertree were, and as much fun as he was having with helping them out, Cael still had a job to do. He could scarcely ignore his responsibilities any longer.

Cael flexed his shoulders, testing the muscles there. If there was going to be a time to go after Dartain, now was it. Yes, best to do go ahead before he had the chance to talk himself out of it. He sat up and swung his legs over the edge of his cot. He buried his face in his hands, letting the cold of the titanium one bring him to full wakefulness.

With a path to follow, Cael pulled on his boots and set off to find Zander. He located the white wolf in the mess hall tearing into a bowl of pot roast. He sat down across the table from Zander and was suddenly unsure of how to begin his farewells.

Their silence stretched to the point of being uncomfortable, at least for Cael, Zander had taken a large chunk of bread and was mopping up the gravy from his pot roast. He looked up, gravy sodden bread halfway to his mouth, and frowned. "There something wrong?"

"Well, yes and no I guess," Cael began, "The time has come for me to move on, get back to completing my task. But that means I have to leave." It sounded obvious and dumb when he said it, but he couldn't think of a better way to explain his reluctance to say goodbye.

On the other hand, Zander nodded knowingly, "you'll just have to come back and visit us once you're done with your task. We'll hold a great revel, and you can sing the songs of your victory."

Cael considered the option and felt suddenly better, "you're right, I just may have to do that."

"So when are you heading out?" Zander asked.

"As much as I would like to say goodbye to Dane as well, I think I ought to go as soon as possible," Cael replied, standing up.

Zander stood as well and gave Cael the knight's salute of placing one fist on his heart and bowing at the waist.

Unsure if he was allowed to return the gesture Cael simply offered a hand to Zander who clasped it with a wolfish grin. "Until next time then."

Zander nodded, "see you then."

The champion turned and clawed a portal open to the Illuminated Mists and exited through it. Once on the other side he simply began walking, he wasn't entirely sure how he knew where to go, but he assumed it was once again some part of him that was Darius leading the way.

Cael had to admit now that he was comfortable with the Mists, it was actually quite a lovely place. Even though he couldn't actually see it, he was currently walking through a forest, there were trees all around him and grass springing from soft soil under his feet he even felt a slight breeze ruffling his hair. After a while of walking, he thought he heard birdsong, and he wondered if he was hearing someone's familiar. Darius had said that the Illuminated Mists is where he had lived for Cael's first eighteen years so it did stand to reason that there would be other familiars here as well.

He came upon a stream burbling its way across his path, and the smell of damp soil and the water rose up to his nose. He breathed in deeply and couldn't help but smile. This place was just so peaceful.

When Cael reached his destination, he clawed his way back out of the Mists and found himself on the side of a mountain. He shivered in the cold and looked around for some kind of door. He spotted something promising a few dozen yards ahead, so he set off in that direction. A short cliff that rose up to the level of his chin blocked his way. Cael had to grip the cliff's edge while pushing up off of footholds to get to the point where he could simply hoist himself up and over.

Past the cliff, he came across an actual pathway that took him the rest of the way to what was, in fact, the door to Argentcloud. Inside Cael stamped his feet and blew into his hands in an effort to warm up.

It was a minute or two before he actually noticed any of his surroundings. An old woman with white hair and a sardonic grin stood in front of him. She was leaning against a wall with her arms crossed over her chest.

"What kind of idiot comes to the top of a mountain without so much as a coat?" she asked with a raised eyebrow.

"I was not aware of the elevation issue," Cael answered defensively.

The old woman rolled her eyes and turned, beckoning for him to follow, "well come on then let's get you warmed up." she took him down a hallway and into a small side room inside there was a number of bookshelves and a large couch. She sat him down on the couch and conjured a large blanket. "Here I'll have one of my acolytes bring you something hot to drink. Come see me in the atrium when you are ready, Champion."

"Your acolytes? Wait, you're the temple master?" Cael asked rising slightly to look over the back of the couch at the woman's retreating back.

She looked back, "who did you think I was? Yes, I'm Agatha Argentcloud." And with that, she disappeared through the doorway.

Cael sat there, a little stunned, none of the other temple masters had been so...coarse. He had expected Agatha Argentcloud to be just as friendly and helpful as the others had been but that certainly seemed to not be the case. He wrapped the blanket tighter around himself and tried to get warm. Not long after a young dark-haired boy of maybe ten years came in wearing a white leather jerkin with a purple cloud-topped mountain insignia on the back and purple linen trousers, he was carrying a tray with a teapot and cup.

The acolyte set the tray on a small table in front of the couch and fixed a cup of the tea with milk from a little pitcher and a few spoonfuls of sugar. The boy offered Cael the mug with a cheerful smile, then turned and skipped out of the room.

Cael chuckled and shook his head before taking a sip of the tea. It was richer in flavor and body than the tea he had tried at Redearth it was also a great deal sweeter. It was not long before the tea and blanket had done their jobs. Cael was feeling downright toasty. In truth he was not all that cold, to begin with, he had not been stuck outside in the elements for all that long.

Once the cup was drained Cael stood and folded the blanket to set it down on the seat of the couch. He stepped out the door and wandered back toward the entrance. Argentcloud seemed to be designed in such a way that all hallways led to one central chamber. This central chamber had to be the atrium that Agatha spoke of with a vast ceiling of stained glass throwing a dissonance of color against the walls and the white marble columns that lined the room. The back wall was covered mostly by a huge brass organ.

Agatha stood in the middle of the chamber, her hands clasped behind her back. She was gazing up at the ceiling with a thoughtful expression. As Cael approached her gaze shifted to him. "You certainly look warmer now."

Cael grinned, "yes thank you."

"Now, what is it you need?" the temple master demanded.

"I thought Marina had arranged with you to get me to the Demon King Dartain's domain?" Cael answered.

Agatha was silent for a time, clearly scrutinizing Cael. Her sharp eyes studying him from top to bottom and lingering on the scars he'd already sustained on this journey. Cael was beginning to worry that this wizened old woman thought that he wasn't up to the task.

"If you're going to dive headlong into the Obsidian Palace there are a few things you're going to need before I send you there," Agatha finally declared.

"Like what?" Cael demanded, indignant.

She frowned at his response, "first of all, idiot, you certainly need a better attitude. You'll get yourself killed if you arrogantly charge off thinking you already have victory in hand. Secondly, your armor is crap. Is that really all you have? A temple jerkin and some chainmaille? You're an alchemist, right? Conjure up some plate armor, and then you might have something. And lastly, you're going to need a good meal and a whole lot of water in you. The Fire Desert is extremely hot, and you need to be hydrated."

Cael was taken aback by Agatha's tirade, and he was a little annoyed that she had insulted his armor, it had served him well up to this point, and his friends had provided it for him which made it extra special. He said as much to the temple master, and she looked at him like he had grown a second head as they were standing there.

"Are you serious? Do you honestly think that when you go up against the currently most powerful king of demons that your warm fuzzy feeling from your friends is going to keep you safe? Because I can tell you how that would go right now, he will burn you to ashes where you stand without a second thought, and then he's going to laugh at you."

Cael snarled, he didn't like hearing it, but she had a point. "Fine," he said in a huff, "I'll make better armor, but I'll need a space to work."

For the first time since arriving, he saw Agatha smile openly, "Good, right this way." she led him to another small room down a different hallway than the first, inside was a work table and a stool and not much else. "Will this suffice, Champion?" she asked with mock sweetness.

Cael raised an eyebrow at her, "yes, thank you," he responded dryly.

She left him alone, and he perched on the edge of the stool and stared at the work table for a moment, waiting for inspiration. Eventually, he ran a hand through his hair and brought his hands up to work. He figured he would start with one piece and go from there. The helmet seemed like the best choice. Start from the top and work his way down. He tried to picture how he wanted it to fit onto his head, and he began to conjure the steel and started to form it.

He ended up with a close helm style that he shaped to look more like a wolf's head. He was going to be wearing this in combat while using lots of magic and it would need to fit Darius's form more than his usual face, and he figured he might as well go all the way in making it look like Darius's face too. The rest of the armor was reasonably straightforward but well-articulated. He wanted to be able to move as much as possible. The knee and elbow cops alone were fashioned from seven different segments each, which may have been going a bit overboard but he wanted to err on the side of caution.

Besides the helmet, the only addition Cael gave the armor purely for an aesthetic reason was to finish the edge of each separate plate with brass. He stepped back and regarded the effect that made and decided to also change all of the rivets to brass as well.

He padded and strapped each piece with Kevlar, which in truth, was the more difficult part since he had to get the fibers just right for it to behave like a textile. Then he had to put the whole suit on to ensure that it fit right and moved the way he wanted to. The helmet fit perfectly over his transformed, wolfish features, but he was uncomfortable with the way the helmet limited his field of vision. He supposed, though, some things had to be sacrificed in exchange for the protection it provided.

It was dark by the time Cael finished creating his armor. He left the pile of metal in the workroom and went in search of Agatha, going down each hallway that radiated out from the atrium in turn. He eventually found her and everyone from the temple past a corridor that sloped down and curved back on itself and opened up to a massive feast hall.

The temple master sat in the middle of a long table sitting at the center of the hall. She beckoned him with one hand as he entered. "I don't see any armor," she admonished when Cael came near.

"It's done, I just left it in the workroom," Cael explained.

"Hmm... well, I guess I shall simply have to inspect it later. In the mean-time sit have some beef stew, you look tired."

The nearest empty seat was several paces away, so Cael took his leave of Agatha and retreated to sit amongst the acolytes. He found his spot in between a red-haired woman and a large man with a shaved head. There were several platters and pots of food and pitchers of drink sitting in the middle of the table, so Cael helped himself and began to eat.

He was almost instantly interrupted from his meal when the red-haired woman asked him, "So what brings you here? It must be pretty complicated; most Runners don't travel to the temple directly."

"They don't?" Cael questioned, confused.

"No we can transport remotely using the map on the floor of the Atrium, didn't you know that? I thought Greenwood went over this with all the Runners they train." the bald man explained.

Cael had to speak around a mouthful of beef stew and mashed potatoes, "I'm not really a Runner, I'm a champion. It would be too dangerous to fight my way through all of the demon king's territory to get to his front gate so I'll need a little bit of help getting there."

"Oh," the redhead began, drawing out the word, "So you're Marina's champion."

Cael nearly choked on the carrot he'd been chewing, the bald man let out a boisterous laugh and a "careful there, lad."

"How do you know about that?" Cael exclaimed once he could breathe again.

"I expect all the temples have known since her little crush started, really. You see every few months, or so all the temples convene and report on what they've been doing. Sablewater reports possible threats to the multiverse that she's monitored so that Greenwood knows which Runners to prepare for their missions and Redearth offers what wisdom or newly discovered technique might help and then lastly Argentcloud sends the Runners out at the proper moment.

"Anyway, what I'm getting at is that every time Marina reported on the progress of the latest champion's training, she would always get a bit flustered and go all red. It wasn't hard for everyone to figure out why" the redhead chortled.

Cael grinned a bit himself and felt a blush rising in his own cheeks. The large bald man next to him scoffed, "what I'm more curious about is the content of those reports, honestly. It's not every day you hear about a teenager putting his skin on the line to protect strangers in a big city, even if he is a champion."

"I don't know it just sort of happened, the first time. I couldn't help it. This man was getting mugged, and when I heard him cry out for help, I knew I could do something, so I had to intervene. I couldn't just stand by and do nothing. After we saved him any time my pack and I went somewhere, I kept an ear out for others that might need help. I think my friends got so tired of me running off every other time we walked somewhere that they endeavored to learn ways they could help me and our patrols grew from that." Cael smiled at the memory.

"Hmm," the man grunted thoughtfully but made no further comment.

Cael was able to finish his meal with little more interruptions and when everyone rose to go to bed the bald man directed Cael to a room for him to sleep. He guessed that Agatha would give her final say on whether or not his armor was good enough to properly outfit him for his attack on the Obsidian Palace in the morning. So, Cael geared down and tried to settle into sleep.

In the quiet, Cael tried not to think about what would come in the morning. This was the moment he had trained his whole life for. But at the same time, he had clashed with Dartain twice before and had not come out better for it; though neither time could actually be considered a real fight. Maybe his best chance was to go in swinging and not stop. Before he hadn't been able to get a shot in, this time, Cael asserted, would be different.

* * *

Light came spilling in through the window of Cael's room. He squeezed his eyes shut tighter, trying to block it out but it was no use; he was decidedly awake now. With a groan, he sat up and rubbed his eyes to wakefulness. He tumbled out of bed and was beginning to get ready when there came a knock at the door.

It was another acolyte, "uh sir? Are you awake?" she asked timidly and only continued after Cael called out affirmatively. "Mistress Agatha wishes to speak with you in the workroom you were using yesterday."

Cael thanked the girl and assured her that he was on his way. Though, the fact that Agatha decided to critique his armor making skills first thing in the morning seemed a bit ominous to Cael, like she expected to find nothing but flaws in his work. With that cheery thought, Cael opened the door of the workroom.

Agatha was standing facing the door with one of the greaves in her hand. "what's with the plastic padding on this? You know the Fire Desert is hot right? And plastic melts."

Cael took a slow deep breath, trying to retain his composure, "well, any organic material like cotton or leather would be far too complex for me to conjure, so I went with something that has a simpler atomic structure. And while Kevlar does lose some of its strength at higher temperatures, I'm confident that it will hold up considering it is not the main part of the armor."

Agatha narrowed her eyes and looked down again at the armor in her hands, "very well this will suffice." She set down the greave on the table and marched past Cael out the door, "Come on you should get one last meal in you before we send you off."

"Did she have to say last meal?" Cael muttered as he followed her back down to the dining hall.

Cael was surprised to find the hall full of people this early in the day. He was grateful for it though, the indistinct sound of human chatter was strangely calming. Cael sat down next to Agatha this time and was given a large bowl of oatmeal with blueberries and banana slices along with toast, a tumbler of orange juice and one of water. Cael found that he rather enjoyed the meal and once he drained the glass of water he reached for a nearby carafe of coffee.

"That won't really help you, you know," Agatha admonished. Cael looked at her wryly with a raised eyebrow, "on the off chance that this is indeed my last meal, I'm going to have some expletive coffee."

The meal ended soon after and people began cleaning up. Agatha led Cael back to his armor. Once there, she surprised him by actually helping him get everything on. Altogether the suit was a fair bit heavier than he expected. It dragged down his shoulders and, despite his meticulous articulation; it did limit his range of motion.

Agatha could sense Cael's difficulty, "take it easy. Bend with it. Find its limits. Get used to its weight on your body. You'll be okay."

Cael exhaled slowly and did as the temple master advised. He slowly moved around in the armor and familiarized himself with the way it moved. He bent and stretched and jogged in place before too long he grew accustomed to wearing it. Its weight didn't seem to encumber him as much now.

"Good," the old woman nodded, "are you ready?"

"It's either now, or never I guess, let's go," Cael answered flipping the visor of his helmet up so he could see her better.

"Let's go," she agreed and led him back out to the atrium. She positioned him in a specific part of the atrium floor. Cael looked down at the sprawling map on the ground that he hadn't noticed when he first arrived. Agatha stood a few steps away from him and lifted up her hands towards him. Light seemed to coalesce from the stained glass above them around her hands. This light shot forward and enveloped Cael, and he instantly disappeared from the room to reappear in front of a wall made of a solid block of mahogany obsidian.

Chapter XIV:
Infiltration

He was standing at the outside corner of Dartain's palace, he knelt down and peered around the corner to see two guards, men in centurion armor, standing on either side of a gargantuan archway, sealed with a portcullis. Cael supposed fighting two guards was better than an army, but he still had to try and contend with them as quickly and quietly as possible. He scanned the area in front of the palace to ensure that there was no one else in the vicinity.

The area was clear, so he drew Howling Wolf with one hand and one of his clawed gauntlets with his off hand and charged forward. He caught the first one by surprise and downed him with a single slice. Flames erupted from the wound, and soon there was nothing more than a pile of ash where he had once stood. The second one had time to bring the spear in his hand into play. The demon tried to keep Cael at the end of his spear's reach, but Cael hooked it with his clawed gauntlet and pushed it aside as he rushed passed the length of the weapon. Once inside his opponent's range

Cael infused Howling Wolf with magical energy and punched the now glowing blade through the bronze breastplate of the second demon, and he too was soon consumed by the very fire that ran through his veins.

Cael wrenched the blade free and was at the portcullis before the second demon disappeared. He sheathed Howling Wolf to free his right hand but kept the clawed gauntlet ready just in case. With his free hand, he transformed the steel of a section of the portcullis into the air and slipped inside the Obsidian Palace. He found himself in the courtyard, and there was nothing but open ground between him and the main keep.

Cael was reasonably confident that somewhere in the keep is where he would find Dartain but he had to get there first. He ran, skirting the shadow of the wall, searching for an area that looked like a blind spot to the guards who were watching from the walls so he could cross to the keep. He found a likely area just past where the corner of the keep aligned with the corner of the outer wall.

Footsteps sounded nearby and panicked, Cael dived behind a wagon overloaded with barrels. He sat in the hot dirt, not daring to breathe, with his knees up against his chin watching the feet of some demon minion as it lumbered past. Cael did have the option of fighting the beast but he wanted to avoid leaving too an obvious a trail of defeated enemies behind him, nor did he feel the need to waste energy on every demon in the palace.

Cael waited until long after he could no longer hear footsteps to sprint across to the wall of the keep. He next had to find a door and fast. It would be much easier for the guards on the wall to see him on this side of the courtyard. His best chance of success was to get into the cover of the building beside him with all expedience.

As he went, he ran his right hand along the smooth surface of the obsidian wall. He finally came to a door, and he slipped quickly inside. He began to deliberately take stock of his surroundings only to discover that he had so carefully infiltrated... Dartain's tool shed. With rakes and shovels and the like heaped up into one corner. Still, it was an excellent place to stage his next sprint along the wall.

He watched cautiously from the doorway as one guard, this one a woman in thick furs and other leather armor carrying massive great-sword on one shoulder, marched along the top of the ramparts. Cael waited until her back was to him before dashing out along the wall of the keep. The clanking of his armor sounded far too loud to his paranoid ears as he went along but in truth, it wasn't any louder than the guards' armor, and it would not have seemed out of place had any of them heard it.

He came to another door, this time he opened it a crack and peered inside. It looked like this one opened up into a corridor, lit up by oil lamps placed in sconces set at measured intervals. The passage was empty, so Cael slipped inside and shut the door quietly behind him. The fire from the lamps glinted madly off the glossy red walls, and the shadows skipped erratically down the hall.

Cael wondered what he should be looking for, a throne room? Dartain's personal chambers? Maybe he had a study or a war-room? In the end, he supposed he should just be looking for the demon king himself, and he would have to search each room as he came to it.

As fortune would have it most of the doors down the corridor had a small rectangular opening towards the top, covered in iron bars. Cael quickly glanced into each opening and found the majority of them occupied by still sleeping residents. It had been relatively early when Cael had set out. Then there was the demon who was doing chin-ups from a bar that stretched the length of the room with his back to the door. And the one who was reading in an armchair by a narrow window.

Cael came to a split in the hallway with paths stretching out to his left, his right and straight ahead. After a moment's deliberation, he took the right-hand turn reasoning that he would follow the wall on his right all the way through the palace so that he wouldn't get lost.

One of the doors a few feet ahead suddenly opened and a demon with a multitude of scars on his arms and was wearing a shirt of scale mail stepped out. He looked at Cael and froze, shocked to find that he was not alone in the corridor. Cael had been ready for this inevitability and jumped at the demon without a second's hesitation.

Clawed gauntlet still in hand, Cael slashed directly at the demon's throat but not before the demon let out a warning yell. Cael cursed his luck even as his opponent fell to the ground and was burned to cinders by his own flaming blood. Cael rushed into the room the demon had left, assuming that it would now be empty.

He was wrong.

Cael found himself face to face with yet another demon. This one had a small sickle in hand and moved with the air of someone investigating a strange noise, this action made all the more difficult by his missing eye covered by a brown leather eye patch. This demon wore no armor and Cael rushed forward to take advantage of that fact, aiming for the demon's stomach, magical energy enveloping Cael's whole arm up to the elbow. The demon blocked his strike and hooked one of the claw blades in the curve of the sickle he then twisted the gauntlet, and Cael's arm along with it, off to the side and brought Cael down to one knee.

"That's right, whelp, bow before me!" the demon snarled, "did you think you could overpower me? Ha! I am Cormund, one of Dartain's own lieutenants."

Cael growled, he could feel his teeth growing into fangs and his ears lengthening; his clean-shaven face suddenly sprouting iron hued fur. Halfway through his transformation, he stood up and pushed back against Cormund's sickle and shoved him away. "And I am Cael Ivywood, champion of the creation temples. What makes you think you're stronger than me?" his words were only slightly muted by the visor on his helmet.

Cormund's eye widened, and then he smiled, "you're the threat Dartain has been so scared of all this time?" He laughed before continuing, "do you think you're some kind of epic hero? 'champion of the creation temples' do you know what I see when I look at you? A joke. The only reason that you're not standing at my side saluting me is that Dartain assumed the portion of his essence that he grafted to your soul was enough to corrupt you even though the ritual was interrupted. Still, I wonder if it wasn't enough that we can work with it, yet."

Cormund pulled Cael closer to him with his sickle. The only way out that Cael saw was to drop the weapon. He stepped away and drew the other clawed gauntlet and one of the throwing knives from Max that Dorothy had tucked in the baldric of Howling Wolf. He flung the blade at Cormund, and even though he ducked out of the way, it did leave a cut on his shoulder.

"How many weapons do you have?" Cormund exclaimed in alarm.

Cael smirked, "buddy I'm armed for bear, or I suppose more accurately, for lion."

Cormund didn't seem to like that, "impudent WELP!" he roared. With his free hand, he gathered a ball of pure energy, his was a dark, sinister purple color, more like shadow than light. As soon as it was big enough he hurled it at Cael.

Cael infused his clawed gauntlet with his own energy and moved to block the ball. Instead of fizzling out like he expected, he absorbed it. The instant the malevolent energy saturated him every muscle in his body clenched sending an unpleasant shock-wave through him. Involuntarily, his form changed from iron hued wolf to crimson mountain lion. With this change also came a compelling urge to harm. Maim. Kill. The sheer abruptness and intensity of the compulsion, however, was enough to shock Cael out of whatever state the malevolent energy put him in.

"Well, well, it seems we can draw the beast out," Cormund remarked.

"What did you just do to me?" Cael demanded.

"Not much. Right now at least. All I did was throw some of my own magical energy at you. Though, that energy seemed to have awoken the demon essence that his majesty grafted to your soul. He may not have been able to turn you that day, but it looks like we may still be able to, shall we say, bring you around to our way of thinking." Cormund stepped closer and reached out a hand.

Cael took a step back and slapped the hand away, "I will never be anything like you!" He spat the words out as if to also expel the horrible murderous way he'd felt moments before. He may have accepted the fact that he would have to kill Dartain and even some of his followers in the name of protecting innocent lives, but he would absolutely never take any kind of satisfaction from it.

"No? We'll see about that, I think," Cormund summoned more raw energy, a great deal more than before and this time instead of throwing it he wove a cage around Cael. He tried to avoid being ensnared, but the enclosure stretched out to meet him at every turn.

Once it had closed around Cael, the cage began to shrink. Cael slowly sank down, trying to avoid the walls for as long as possible. Eventually, however, with Cael on his hands and knees on the floor, the malevolent energy cocooned him and soaked into him. The sensation was exponentially worse than before.

Cael looked up at the demon standing triumphantly above him and felt rage and hatred consume his heart. He wanted nothing more than to see the creature before him writhing at his feet in torturous agony. He wanted to delight in the spectacle of Cormund screaming out in excruciation. Then he could show everyone just how pathetic this demon lieutenant really was.

Everyone.

He could see their faces now, he knew how they would react. Dorothy would turn her face away, dismayed. Abby's almost perpetual smile would fall and turn to a look of horror. Gavin would angrily shove Cael out of the way to stop him from attacking an opponent who was clearly already beaten, and Jim would be right behind him. Brock would have something poignant and poetic to say about how doing nothing but inflicting pain was not the answer. And Max. The very same Max who argued against his father from using violence would turn those arguments against Cael himself.

The temple masters, especially Marina, who were all so helpful on his journey and did so much to help, not just him but everyone across the multiverse, would hang their heads in disappointment. Ferdinand and his friends would be heartbroken. The runners he'd met in Greenwood, women, and men who voluntarily put their lives in harm's way for the sake of strangers would be appalled. The Knights of the Silvertree would turn their swords against him. His friends, people that he looked up to and admired, people that inspired him to continue on his own path to help people, would not be impressed by such an act. They would be ashamed.

This was not who Cael was.

Cael stood up and looked Cormund straight in his one remaining eye, "I told you already; I will never be anything like you. This scar on my soul will not define me."

He felt the roaring, hateful monster inside his chest, felt it in stark contrast to the wildly playful beast right next to it. He shut the evil thing behind an iron door never to be so much as thought of again.

Cormund snarled angrily and began to summon more energy, but Cael wasn't going to give him time to finish. Cael used his magic to drag his weapons to him from where they had fallen across the chamber. He pounced on the demon with no warning and slashed at his chest. Caught by surprise, all Cormund had time to do was bring his glowing hands up to defuse some of the force of Cael's strike. So steadfast was Cael's resolve in this moment, so sharp was his focus that the malevolent energy had no effect on him this time.

Even with Cormund's block, Cael's clawed gauntlets found their mark and fire began licking at the demon's wounds, and flames clung to Cael's blades. He followed up his first strike quickly with one to his adversary's face. The blow struck hard and sliced through the straps of Cormund's eye-patch revealing the melted flesh beneath.

Cormund picked his sickle back up, abandoning the tactic of using raw magical energy and tried to catch the edge of Cael's breastplate in an attempt to rip it off. He succeeded in catching the edge of the armor with his weapon, but Cael moved with the blow and used its force to drive his claws into Cormund's mid-section, and a great tongue of flame spit forth when he pulled the blades free. A look of shock crossed Cormund's features before he fell back, the sickle slipping from his grip. And all that hit the floor was ash.

Cael looked down at his clawed gauntlets to see a fire on each as bright as a torch. Momentary panic flared up in Cael's throat, but he suppressed it. He put out the fire by magically starving it of oxygen with a flick of his wrists. Then he slipped them back into their sheaths behind him. He looked around in search of the knife he'd thrown at Cormund and found it sticking in the back of an armchair.

The sickle was still hooked into his armor. It seemed to have bit into the edge of the steel about an inch or so deep. It took a moment, but he managed to wrench the weapon free with a terrible squealing noise and dropped it on the pile of ash that was its former owner.

Cael peered out of the small window at the top of the door to ensure that the hallway beyond was still empty. He saw a guard marching down the corridor in a routine sort of way. He ducked out of sight of the window and waited for her to pass. Then, quietly as he could, he slipped out of the room and continued on with his search pattern.

Cael slowly worked his way through the palace, ducking and hiding whenever a guard came into view. As he went, he contemplated his situation. Ever since his encounter with Dartain in the Fire Desert he had known that the demon king's ritual must have at least partially worked. Especially after his time in Athanor, he could definitely tell the difference between the energy that Darius had left behind and whatever Dartain had done to him.

He hadn't wanted to examine it at the time. If he simply didn't acknowledge the demon essence then it couldn't affect him, right? Cael scoffed at his own foolishness as if ignoring the problem could make it disappear. He had just been so afraid of the prospect of his adversary succeeding in turning him into some kind of horrible demon hybrid or whatever it was that had been the lion man's actual goal.

Still, in the end, Cael was glad that he was forced to face the demon essence that now resided within him. The truth was nowhere near as bad as he had feared. Knowing that it was too small a portion and too weak a power to influence his actions unless he was directly exposed to malevolent energy was something he could probably live with. He couldn't help but feel a bit tainted, though.

And it did make the impending conflict a bit more complicated. Sure, he was able to rise above the sadistic compulsion that had accompanied Cormund's magical attacks, and he had achieved some measure of success in clamping down on the demon. But that didn't guarantee he'd be as successful with Dartain who was more powerful and thus had to have stronger malevolent energy. Cael supposed he would just have to trust that his experiences thus far had sufficiently prepared him and that he would not succumb to the demon essence within him.

He would strive to be worthy of standing beside the people he so much admired as an equal.

It was with a renewed resolve that Cael continued on to the next section of the Obsidian Palace. There was a large open chamber up ahead. The archway at its front was flanked, not by more guards, but by a pair of fire cats. Further in the chamber's depths, sitting on a throne of masterfully and strategically chipped smoky obsidian was the Demon King Dartain himself.

Chapter XV:
The Task at Hand

His enemies before him, Cael wasted no time. He marched forward with purpose in his stride, pulling Howling Wolf free from its sheath as he went. The fire cats charged forward to engage with much angry roaring. Dartain himself had stood up and stilled his minions with a single command.

"Settle down! I will require no assistance with this one." The feline demon king beckoned for Cael to come forward.

He stomped under the archway and into the throne room. Dartain greeted his approach with his arms spread wide open in welcome and a self-satisfied grin on his lion-like features. Cael felt his scowl deepen under the visor of his helmet. "You certainly seem very accommodating."

Dartain lowered his hands, but his smile never left his face, "Well certainly, you've come into my home, and I will never let it be said that I am not a good host. After all," his grin twisted into something sinister, "these are your final moments, you should be comfortable."

"I haven't taken my last breath yet, we'll see whose final moments will be spent here," Cael retorted.

Dartain laughed, "we've already done this dance twice before. We both know how this is going to end."

"The difference is, you don't have any advantage to hang over my head this time. Now it's just you and me, and I'm ready for you," Cael readied his fighting stance and lifted his sword into position.

"Oh, don't I?" Dartain answered. He reached back and grabbed the massive double-bladed ax that leaned up against the arm of his throne. When he brought it up into his own fighting stance, he infused the weapon with his magical energy. The light that now came from the ax-head flickered like an ethereal fire. He lifted the battle ax high and stepped into his first swing, but Cael was already on the move.

He had come around, far outside the range of the demon's swing. Dartain was wearing black enameled plate armor, so Cael aimed his strike for just above his elbow protection. The demon could not block because of the momentum of his own missed strike; so instead, he rolled into it and away from Cael so that the champion's attack bounced off of his back armor.

Dartain recovered from his roll and spun back around to face Cael, swinging his ax as he went. The blade did not touch him, but the magical energy that surrounded the weapon was launched forward and hit Cael square in the chest, knocking him off his feet. It came over him like a wave, both the physical change that made him briefly look like a crimson fire cat and the emotional change that gave Cael the notion that he'd like to set Dartain on fire. Cael shook his head to clear this thought and got back to his feet.

"Your lieutenant, Cormund, already tried that, it didn't work for him either," Cael spat, his features returning to their lupine form.

"You fought Cormund? And yet you're still standing?" Dartain questioned, but he did not pause in his assault. He took his ax in both hands and jabbed at Cael with the blades' points. Cael answered this attack by slamming the pommel of Howling Wolf into the center of the ax head with one hand. He followed the parry up by slashing at Dartain's neck with a flick of his wrist. The strike hit home but was not particularly effective; the force of the blow was mostly defused by the lion man's mane.

"He wasn't as tough as he thought he was," came Cael's eventual answer as Dartain stepped back with a twirl of his weapon, he stalked around Cael like the great cat he so much resembled.

Dartain's eyes narrowed, calculating, "you may be stronger than I've given you credit for," he shook his head, "but that doesn't mean you can win." He called a mass of fire to his free hand much like he had during their first encounter, but this time instead of throwing the fireball directly at Cael, he threw it sideways in an arch around the alchemist the flames then grew and spread into a circle around Cael, trapping him.

Everywhere Cael looked there was a flaming wall blocking his path. He could feel panic rising in his chest. His breathing quickened, making it difficult to think. The adrenaline coursing through his veins demanded swift and immediate action, everything was happening too fast. If Cael didn't get control of the situation, and more importantly his response to it, he was going to die; without even much of a fight. Cael took a step back and stared at the fire and let himself feel the fear in his heart then he forced his breathing to slow and his mind to calm. The fear was still there, but he had a tight rein on it now.

He could see Dartain beyond the flames. It seemed to Cael that the demon was highly entertained by the spectacle that was his current predicament. At some point, though he didn't remember doing it, Cael must have torn his helmet off, perhaps to make it easier to breathe, the air was getting thin. He'd have to do without it, there was no time to put it back on.

He had to do something to get rid of this fire. Cael reached out and with his magic tried to starve a section of the conflagration by removing all the oxygen around it. He succeeded in clearing that section, but before he could leap through, the surrounding fire rushed in to fill the void. He could try removing the oxygen from the whole area, but that would result in killing not only the fire but himself along with it, so that was not the solution.

Cael looked around him searching for a way out. His eyes came to rest on the floor at his feet he crouched down and placed a hand on the smooth ground beneath him. He created a tunnel going underneath the wall of fire and, almost desperately, pushed himself through sword first.

Once on the other side, he had to take a second to catch his breath. He was not so occupied by this, though, that he was not ready when Dartain came charging at him. He side-stepped the demon's swing and brought his blade crashing down on Dartain's forearm just above the bracer. The edge bit deep, and a surprisingly weak flame started from the wound.

The lion man roared out in pain and back-handed Cael away. Cael stumbled backward and touched his jawline gingerly; he could tell there would be a nasty bruise there later. He returned his attention to his adversary and noticed that something about Dartain's posture had changed. He had become stiffer and his expression hardened. The effect was a bit intimidating.

"Fine if I can't avoid an all-out fight with you I guess it's time to get serious about this," the demon snarled.

"Trying to set me on fire was you playing around?" Cael questioned incredulously.

The demon king gave no reply, he roared out angrily and charged forward with his ax raised. Cael stood his ground, and when the demon king sent the heavy blade crashing down towards his head, he met it with his own weapon and deflected it off to the side. Dartain's attack still held some power though and landed, jarringly, on the spaulder protecting Cael's right shoulder. In fact, as he pulled the weapon away for another strike a piece of the plate metal went with it. Cael didn't even want to think about how bad it would have been if the armor had not been there and made a mental note to thank Agatha for her insistence.

The two combatants stepped back from one another. Dartain circled around again, but this time Cael countered him. He then struck out twirling his blade and launching it into a slash at the lion man's chest, at the peak of his swing's arch he poured his raw magical energy into Howling Wolf. The blade tore a path through the black enameled breastplate before Dartain could block the strike.

"You certainly have an awful lot of nerve, Champion. Do you have any idea how many battles I have won before this? How much territory I have seized with the edge of this very ax? What makes you think one man can hope to stand the slightest chance against me?" the demon king spat, one hand on his chest as if that could stop the hemorrhage that had begun there.

"It seems to me, demon, that the odds are more than even, and I'm the one who drew first blood," Cael snarled, "so don't start now trying to tell me I'm in over my head."

This was evidently the wrong thing to say for it only prompted Dartain to roar out in fury and bring his ax up once more with far greater ferocity than before. He charged forward dragging the edge of his ax across the floor as he went. In the wake of the blade, the smooth surface of the floor fractured into large shards.

Dartain flung these shards at Cael with a flick of his ax head. The sharp chunks of obsidian skated along the ground followed closely by a large fissure.

Before Cael had time to get out of the way, the glassy debris bit through the black leather boot on his left foot and the growing crack yawned wide, swallowing up the appendage. Quick reflexes prevented both feet from becoming ensnared, but Cael was still firmly trapped. Before he knew it, the demon king was bearing down on him.

Dartain lifted his weapon high above his head, and with an angry roar, he brought it crashing down. Cael blocked with Howling Wolf, and the force of the blow sent a shock-wave down his arm, throwing him off balance. He fell back, his foot twisting painfully, and landed hard on his backside. Cael snarled in pain and slashed out wildly in reflexive anger. The suddenness of the strike caught Dartain off guard, and he cut the demon across the thighs.

Dartain loomed over Cael menacingly, and Cael felt his heart jump to his throat, this was not a good position to be in at all. The demon king raised his ax above his head once more. Cael tugged at his foot frantically, and with each pull, he could feel the sharp edges of the obsidian cutting into him. This tactic wasn't getting him anywhere at the moment, and just then, Dartain started to bring the edge of his weapon down onto Cael's head. The champion had to make sure he wasn't there when it landed.

Cael sat up, narrowly missing the ax on its way down, and launched forward head-butting Dartain in the groin. It was a low blow, but Cael was desperate. The lion man stumbled away and dropped his weapon. Cael tried once more to pull his foot free, but the shards of obsidian held it fast. In a half-blind panic, Cael decided to use his magic, not with his hands but with his foot, to transform the obsidian into air. To his infinite relief, he managed it, and he was finally able to pull free.

As he scrambled out of the fissure, his shredded boot came free of his foot, but he had no time to waste worrying about it. There were a series of pillars on either side of the throne room and Cael bolted for one of them off to his right. He hid behind the pillar and sat with his back against it for a moment, trying to catch his breath.

"I was under the impression that you were above such lowly tricks!" Dartain roared, "evidently, I was mistaken." The demon king's voice got louder and clearer with every word until he appeared at Cael's right side making the young alchemist jump in surprise. "It is also evident that you aren't particularly bright when you try to hide behind a column after leaving a trail of bloody footprints right to it." He gestured casually to Cael's torn up foot.

Cael jumped up to a standing position and glared at Dartain with a lupine growl. "I wasn't really trying to hide, just protecting my back while I caught my breath."

"Oh really? Well, let's see how ready you are to rejoin the fight!" Dartain summoned a fireball halfway through his sentence and punctuated its end by lobbing it right at Cael.

He responded by crouching down on one knee and manipulating the molecules in the floor, bringing them up in a wall to block the fireball. Once the attack fizzled out, he brought the floor back down while simultaneously leaping over it and letting his blade bite deep into the demon king's shoulder.

The lion man roared in pain and fury and jerked away from the champion. This reflexive action wrenched Cael's sword from his hands, his breath caught in his throat as the hilt slipped from his grasp.

Dartain retreated several paces he shook his head violently and then turned to glare at Cael with more fire and hatred in his eyes than Cael had ever seen. With a furious growl Dartain pounced, knocking Cael to the ground. In the process, the demon king had forsaken his ax in the attack and begun to strike at Cael with only his claws. But the sheer intensity of the onslaught was overwhelming.

Cael did his best to protect his face and chest with his titanium arm while trying to push Dartain off of him with his other hand. He wasn't having much success in moving the lion man's considerable bulk. Dartain actually began to rip apart Cael's breastplate as easily as if it were an aluminum can. Eventually, Cael's hand found the blade of Howling Wolf. The hilt of the weapon was blocked by Dartain's arm, but Cael managed to carefully slide his hand down to the ricasso, where he could grip it without fear of cutting himself. There was no room for finesse, so he merely jerked the blade down, cutting deeper into Dartain's shoulder. Two things happened in quick succession, first the blade came free and clanged against the floor and second Dartain howled in agony and fell to one side, clutching his shoulder.

Cael scrambled back up to his feet and regained a proper hold on his sword and trained it on the demon king's writhing form. Huffing, Dartain first got up to his knees, and then struggled to his feet; All the while clutching an arm that hung limp and useless at his side. He advanced slowly on Cael who matched each advancing step with a retreating one of his own.

Dartain abruptly increased his pace and batted away the point of Cael's sword. He grabbed hold of the back of the champion's neck and forced him to look directly into Dartain's eyes. "It's okay you can put the weapon down now."

Cael's initial thought was how absurd the statement was, he was in the middle of the most significant battle of his life, and he had just regained hold of his sword. There was no way he was letting it go. But almost of their own volition, Cael's fingers relaxed their grip, and the blade clattered to the floor. He also felt the now familiar burn of hatred that he had begun to associate with malevolent magical energy, Cael would have liked nothing more than to sink his fangs into Dartain's throat and rip it out, but he couldn't move, his limbs felt suddenly heavy, and his thoughts began to gain a fogginess to them.

Dartain gave a laugh that ended in a grimace, the flames of the demon's blood licked at the sliced edges of this black armor slowly turning it into a glowing red. "Go ahead, have a seat. Make yourself comfortable." The demon king's voice had taken on a sultry quality to it. It was far different from the tone he'd used thus far. Dartain maintained eye contact as once again Cael's body moved of its own accord, he sank down to the ground and sat cross-legged at Dartain's feet, looking up at him.

He spoke again, this time more to himself than anything, "you're just a child. Never in my thousands of years ruling this place, has anyone managed to wound me this severely. I have conquered scores of armies of powerful demons nearly single-handed! Demons that were certainly more powerful than you! Who do you think you are? I have achieved the impossible countless times, and I will continue to do so until the entire Lowest Plane is under my command. You will not be the end of me. You will not!"

All throughout Dartain's tirade, he did not look away from Cael's eyes once, in the back of Cael's mind he knew this was an important detail, but for the life of him, he could not grasp the thought. The only thing Cael had attention for was the dreamlike feeling that had blanketed his entire being, well, everything but the burning hatred that bubbled up within him, the combination was a surreal experience.

Suddenly something cut through Dartain's ranting, a nudge on his mind. There was something familiar about this new presence. *"Hey! Snap out of it Cael! He's going to kill you!"* It was Marina speaking to him from a mental connection. Cael focused inward on her presence in his mind, he clung to it like the last lifeline he would ever see. *"Listen to me Cael, all you have to do is look away! Break your eye contact!"* Cael struggled to comprehend her meaning; his mind was even more sluggish and foggy than before.

Dartain chuckled, shifting Cael's attention, "it seems the sacrifice of my essence was not a complete waste after all. I wasn't able to graft as much as I had planned onto your soul, when it didn't corrupt you I chocked it up to a failed experiment. Then when you were able to resist its effects even after being hit with more malevolent energy, I must say I was quite annoyed, but at least it seems to make my powers of suggestion a great deal more effective. I wonder if it only works for me since it's my essence, or if it would work if another demon tried it."

He gestured behind him to the entrance of his throne room, "Maybe we should test it," his laugh turned cruel, "we could try getting you to fall on your own sword; that would be rich. Then the problem you pose would finally be over."

"Cael! You have to come to your senses! You don't have much time. Please, Cael!" The desperation in Marina's voice tore at Cael's heart. That, above anything else, was enough to shake Cael from the grip of Dartain's suggestion.

"I'm okay, thank you, Marina. You saved me." It was all Cael had time to say, he hoped he had conveyed his relief and gratitude adequately.

Dartain was still talking, musing over which of his lieutenants he should call in to help toy with Cael. The young alchemist meanwhile, was taking quick mental stock of his surroundings. He kept his eyes focused not on Dartain's eyes but his nose, Cael hoped the demon wouldn't notice until it was too late. He also sensed out the exact location of Howling Wolf using a similar technique to how he navigated the Illuminated Mists. The second he was sure he could regain his weapon and strike fast enough he moved.

The champion grabbed his sword and used the momentum of rising to his feet to add power to his lunge. Cael plunged the blade straight through armor, muscle, bone, and finally through the demon king's heart. Dartain looked at him with a bewildered look frozen on his face. Cael pulled his blade free, and the demon fell to his knees.

"But you were subdued, I had won," a great conflagration burst from the gaping hole in Dartain's chest, and he fell face first onto the dais his throne sat on. Cael stayed long after he had reverted to his more human appearance and watched as the flames consumed Dartain's entire body. He had to be certain this was over. Cael glanced over at the entrance of the throne room, worried that the fire cats guarding the archway would come rushing at him since Dartain was not there to stop them. Cael's fears proved to be unfounded; however, the fire cats were retreating in the opposite direction as fast as their four paws could take them.

Not until there was nothing but charcoal left did Cael claw a portal open to the Illuminated Mists. His hike back through the middle plane was slow going, his foot sent shock-waves of pain with every step and every other part of his body hurt in varying degrees of intensity.

He headed for Greenwood in the hopes that they might be able to patch him back up before returning home. Mostly, he kinda just wanted to sleep.

Chapter XVI:
The Wolf Den

A mostly recovered Cael walked down the halls of Sablewater towards the viewing chamber. He wanted a proper chance to thank the temple's captivating master for pulling his butt out of the fire. He was barely across the threshold before Marina collided with him in an exuberant embrace.

Cael grunted softly in discomfort as she pressed against his still healing chest, "profanity Marina! Did you save me from Dartain just so you could kill me off yourself?" he teased.

"Oh! I'm so sorry, are you okay?" Marina had jumped back and covered her mouth with both hands.

Cael chuckled, "I'd be a lot worse off if it weren't for you. I came here to thank you, actually. I owe you my life."

The temple master smiled sweetly at him, "perhaps there will come a day when I can take you up on that offer, for now, though I will settle for your occasional presence."

Cael grinned, "not quite what I meant, but I'm not going to argue against that interpretation."

"Ugh, you guys are gonna make me vomit," Cael had not noticed the purple haired youth standing by the stone basin in the middle of the room until she spoke. The girl, dark skinned and maybe fifteen or so rolled her eyes as she walked toward the pair.

"Ah yes, Cael allow me to introduce you to Reanne, she's my new apprentice," Marina offered.

Reanne looked him up and down with her arms crossed against her chest, "so you're her champion huh?" She spoke with a particular teasing emphasis with a smirk at her teacher.

Cael grinned at Marina in kind with only the tiniest bit of a snort of laughter, "I guess you could say that."

"Oh shut up both of you," Marina huffed and turned to the bay window at the back of the chamber with her arms crossed.

"But my lady!" Cael began in an exaggeratedly gallant tone, "I have crossed entire dimensions from my place of recuperation to swear my undying loyalty and gratitude to your most illustrious self! I would be absolutely devastated if you were to spurn my affection and admiration!"

Marina turned her head slightly to glare at him out of the corner of her eye for a moment before turning back away from him.

"Ah! See now! The object of my fondness refuses me! I shall henceforth live out a desolate existence of solitude and sorrow!" Cael dropped to his knees and held a wrist up to his forehead.

At this point, Marina's shoulders were shaking, and the sound of her barely contained giggles could faintly be heard from her position at the window before she gave up and dissolved into a fit of full-blown laughter. She turned back around to face them both. "You're ridiculous!" she choked out tears beginning to form at the corners of her eyes.

Reanne rolled her eyes, "you guys are so weird." she moved back over to the basin and resumed whatever exercises Cael had interrupted.

Marina slowly recovered from her fit of giggles, "perhaps, we could take a walk? Reanne, continue practicing until I return. If you have any questions, Lyris should be able to help you."
In response, the girl merely waved the temple master off.

The pair exited the chamber and wandered back through the temple for a while in comfortable silence. They followed their feet out the main doors and deep into the jungle beyond. The distant sound of rustling vegetation and the songs of tropical birds accompanied their stroll.

"So, she seems nice," Cael commented.

"Ah, yes well, she seems, maybe not to resent her talent exactly, but she does seem a bit exasperated with it. Her parents were very excited when we took her into the temple. Through her acolyte training she liked to rebel here and there, but overall her heart is in the right place." Marina explained in a fond tone.

"I hope she doesn't give you too much trouble," Cael expressed.

"Oh no. Not more than I can handle anyway," Marina laughed.

"And where do you even get purple hair dye in the middle of the jungle?"

"Abby."

Cael snickered, "of course she did."

They reached the clearing where they had spent much of Cael's last day at Sablewater on his previous visit and sat once again of the fallen log.

"Have you been to see Dorothy yet?" Marina asked.

"I was planning on going there next, why?" Cael asked.

"She might just have something to show you once you get there," Marina smiled conspiratorially.

* * *

For once the gates of Purple House were actually open. Cael was able to stroll along the path to the front door uninhibited. It was the middle of the afternoon, yet the grounds were strangely quiet. There was only one reason that the area surrounding the house would be this silent. There was someone here doing interviews for adoption.

Cael didn't want to disturb such a crucial interview, so he slipped into the parlor and took a seat to wait. Some forty minutes later, a couple of women came down the hallway behind Zack. He was carrying a suitcase that was as tall as he was. As they passed Cael on their way to the door, Cael gave Zack a smile and a thumbs up which Zack returned enthusiastically.

"Thank you Mrs. Andlor," Dorothy was saying as she opened the door for the trio. "And if you have any more questions from me or need anything else don't hesitate to contact me. Good luck you three!" The orphanage director waved them out of the door.

She softly let the door snap shut and then turned a scrutinizing eye on Cael. He was currently wearing brown leather boots from Greenwood and a fresh black leather jerkin and the blue linen trousers of Sablewater. Only the bandages from his shoulder wound were visible and even then barely so. Cael hoped Dorothy would not be too worried about him.

"So you did it already huh?" Dorothy grinned, she stood before him with her hands on her hips, "I could kick you, it took me years to complete my task, but then mine was a little bit trickier."

Cael grinned sheepishly, "Yeah." he ran a hand through his short brown hair, "Dartain is gone."

Dorothy beamed, "I'm so proud," she stamped her foot in response to Cael's raised eyebrow, "no really, I am! You've accomplished much in such a short time; though it looks like you nearly killed yourself doing it."

"Mom I'm fine, I promise. As you can see I am all in one piece." Cael stood and held his arms out to give a clear view of himself.

Dorothy nodded sympathetically, "ours is a dangerous job. But now there is something you need to see. Come with me."

She led Cael out the front door and over to the garage where she opened the garage door to reveal her old sedan. "You're showing me your car?" he asked.

"Don't be so facetious. No, we have to drive there." Dorothy stuck her tongue out at him.

"And we're just going to leave the children here by themselves?"

"Well since you left and I lost my built in babysitter I hired an assistant, his name is Mitch," as soon as they were in the car an on their way, Dorothy continued, "he might even be better with the kids than you were."

"That's not saying much, mostly I just encouraged them to horse around," He looked at his mother slyly, "but tell me about this Mitch. Is he handsome?"

The orphanage director raised an eyebrow at him, "I don't know why that would be important."

"No? No potential there then huh?" Cael asked, still teasing.

"I don't know, it's too early for any of that," she began, "for now it's just good to have help running Purple House."

Before long, Dorothy did finally pull the car up to the gate of another estate several miles away. She reached a hand out to an electronic pad set into the stone of the surrounding wall and pressed her palm against it. A light flashed green, and the gate began to open allowing them to drive right up to the manor. It was gray with blue and black trim. It stood three stories high and had a massive porch that wrapped around two walls. The grounds were almost completely covered in a densely wooded area with a space cleared around the manor itself.

"So what do you think?" Dorothy asked.

"It's really nice, but why are we here?" Cael responded.

"It's yours. Each blooded champion is awarded an estate in exchange for their services. I distinctly remember telling you this before." His mother explained.

"I just wasn't expecting it this soon, I guess. This whole place is really mine?" Cael was dumbfounded. He knew Purple House had been given to Dorothy when she completed her task, but for some reason, he had never really thought about having his own.

"Yep, all yours. Do you want to go inside and have a look around?" She opened the door and then handed over the keys.

The front door opened up to a parlor with a staircase against the right-hand wall. Through an archway to the left there was a kitchen followed by a spacious dining hall and beyond that a den. The second and third floors held multiple bedrooms. The manor was also completely furnished with chairs and couches of hardwood and leather and several beds. The dining room had a huge oak table and matching chairs.

"I notice there's no fireplace," Cael chuckled, "was that on purpose?" With Purple House having two of the structures, the omission was a bit odd.

"Agatha thought with your rather unsavory experience with fire that you wouldn't much care for one." the other champion explained.

"I'll have to remember to thank her for that as well the next time I see her," Cael smiled.

"There is one last thing," Dorothy pulled out a silver coin with the cloudy mountain peak insignia of Argentcloud and placed it into Cael's hand. The coin transformed into a twenty dollar bill the moment it touched Cael's hand. "There is a treasury vault in the basement full of these temple coins. They use them mostly to pay the runners so that no matter what plane of existence they are in they can buy things with an equal value of the local currency. They just also happen to pay blooded champions with them as well. I guess because that's what they have on hand."

"They really make it easy to travel between the planes of existence don't they?" Cael asked with a grin.

"I should hope so, it is the main function of the temples after all," Dorothy said. "But I think it's getting to be about time for me to head back, I don't want to leave the Orphanage solely in Mitch's hands for too long."

"Yep you go see your man," Cael joked.

Dorothy sighed exasperatedly, "he's not my man he's my assistant." she paused to glare at him and poked a finger into his chest, "stop that."

On her way out Dorothy programmed the gate's locking mechanism to recognize Cael's hand-print. As a joke, he tried to use his left hand, but the pad didn't register that there was anything on it, so the joke fell a little flat.

When Dorothy left, Cael locked up the front door and brought his Communicator Watch to his face, "hey are you guys by any chance at the base?"

Abby's face appeared on the screen, "We're actually at Tony's, why?"

"Oh perfect, I'm starving. I'll see you guys there in a bit!" it was only after he shut down the connection that Cael realized that it would take a great deal longer than 'a bit' to take the subway into town and all the way to Tony's.

Cael scratched the back of his neck. He didn't generally like to use magic in town it tended to draw unwanted attention, but maybe if he came out the other side in a back alley, it would be discrete enough. It seemed to Cael like the only way to get there in time, was to go through the Illuminated Mists the compressed space of the Mists would make the trip much shorter. He clawed open a portal and came out the other side in barely any time at all.

Of course, Cael realized too late that his current attire was a bit strange for the middle of Charnley, Illinois. As he walked down the street, a woman pushing a stroller looked at him like he had lost his mind. "Just came from a renaissance fair!" Cael called out in her direction with a self-conscience laugh.

He stepped through the glass door and into the pizzeria. Sitting at their usual table was his pack the one who had his back through anything. As Cael watched; Jim blew the wrapper off his straw into Brock's face. Brock retaliated by throwing an ice cube down the front of Jim's shirt.

As Cael was about to make his way to the table, Tony came from around the counter. "There-a you are we have-a not seen you in-a quite a while. Where-a have you been? You look-a like you've had a rough time. You have-a not been into any-a trouble have you?"

"Nothing I couldn't handle Tony, and I'm fine now. Things are really looking up," Cael assured.

Tony smiled, "well-a that's good to-a hear. I won't keep-a you any longer go, sit! eat!"

Cael laughed to himself and navigated through the restaurant to his friends. He greeted them with a smile and Max leaped up from his seat to embrace Cael with a crushing hug. Everybody else got up and gathered around him.

Gavin stood directly in from of Cael with a calculating gaze, then his face broke out into a grin, "Well, you certainly don't look dead."

"No, but I sure tried my hardest to make it happen. Unfortunately, the other guy got that honor," Cael crossed his arms across his chest and shook his head in a dejected manner.

"So, he's really gone?" Abby asked, "your task is finished?" they all settled back into their seats around the table, and everyone looked at Cael.

Cael nodded, "Yep, It's really over, Dartain is done for. It wasn't easy by any stretch of the imagination, and I did legitimately almost die in the process, but yeah, I did it."

Max shook his head, "man, that's such a relief. We were so worried about you these last few months."

"Sure it was touch and go there for a while but, hey I'm alright now," Cael consoled.

The rest of the Pack demanded that he tell them everything that had happened since they had seen each other last. Cael told them all about Athanor and Zander and Dane and everything about the Knights of the Silvertree. Then he told them about Agatha and her demands for Cael's preparation.

"So, you have a suit of armor now? That's pretty cool," Jim commented.

"Not as such, no. Let me tell you what became of that suit of armor," Cael hedged.

So he told them about sneaking into Dartain's palace and his encounter with Cormund and then he described the actual battle with Dartain himself and how severely his armor was torn up in the process of defying the demon king.

"There's one more thing," Cael said leaning forward over his finished plate of pizza.

"Are you kidding?" Brock demanded, "There's more?"

"This part's good I promise," Cael chuckled, "as a reward for destroying Dartain I have been awarded an estate. And I'm telling you this place is gigantic, way too big for just me to stay there. So I was thinking that we move our base of operations. When do your semesters end?"

"About a month and a half and then we're off for the summer," Gavin answered.

"But you're still living with your uncle though right? You just commute to Rockfield don't you?" Cael asked, and Gavin nodded in confirmation. "so the only ones still stuck in the dorms until summer is you two." He looked at Max and Brock.

"Yeah but after that, it would be a really good thing to have somewhere to go besides my dad's house," Max assured.

"And I think I've had enough of a taste of the 'full college experience,'" Brock added.

"All of us living together sounds kinda fun," Jim commented.

"That's kinda what I was thinking too," Cael agreed.

Abby jumped up with her usual exuberance, "So let's go see this place!"

So they settled their bill with Tony and headed down to the subway and grabbed a train outside of the city. The ride didn't take too long, and on the way, they took the opportunity to catch Cael up on what the rest of the Wolves had been doing over the past year. Jim was getting high praise at his job for the quality of work he was putting out. Abby was helping out at her uncle's garage they had just gotten in an old '67 Corvette that she had been drooling over as they overhauled the transmission. Gavin was learning how to make soufflés in class, and they were a lot harder than they looked. Brock had written half an album instead of listening to his history of art lectures but was able to use the schools recording studio, and the difference in quality for his music was impressive. Max in that same history of art class was quite enjoying learning about the neoclassical era and was taking notes for the both of them.

Eventually, they made it to the gates of Cael's estate, and he opened the gate with a press of his palm and went ahead and added the rest of the Pack to the system as well. They walked down the path through the woods to the front entrance. He unlocked the solid mahogany door to reveal the space within.

"Welcome," Cael said, "to the Wolf Den."

-37658159R00168

Made in the USA
San Bernardino, CA
01 June 2019